"I'll want

"Of course,"

"I'll take care of it tomorrow."

"What?" She shook her head, looked at him and asked, "Don't you have to wait until we're back in San Pedro?"

"No, I'm not going to wait. I want this question settled as quickly as possible." He continued to eat, as though what they were discussing wasn't affecting him in the slightest. "We dock at Cabo in the morning. You and I will go ashore, find a lab and have them fax the findings to the lab in San Pedro."

"We will?" She hadn't planned on spending a lot of time with Nick, after all. She'd only come on board to tell him about the twins and, frankly, she'd thought he wouldn't want anything more to do with her after that. Instead, he'd moved her into his suite and now was proposing that they spend even more time together.

"Until this is taken care of to my satisfaction," Nick told her softly, "I'm not letting you out of my sight. The two of us are going to be joined at the hip. So you might as well start getting used to it."

For Blackmail...or Pleasure
by Robyn Grady

ᴉ ✿ ᴄ

"I hate you."

His jaw tensed. "Then I'm no worse off."

She despised giving in. She'd much rather tell him to go straight to hell. But that had never been an option. "Where and when?"

Tate's chest inflated. Battle won.

"At my television studios. Monday at ten. Don't be late." So unforgettable and debonair in that tux. "One more thing."

His kiss was swift, overwhelming – the same skill she remembered, yet strangely so much more. Her mind hurtled back and the years slipped away. In this surreal moment she was Tate's again and, incredibly, nothing else mattered.

Brutal reality – where they were, what she'd done – finally kicked in. Shoving at his rock-hard chest, she managed to break free.

The dimple she'd once adored appeared as he genuinely smiled. He was so damn superior. "Just wanted to let you know how sexy you are when you're mad."

Available in May 2009
from Mills & Boon® Desire™

Bedded by the Billionaire
by Leanne Banks
&
Tycoon's One-Night Revenge
by Bronwyn Jameson

Baby Bonanza
by Maureen Child
&
For Blackmail…or Pleasure
by Robyn Grady

The Desert Lord's Baby
by Olivia Gates
&
Seduced for the Inheritance
by Jennifer Lewis

Baby Bonanza
MAUREEN CHILD

For Blackmail...or Pleasure
ROBYN GRADY

MILLS & BOON®
Pure reading pleasure™

*First published in Great Britain 2009
by Harlequin Mills & Boon Limited,
Eton House, 18-24 Paradise Road, Richmond, Surrey TW9 1SR*

The publisher acknowledges the copyright holders of the
individual works as follows:

Baby Bonanza © Maureen Child 2008
For Blackmail...or Pleasure © Robyn Grady 2008

ISBN: 978 0 263 87099 2

51-0509

*Printed and bound in Spain
by Litografia Rosés S.A., Barcelona*

BABY BONANZA

by
Maureen Child

Dear Reader,

Is there anything sweeter than watching a strong man be completely befuddled by a baby? Just as there's something elemental about seeing a father meet his child for the first time. Something powerful and touching.

In *Baby Bonanza*, Nick Falco does just that. He finds out he's a father and meets his twin sons for the first time. Everything changes for him – and because it does, everything also changes for the mother of his babies, Jenna Baker.

I hope you enjoy reading their story as much as I enjoyed writing it!

Happy reading,

Maureen

MAUREEN CHILD

is a California native who loves to travel. Every chance they get, she and her husband are taking off on another research trip. The author of more than sixty books, Maureen loves a happy ending and still swears that she has the best job in the world. She lives in Southern California with her husband, two children and a golden retriever with delusions of grandeur.

To the ladies at Long Beach Care Center –
Christabel, Barbara and all of the others who
give such loving care to the patients – including
my uncle – who need it the most. You really
are amazing.

One

"Ow!" Jenna Baker hopped on her right foot and clutched at the bruised toes on her left one. Shooting a furious glare at the bolted-down table in her so-tiny-that-claustrophobics-would-die cabin, she called down silent curses on the head of the man who was the reason for this cruise from hell.

Nick Falco.

His image rose up in her mind, and just for a second Jenna enjoyed the nearly instant wash of heat that whipped through her. But the heat was gone a moment later, to be replaced by a cold fury.

Better all around if she concentrated on *that* particular emotion. After all, unlike every other passenger aboard *Falcon's Pride,* she hadn't come aboard the floating orgy to party. She was here for a reason. A damn good one.

While her aching toes throbbed in concert with her heartbeat, Jenna cautiously stood on both feet and took the step and a half that brought her to a minuscule closet. She'd already hung up her clothes, and the few outfits she'd brought with her looked crowded in the narrow wardrobe. Snatching a pale yellow blouse off the attached-to-the-rod hanger, she carried it to the bathroom, just another step away.

It was the size of an airplane bathroom, only it also contained a shower stall designed to fit pygmies. In fact, the opening of the sliding door was so slender, Jenna had slapped one arm across her breasts when leaving the shower, half-afraid she'd scrape her nipples off.

"Really nice, Nick," she muttered, "when you upgraded this old boat and turned it into your flagship, you might have put a little extra thought into those people who *aren't* living in the owner's penthouse on the top deck."

But she told herself that was typical enough. She'd known what Nick was like even before she'd met him on that sultry summer night more than a year ago. He was a man devoted to seeing his cruise line become the premier one in the world. He did what he had to do when he had to do it. And he didn't make apologies for it.

She'd been working for him when she met him. An assistant cruise director on one of the other cruise ships in the Falcon line. She'd loved the job, loved the idea of travel and stupidly, had fallen in love with the boss. All because of a romantic moonlight encounter and Nick's undeniable charm.

Jenna had known darn well that the boss would never get involved with an employee. So when the sexy, gorgeous Nick Falco had stumbled across her on the Pavilion Deck and assumed she was a guest, she hadn't corrected him. She should have and she knew it, but what woman wouldn't have been swept away by a chiseled jaw, ice-blue eyes and thick black hair that just tempted a woman to tangle her fingers in it?

She sighed a little, set her hands on the sides of the soapdish-size sink and remembered how it had been from the first moment he'd touched her. *Magic.* Pure and simple. Her skin had sizzled, her blood had sung and her heart had beaten so frantically, it had been hard to breathe. He'd swept her into a dance, there in the starlight, with the Hawaiian breeze caressing them and the music from the deck below floating on the air like a sigh.

One dance became two, and the feel of his arms around her had seduced Jenna into a lie that had come back to haunt her not a week later. She fell into an affair. A blistering, over-the-top sexual affair that had rocked her soul even as it battered her heart.

And when, one week into that affair, Nick had discovered from someone else that she actually worked for him, he'd broken it off, refused to hear her out, and once they were back in port, he'd fired her.

The sting of that…dismissal felt as fresh as the day it had happened.

"Oh, God. What am I doing here?" She blew out a breath as her stomach began to twist and ripple with the nerves that had been shivering through her for months. If there were any other way to do this, she would have. After all, it wasn't as if she were looking forward to seeing Nick again.

Gritting her teeth, she lifted her chin, turned sharply and cracked her elbow into the doorjamb. Wincing, she stared into her reflection in the slim rectangular mirror and said, "You're here because it's the right thing. The *only* thing. Besides, it's not like he left you any choice."

She had to talk to the man and it wasn't exactly easy to get access to him. Since he lived aboard the flagship of his cruise line, she couldn't confront him on dry land. And the few times he was in port in San Pedro, California, he locked himself up in a penthouse apartment with tighter security than the White House. When she couldn't talk to him in person, she'd tried phone calls. And when they failed, she'd taken to e-mailing him. At least twice a week for the last six months, she'd sent him e-mails that he apparently deleted without opening. The man was being so impossible, Jenna'd finally been forced to make a reservation on *Falcon's Pride* and take a cruise she didn't want and couldn't afford.

She hadn't been on board a ship in more than a year and so even the slight rolling sensation of the big cruise liner made her knees a little rubbery. There was a time when she'd loved being on ship. When she'd enjoyed the adventure of a job that was never the same two days in a row. When she'd awakened every morning to a new view out her porthole.

"Of course," she admitted wryly, "that was when I *had* a porthole." Now she was so far belowdecks, in the cheapest cabin she'd been able to find, she had no window at all and it felt as though she'd been sealed up in the bowels of the ship. She was forced to keep a light on at all times, because otherwise, the dark was so complete, it was like being inside a vacuum. No sensory input at all.

Weird and strangely unsettling.

Maybe if she'd been able to get some sleep, she'd feel different. But she'd been jolted out of bed late the night before by the horrific clank and groan of the anchor chain being lifted. It had sounded as if the ship itself was being torn apart by giant hands, and once that image had planted itself in her brain, she hadn't been able to sleep again.

"All because of Nick," she told the woman in the glass and was gratified to see her nod in agreement. "Mr. Gazillionaire, too busy, too important to answer his e-mail." Did he even remember her? Did he look at her name on the e-mail address and wonder who the heck she was? She frowned into the mirror, then shook her head. "No. He didn't forget. He knows who I am. He's not reading the e-mails on purpose, just to make me crazy. He couldn't have forgotten that week."

Despite the way it had ended, that one week with Nick Falco had turned Jenna's life around and upside down. It was simply impossible that she was the only one affected that strongly.

"So instead, he's being Mr. Smooth and Charming," she said. "Probably romancing some other silly woman, who, like me, won't notice until it's too late that he's *nobody's* fantasy."

Oh, God.

That was a lie.

The truth was, she thought with an inner groan, he actually *was* any woman's fantasy. Tall, gorgeous, with thick, black hair, pale blue eyes and a smile that was both charming and wicked, Nick Falco was enough to make a woman's toes curl even *before* she knew what kind of lover he was.

Jenna let her forehead thunk against the mirror. "Maybe this wasn't such a great idea," she whispered as her insides fisted and other parts of her heated up just on the strength of memories alone.

She closed her eyes as vivid mental images churned through her mind—nights with Nick, dancing on the Pavilion Deck beneath an awning of stars. A late-night picnic, alone on the bow of the ship, with the night crowded close. Dining on his balcony, sipping champagne, spilling a few drops and Nick licking them from the valley between her breasts. Lying in his bed, wrapped in his arms, his whispers promising tantalizing delights.

What did it say about her that simply the memories of that man could still elicit a shiver of want in her, more than a year later? Jenna didn't think she really wanted an answer to that question. She hadn't boarded this ship for the sake of lust or for what had once been. Sex wasn't part of the equation this time and she was just going to have to find a way to deal with her past while fighting for her future. So, deliberately, she dismissed the tantalizing images from her mind in favor of her reality. Opening her eyes, she stared into the mirror and steeled herself for what was to come.

The past had brought her here, but she had no intention of stirring up old passions.

Her life was different now. She wasn't at loose ends, looking for adventure. She was a woman with a purpose, and Nick was going to listen to her whether he wanted to or not.

"Too busy to answer his e-mail, is he?" she muttered. "Thinks if he ignores me long enough I'll simply disappear? Well, then, he's got quite the surprise coming, doesn't he?"

She brushed her teeth, slapped some makeup on and ran a brush through her long, straight, light brown hair before braiding it into a single thick rope that lay against her back. Inching sideways out the bathroom door, she carefully made her way to the built-in dresser underneath a television bolted high on the wall. She grabbed a pair of white shorts, tugged them on and then tucked the ends of her yellow shirt into the waistband. She stepped into a pair of sandals, grabbed her purse and checked to make sure the sealed, small blue envelope was still inside. Then she took the two steps to her cabin door.

She opened her door, stepped into the stingy hallway and bumped into a room service waiter. "Sorry, sorry!"

"My fault," he insisted, hoisting the tray he carried high enough that Jenna could duck under it and slip past him. "These older hallways just weren't made for a lot of foot traffic." He glanced up and down the short hall, then back to Jenna. "Even with the ship's refit, there are sections that—" He stopped, as if remembering he was an employee of the Falcon Line and really shouldn't be dissing the ship.

"Guess not." Jenna smiled back at the guy. He looked about twenty and had the shine of excitement in his eyes. She was willing to bet this was his first cruise. "So, do you like working for Falcon Cruises?"

He lowered the tray to chest level, shrugged and said, "It's my first day, but so far, yeah. I really do. But…" He stopped, turned a look over his shoulder at the dimly lit hall as if making sure no one could overhear him.

Jenna could have reassured him. There were only five cabins down here in the belly of the ship and only hers and the one across the hall from her were occupied. "But?" she prompted.

"It's a little creepy down here, don't you think? I mean, you can hear the water battering against the hull and it's so…dark."

She'd been thinking the same thing only moments before and still she said, "Well, it's got to be better than crew quarters, right? I mean, I used to work on ships and we were always on the lowest deck."

"Not us," he said, "crew quarters are one deck up from here."

"Fabulous," Jenna muttered, thinking that even the people who *worked* for Nick Falco were getting more sleep on this cruise than she was.

The door opened and a fortyish woman in a robe poked her head out and smiled. "Oh, thank God," the older blonde said. "I heard voices out here and I was half-afraid the ship was haunted."

"No, ma'am." The waiter stiffened to attention as if just remembering what he'd come below for. He shot Jenna a hopeful look, clearly asking that she not rat him out for standing around having a conversation. "I've got breakfast for two here, as you requested."

"Great," the blonde said, opening the door wider. "Just…" She stopped. "I have no idea where you can put it. Find a place, okay?"

While the waiter disappeared into the cabin, the blonde stuck out one hand to Jenna. "Hi, I'm Mary Curran. My husband, Joe, and I are on vacation."

"Jenna Baker," she said, shaking the other woman's hand. "Maybe I'll see you abovedecks?"

"Won't see much of me down here, I can tell you," Mary admitted with a shudder as she tightened the sash on her blue terry-cloth robe. "Way too creepy, but—" she shrugged "—the important thing is, we're on a cruise. We only have to sleep here, after all, and I intend to get our money's worth out of this trip."

"Funny," Jenna said with a smile. "I was just telling myself the same thing."

She left Mary to her breakfast and headed for the elevator that would carry her up and out of the darkness. She clutched the envelope that she would have delivered to Nick and steeled herself for the day to come. The elevator lurched into motion and she tapped her foot as she rose from the bowels of the ship. What she needed now was some air, lots of coffee and a pastry or two. Then, later, after Nick had read her letter, she would be ready. Ready to face the beast. To beard the lion in his den. To look into Nick's pale blue eyes and demand that he do the right thing.

"Or," Jenna swore as the doors shushed open and she stepped into the sunlight and tipped her face up to the sky, "I will *so* make him pay."

"The sound system for the stage on the Calypso Deck has a hiccup or two, but the techs say they'll have it fixed before showtime."

"Good." Nick Falco sat back in his maroon leather chair and folded his hands atop his belly as he listened to his assistant, Teresa Hogan, rattle off her daily report. It was only late morning and together they'd already handled a half-dozen crises. "I don't want any major issues," he told her. "I know this is the shakedown cruise, but I don't want our passengers feeling like they're guinea pigs."

"They won't. The ship's looking good and you know it," Teresa said with a confident smile. "We've got a few minor glitches, but nothing we can't handle. If there were real trouble, we never would have left port last night."

"I know," he said, glancing over his shoulder at the white caps dancing across the surface of the ocean. "Just make sure we stay one step ahead of any of those glitches."

"Don't I always?"

"Yeah," he said with a nod of approval. "You do."

Teresa was in her late fifties, had short, dark hair, sharp green eyes and the organizational skills of a field general. She took crap from no one, Nick included, and had the loyalty and tenacity of a hungry pit bull. She'd been with him for eight years—ever since her husband had died and she'd come looking for a job that would give her adventure.

She'd gotten it. And she'd also become Nick's trusted right arm.

"The master chef on the Paradise Deck is complaining about the new Vikings," she was saying, flipping through the papers attached to her ever present clipboard.

Nick snorted. "Most expensive stoves on the planet and there's something wrong with them?"

She smirked a little. "According to Chef Michele," Teresa said, "ze stove is not hot enough."

Not a full day out at sea and already he was getting flak from temperamental artistes. "Tell him as long as ze heat is hot, he should do what I'm paying him to do."

"Already done."

One of Nick's eyebrows lifted. "Then why tell me at all?"

"You're the boss."

"Nice of you to remember that occasionally," he said, and sat forward, rolling his chair closer to the desk where a small mountain of personal correspondence waited for his attention.

Ignoring that jibe, Teresa checked her papers again and said, "The captain says the weather outlook is great and we're making all speed to Cabo. Should be there by ten in the morning tomorrow."

"That's good." Nick picked up the first envelope on the stack in front of him. Idly, he tapped the edge of it against his desk as Teresa talked. And while she ran down the list of problems, complaints and compliments, he let his gaze shift around his office. Here on the Splendor Deck, just one deck below the bridge, the views were tremendous. Which was why he'd wanted both his office and his luxurious owner's suite on this deck. He'd insisted on lots of glass. He liked the wide spread of the ocean all around him. Gave him a sense of freedom even while he was working.

There were comfortable chairs, low-slung tables and a fully stocked wet bar across the room. The few paintings hanging on the dark blue walls were bright splotches of color, and the gleaming wood floors shone in sunlight that was only partially dimmed by the tinted glass.

This was the ship's maiden voyage under the Falcon name. Nick had bought it from a competitor who was going out of business, and over the past six months had had it completely refitted and refurbished to be the queen of his own cruise line. *Falcon's Pride,* he'd called her, and so far she was living up to her name.

He'd gotten reports from his employees on the reaction from the passengers as they'd boarded the day before in the L.A. port of San Pedro. Though most of the guests on board were young and looking to party, even they had been impressed with the ship's luxurious decor and overall feel.

Nick had purchased his first ship ten years before, and had quickly built the Falcon Line into the primary party destination in the world. *Falcon's Pride* was going to take that reputation and enhance it. His passengers wanted fun. Excitement. A two-week-long party. And he was going to see that they got it.

He hired only the best chefs, the hottest bands and the greatest lounge acts. His employees were young and attractive—his mind shifted tracks around that thought and instantly, he was reminded of one former employee in particular. A woman he'd let get under his skin until the night he'd discovered her lies. He hadn't seen or spoken to her since, but he was a hell of a lot more careful these days about who he got involved with.

"Are you even listening to me?"

Nick cleared his thoughts instantly, half-irritated that he was still thinking about Jenna Baker more than a year since he'd last seen her. He glanced up at Teresa and gave her a smile that should have charmed her. "Guess not. Why don't we take care of the rest of this business after lunch."

"Sure," she said, and checked her wristwatch. "I've got an appointment on the Verandah Deck. One of the cruise directors has a problem with the karaoke machine."

"Fine. Handle it." He turned his attention to the stack of hand-delivered correspondence on his desk and just managed to stifle a sigh. Never failed. Every cruise, Nick was inundated with invitations from female passengers to join them for dinner or private parties or for drinks in the moonlight.

"Oh," Teresa said, handing over a pale blue envelope. "One of the stewards gave me this on my way in." She smiled as she handed it over. "Yet another lonely lady looking for companionship? Seems you're still the world's favorite love god."

Nick knew she was just giving him a hard time—like always—yet this time her words dug at him. Shifting uncomfortably in his chair, he thought about it, tried to figure out why. He was no monk, God knew. And over the years he'd accepted a lot of invitations from women who didn't expect anything more than a good time and impersonal sex.

But damned if he could bring himself to get interested in the latest flurry of one-night-stand invitations, either. The cards and letters had been sitting on his desk since early this morning and he hadn't bothered to open one yet. He knew what he'd find when he started going through them.

Panties. Cabin keys. Sexy photos designed to tempt.

And not a damned one of them would mean anything to him.

Hell, what did that say about him? Laughing silently at himself, Nick acknowledged that he really didn't want to know. Maybe he'd been spending too much time working lately. Maybe what he needed was just what these ladies were offering. He'd go through the batch of invites, pick out the most intriguing one and spend a few relaxing hours with a willing woman.

Just what the doctor ordered.

Teresa was still holding the envelope out to him and there was confusion in her eyes. He didn't want her asking any questions, so he took the envelope and idly slid his finger under the seal. Deliberately giving her a grin and a wink, he said, "You think it's easy being the dream of millions?"

Now Teresa snorted and, shaking her head, muttering something about delusional males, she left the office.

When she was gone, he sat back and thoughtfully looked at the letter in his hand. Pale blue envelope, tidy handwriting. Too small to hold a pair of lacy thong panties. Too narrow to be hiding away a photo. Just the right size for a cabin key card though.

"Well, then," he said softly, "let's see who you are. Hope you included a photo of yourself. I don't do blind dates."

Chuckling, Nick pulled the card from the envelope and glanced down at it. There was a photo all right. Laughter died instantly as he looked at the picture of two babies with black hair and pale blue eyes.

"What the hell?" Even while his brain started racing and his heartbeat stuttered in his chest, he read the scrawled message beneath the photo:

"Congratulations, Daddy. It's twins."

Two

She wasn't ready to give up the sun.

Jenna set her coffee cup down on the glass-topped table, turned her face to the sky and let the warm, late-morning sunshine pour over her like a blessing. Despite the fact that there were people around her, laughing, talking, diving into the pool, sending walls of water up in splashing waves, she felt alone in the light. And she really wasn't ready to sink back into the belly of the ship.

But she'd sent her note to Nick. And she'd told him where to find her. In that tiny, less-than-closet-size cabin. So she'd better be there when he arrived. With a sigh, she stood, slung her bag over her left shoulder and threaded her way through the crowds lounging on the Verandah Deck.

Someone touched her arm and Jenna stopped.

"Leaving already?" Mary Curran was smiling at her, and Jenna returned that smile with one of her own.

"Yeah. I have to get back down to my cabin. I um, have to meet someone there." At least, she was fairly certain Nick would show up. But what if he didn't? What if he didn't care about the fact that he was the father of her twin sons? What if he dismissed her note as easily as he'd deleted all of her attempts at e-mail communication?

A small, hard knot formed in the pit of her stomach. She'd like to see him try, that's all. They were on a ship in the middle of the ocean. How was he going to escape her? Nope. Come what may, she was going to have her say. She was going to face him down, at last, and tell him what she'd come to say.

"Oh God, honey." Mary grimaced and gave a dramatic shudder. "Do you really want to have a conversation down in the pit?"

Jenna laughed. "The pit?"

"That's what my husband, Joe, christened it in the middle of the night when he nearly broke his shin trying to get to the bathroom."

Grinning, Jenna said, "I guess the name fits all right. But yeah. I have to do it there. It's too private to be done up here."

Mary's eyes warmed as she looked at Jenna and said, "Well, then, go do whatever it is you have to do. Maybe I'll see you back in the sunshine later?"

Jenna nodded. She knew how cruise passengers tended to bond together. She'd seen it herself in the time she'd actually worked for Falcon Cruises. Friendships formed fast and furiously. People who were in relatively tight quarters—stuck on a ship in the middle of the ocean—tended to get to know each other more quickly than they might on dry land.

Shipboard romances happened, sure—just look what had happened to her. But more often, it was other kinds of relationships that bloomed and took hold. And right about now, Jenna decided, she could use a friendly face.

"You bet," she said, giving Mary a wide smile. "How about margaritas on the Calypso Deck? About five?"

Delighted, Mary beamed at her. "I'll be there."

As Jenna walked toward the elevator, she told herself that after her upcoming chat with Nick, she was probably going to *need* a margarita or two.

Nick jolted to his feet so fast, his desk chair shot backward, the wheels whirring against the wood floor until the chair slammed into the glass wall behind him.

"Is this a *joke?*"

Nick held the pale blue card in one tight fist and stared down at two tiny faces. The babies were identical except for their expressions. One looked into the camera and grinned, displaying a lot of gum and one deep dimple. The other was watching the picture taker with a serious, almost thoughtful look on his face.

And they both looked a hell of a lot like *him*.

"Twins?"

In an instant, emotions he could hardly name raced

through him. Anger, frustration, confusion and back to anger again. How the hell could he be a father? Nobody he knew had been pregnant. This couldn't be happening. He glanced up at the empty office as if half expecting someone to jump out, shout, "You've just been punk'd," and let him off the hook. But there were no cameras. There was no joke.

This was someone's idea of serious.

Well, hell, he told himself, it wasn't the first time some woman had tried to slap him with a paternity suit. But it was for damn sure the first time the gauntlet had been thrown down in such an imaginative way.

"Who, though?" He grabbed the envelope up, but only his name was scrawled across the front in a small, feminine hand. Turning over the card he still held, he saw more of that writing:

"We need to talk. Come to cabin 2A on the Riviera Deck."

"Riviera Deck." Though he hated like hell to admit it, he wasn't sure which deck that was. He had a lot of ships in his line and this was his first sail on this particular one. Though he meant to make *Falcon's Pride* his home, he hadn't had the chance yet to explore it from stem to stern as he did all the ships that carried his name.

For now, he stalked across the room to the framed set of detailed ship plans hanging on the far wall of his office. He'd had one done for each of the ships in his line. He liked looking at them, liked knowing that he was familiar with every inch of every ship. Liked knowing that he'd succeeded in creating the dream he'd started more than ten years before.

But at the moment, Nick wasn't thinking of his cruise line or of business at all. Now all he wanted to do was find the woman who'd sent him this card so he could assure himself that this was all some sort of mistake.

Narrowing his pale blue eyes, he ran one finger down the decks until he found the one he was looking for. Then he frowned. According to this, the Riviera Deck was *below* crew quarters.

"What the hell is going on?" Tucking the card with the pictures of the babies into the breast pocket of his white, short-sleeved shirt, he half turned toward the office door and bellowed, *"Teresa!"*

The door flew open a few seconds later and his assistant rushed in, eyes wide in stunned surprise. "Geez, what's wrong? Are we on fire or something?"

He ignored the attempt at humor, as well as the look of puzzlement on her face. Stabbing one finger against the glass-covered ship plans, he said only, "Look at this."

She hurried across the room, glanced at the plans, then shifted a look at him. "What exactly am I looking at?"

"This." He tapped his finger against the lowest deck on the diagram. "The Riviera Deck."

"Uh-huh."

"There are people staying down there."

"Oh."

Pleased that she'd caught on so fast, Nick said, "When the ship came out of refit ready for passengers,

I said specifically that those lower cabins weren't to be used."

"Yeah, you did, boss." She actually winced, whipped out her PDA and punched a few keys. "I'll do some checking. Find out what happened."

"You do that," he said, irritated as hell that someone, somewhere, hadn't paid attention to him. "For right now, though, find out how many of those cabins are occupied."

"Right."

While Teresa worked her electronic wizardry, Nick looked back at the framed plans and shook his head. Those lower cabins were too old, too small to be used on one of his ships. Sure, they'd undergone some refurbishing during the refit, but having them and using them were two different things. Those cabins, small and dark and cramped, weren't the kind of image Nick wanted associated with his cruise line.

"Boss?" Teresa looked at him. "According to the registry, only two of the five cabins are being used."

"That's something, anyway. Who's down there?"

"1A is occupied by a Joe and Mary Curran."

He didn't know any Currans and besides, the card had come from whoever was in the only other occupied cabin on that deck.

So he waited.

"2A is…" Teresa's voice trailed off and Nick watched as his usually unflappable assistant chewed at her bottom lip.

That couldn't be good.

"What is it?" When she didn't answer right away, he demanded, "Just tell me who's in the other cabin."

"Jenna," Teresa said and blew out a breath. "Jenna Baker's in 2A, Nick."

Nick made record time getting down to the Riviera Deck, and by the time he reached it, he'd already made the decision to close up this deck permanently. Damned if he'd house his paying guests in what amounted to little more than steerage.

Stepping off the elevator, he hit his head on a low cross beam and muttered a curse. The creaks and groans of the big ship as it pushed through the waves echoed through the narrow passageway like ghosts howling. The sound of the water against the hull was a crushing heartbeat and it was so damned dark in the abbreviated hallway, even the lights in the wall sconces barely made a dent in the blackness. And the hall itself was so narrow he practically had to traverse it sideways. True, it was good business to make sure you provided less expensive rooms, but he'd deal with that another way. He'd be damned if his passengers would leave a cruise blinking at the sun like bats.

With his head pounding, his temper straining on a tight leash, he stopped in front of 2A, took a breath and raised his right fist to knock. Before he could, the narrow door was wrenched open and there she stood.

Jenna Baker.

She shouldn't have still been able to affect him. He'd had her after all. Had her and then let her go more than a year ago. So why then was he suddenly struck by the turquoise-blue of her eyes? Why did that tight, firm mouth make him want to kiss her until her lips eased apart and let him back in? Why did the fact that she looked furious make his blood steam in his veins? What the hell did *she* have to be mad about?

"I heard you in the hall," she said.

"Good ears," he conceded. "Considering all the other noises down here."

A brief, tight smile curved her mouth. "Yeah, it's lovely living in the belly of the beast. When they raise anchor it's like a symphony."

He hadn't considered that, but he was willing to bet the noise was horrific. Just another reason to seal up these rooms and never use them again. However, that was for another time. What he wanted now were answers.

"Good one," he said. "That's why you're here, then? To talk about the ship?"

"You know why I'm here."

He lifted one hand to the doorjamb and leaned in toward her. "I know what you'd like me to think. The question is, why? Why now? What're you after, Jenna?"

"I'm not going to talk about this in the hall."

"Fine." He stepped inside, moving past her, but the quarters were so cramped, their chests brushed together and he could almost feel his skin sizzle.

It had been like that from the beginning. The moment he'd touched her that first night in the moonlight, he'd felt a slam of something that was damn near molten sliding through him. And it seemed that time hadn't eased it back any.

He got a grip on his hormones, took two steps until he was at the side of a bed built for a sixth-grader, then turned around to glare at her. God, the cabin was so small it felt as though the walls were closing in on him and, truth to tell, they wouldn't have far to move. He felt as if he should be slouching to avoid skimming the top of his head along the ceiling. Every light in the cabin was on and it still looked like twilight.

But Nick wasn't here for the ambience and there was nothing he could do about the rooms at the moment. Now all he wanted was an explanation. He waited for her to shut the door, sealing the two of them into the tiny cracker box of a room before he said, "What's the game this time, Jenna?"

"This isn't a game, Nick," she said, folding her arms over her chest. "It wasn't a game then, either."

"Right." He laughed and tried not to breathe deep. The scent of her was already inside him, the tiny room making him even more aware of it than he would have been ordinarily. "You didn't *want* to lie to me. You had no choice."

Her features tightened. "Do we really have to go over the old argument again?"

He thought about it for a moment, then shook his head. He didn't want to look at the past. Hell. He didn't want to be here *now.* "No, we don't. So why don't you just say what it is you have to say so we can be done."

"Always the charmer," she quipped.

He shifted from one foot to the other and banged his elbow on the wall. "Jenna…"

"Fine. You got my note?"

He reached into the pocket of his shirt, pulled out the card, glanced at the pictures of the babies, then handed it to her. "Yeah. I got it. Now how about you explain it?"

She looked down at those two tiny faces and he saw her lips curve slightly even as her eyes warmed. But that moment passed quickly as she lifted her gaze to him and skewered him with it. "I would have thought the word *daddy* was fairly self-explanatory."

"Explain, anyway."

"Fine." Jenna walked across the tiny room, bumped Nick out of her way with a nudge from her hip that had him hitting the wall and then bent down to drag a suitcase out from under her bed. The fact that she could actually *feel* his gaze on her butt while she did it only annoyed her.

She would not pay any attention to the rush of heat she felt just being close to him again. She would certainly not acknowledge the jump and stutter of her heartbeat, and if certain other of her body parts were warm and tingling, she wasn't going to admit to that, either.

Dragging the suitcase out, she went to lift it, but Nick was there first, pushing her fingers aside to hoist the bag onto the bed. If her skin was humming from that one idle touch, he didn't have to know it, did he?

She unzipped the bag, pulled out a blue leather scrapbook and handed it to him. "Here. Take a look. Then we'll talk more."

The book seemed tiny in his big, tanned hands. He

barely glanced at it before shooting a hard look at her again. "What's this about?"

"Look at it, Nick."

He did. The moment she'd been waiting so long for stretched out as the seconds ticked past. She held her breath and watched his face, the changing expressions written there as he flipped through the pages of pictures she'd scrapbooked specifically for this purpose. It was a chronicle of sorts. Of her life since losing her job, discovering she was pregnant and then the birth of the twins. In twenty hand-decorated pages, she'd brought him up to speed on the last year and a half of her life.

Up to speed on his sons. The children he'd created and had never met.

The only reason she was here, visiting a man who'd shattered her heart without a backward glance.

When he was finished, his gaze lifted to hers and she could have sworn she saw icicles in his eyes.

"I'm supposed to believe that I'm the father of your babies?"

"Take another look at them, Nick. They both look just like you."

He did, but his features remained twisted into a cynical expression even while his eyes flashed with banked emotion. "Lots of people have black hair and blue eyes."

"Not all of them have dimples in their left cheek." She reached out, flipped to a specific page and pointed. "Both of your sons do. Just like yours."

He ran one finger over the picture of the boys as if he could somehow touch them with the motion, and that small action touched something in Jenna. For one brief instant, Nick Falco looked almost…vulnerable.

It didn't last long, though. His mouth worked as if he were trying to bite back words fighting desperately to get out. Finally, as if coming to some inner decision, he nodded, blew out a breath and said, "For the sake of argument, let's say they are mine."

"They are."

"So why didn't you tell me before? Why the hell would you wait until they're, what…?"

"Four months old."

He looked at the pictures again, closed the book and held on to it in one tight fist. "Four months old and you didn't think I should know?"

So much for the tiny kernel of warmth she'd almost experienced.

"You're amazing. You ignore me for months and now you're upset that I didn't contact you?"

"What're you talking about?"

Jenna shook her head and silently thanked heaven that she'd been smart enough to not only keep a log of every e-mail she'd ever sent him, but had thought to print them all out and bring them along. Dipping back into the suitcase, she whipped a thick manila envelope out and laid it atop the scrapbook he was still holding. "There. E-mails. Every one I sent you. They're all dated. You can see that I sent one at least once a week. Sometimes twice. I've been trying to get hold of you for more than a year, Nick."

He opened the envelope as she talked, and flipped quickly through the printouts.

"I—" He frowned down at the stack of papers.

She took advantage of his momentary speechlessness. "I've been trying to reach you since I first found out I was pregnant, Nick."

"How was I supposed to know that *this* is what you were trying to tell me?"

"You might have read one or two of them," Jenna pointed out and managed to hide the hurt in her voice.

He scowled at her. "How the hell could I have guessed you were trying to tell me I was a father? I just thought you were after money."

She hissed in a breath as the insult of that slapped at her. Bubbling with fury, Jenna really had to fight the urge to give him a swift kick. How like Nick to assume that any woman who was with him was only in it for what she could get from him. But then, he'd spent most of the past ten years surrounding himself with the very users he'd suspected her of being. People who wanted to be seen with him because he was one of the world's most eligible billionaires. Those hangers-on wanted to be in his inner circle because that's where the excitement was and it made them feel important, to be a part of Nick's world.

All Jenna had wanted was his arms around her. His kiss. His whispers in the middle of the night. Naturally, he hadn't believed her.

Now things were different. He had responsibilities that she was here to see he stood up to. After all, she hadn't come here for herself. She'd come for her kids. For *his* sons.

"I wasn't interested in your money back then, Nick. But things have changed and now, I *am* after money," she said and saw sparks flare in his icy eyes. "It's called child support, Nick. And your sons deserve it."

He stared at her. "Child support."

"That's right." She lifted her chin even higher. "If I only had myself to think about, I wouldn't be here, believe me. So don't worry, I'm not here to take advantage of you. I'm not looking for a huge chunk of the Falco bank account."

"Is that right?"

"That's right. I started my own business and it's doing fine," she said, a hint of pride slipping into her tone while she spoke. "But twins make every expense doubled and I just can't do it all on my own." Lifting her gaze to meet his, she said, "When you never responded to my e-mails, I told myself you didn't deserve to know your babies. And if I weren't feeling a little desperate I wouldn't be here at all. Trust me, if you think I'm enjoying being here like this, you're crazy."

"So you would have hidden them from me?" His voice was low, soft and just a little dangerous.

Jenna wasn't worried. Nick might be an arrogant, self-satisfied jerk, but physically dangerous to her or any other woman, he wasn't. "If you mean would I hide the fact that their father couldn't care less about them from my sons…then, yes. That's just what I'll do."

"If they are my sons," he whispered, "no one will keep me from them."

A flicker of uneasiness sputtered in Jenna's chest, but she told herself not to react. Physical threats meant nothing, but the thought of him challenging her for custody of their children did. Even as she considered it, though, she let the worry dissipate. Babies weren't part of Nick's world, and no matter what he said at the moment, he would never give up the life he had for one that included double diaper duty.

"Nick, we both know you have no interest in being a father."

"You have no idea what I do or don't care about, Jenna." He moved in close, taking that one small step that brought his body flush to hers. Jenna hadn't been prepared for the move and sucked in a gulp of air as his chest pressed into hers.

She looked up into his eyes and felt her knees wobble a little at the intensity of his stare. He cupped her cheek in one hand, and the heat of his skin seeped into hers, causing a flush of warmth that slid through her like sweet syrup.

"I promise you, though," he murmured, dipping his head in as if he were going to kiss her and stopping just a breath away from her lips, "you will find out."

Three

She ducked her head and slapped his hand away and even *that* contact felt too damn good. Nick stepped back and away from her, which, in that cabin, meant that he was halfway out the door. So once he felt as though he could look at her without wanting to wrap his hands in her hair and pull her mouth to his, he shifted his gaze to hers.

"I don't have the time to go through this right now."

She smirked at him, folded her arms over her chest in a classic defensive posture. "Oh, sure, worlds to conquer, women to seduce. Busy, busy."

"Clever as ever, I see." He didn't even want to admit to himself how much he'd missed that smart mouth of hers. Always a retort. Always a dig, putting him in his place, deflating his ego before it had a chance to expand.

There weren't many people like Jenna in his life. Mostly, those he knew were too busy kissing his ass to argue with him. Everyone but Teresa, that is. And of course, Jenna. But she wasn't a part of his life anymore.

"We'll have dinner tonight. My suite."

"I don't think so."

"You came here to talk to me, right?"

"Yes, but—"

"So we'll talk. Seven o'clock."

Before she could argue, stall or whatever else might come into her too-quick mind, he opened the door and left her cabin. He took a breath in the dark hall, then headed for the elevator that would take him out of the bowels of the ship back into the light.

By five o'clock, she was more than ready to meet Mary for margaritas.

Jenna'd left her tiny, hideous, airless cabin only a few minutes after Nick had. Frankly, his presence had been practically imprinted on the minuscule space and had made the cabin seem even smaller than it actually was. And she hadn't thought that would have been possible.

But he'd shaken her more than she'd thought he would. Just being near him again had awakened feelings and emotions she'd trained herself more than a year ago to ignore. Now they were back and she wasn't sure how to handle them. After all, it wasn't as if she had a lot of experience with this sort of thing. Before Nick, there'd been only one other man in her life, and he hadn't come close to affecting her in the way Nick had. Of course, since Nick, the only men in her life preferred drooling on her shoulder to slow dances in the dark.

Just thinking about her boys brought an ache to Jenna's heart. She'd never left them before, and though she knew the twins were in good hands, she hated not being with them.

"But I'm on this boat for their sakes," she reminded herself sternly.

With that thought in mind, her gaze swept the interior of Captain Jack's Bar and Lounge. Like everywhere else on this ship, Nick hadn't skimped. The walls were pale wood that gleamed in the light glinting down on the crowd from overhead chandeliers shaped like ship's wheels. The bar was a slinky curve of pale wood with a granite top the color of molten honey.

Conversations flowed in a low rumble of sound that was punctuated by the occasional clink of crystal or a high-pitched laugh. First day at sea and already the party had begun.

Well, for everyone but Jenna. She hadn't exactly been in celebration mode after Nick left her cabin.

In fact, Jenna'd spent most of the day lying on a chaise on the Verandah Deck, trying to get lost in the book she'd picked up in the gift shop. But she couldn't concentrate on the words long enough to make any progress. Time and again, her thoughts had returned to Nick. His face. His eyes. The cool dismissal on his face when he'd first seen the pictures of their sons.

She didn't know what was coming next, and the worry over it had gnawed at her insides all day. Which was why she'd decided to keep her margarita date with Mary. Jenna had spent too much time alone today, with too much time for thinking. What she needed now was some distraction. A little tequila-flavored relaxation sounded great. Especially since she had dinner with Nick to look forward to.

"Oh God," she whispered as her stomach fisted into knots again.

"Jenna!"

A woman's voice called out to her, and Jenna turned in that direction. She spotted Mary, standing up at one of the tables along the wall, waving and smiling at her. Gratefully Jenna headed her way, threading a path through the milling crowd. When she reached the table, she slid onto a chair and smiled at the margarita already waiting for her.

"Hope you don't mind. I ordered one for you as soon as I got here," Mary told her, taking a big gulp of her own oversize drink.

"Mind?" Jenna said, reaching for her frosty glass, "Are you kidding? This is fabulous." When she'd taken a long, deep gulp of the icy drink, she sat back and looked at her new friend.

Mary was practically bouncing in her seat, and her eyes were shining with excitement. Her blond hair looked wind tousled and her skin was a pale red, as if she'd had plenty of sun today. "I've been looking for you all over this ship," she said, grinning like a loon. "I had to see you. Find out where they put you."

Jenna blinked and shook her head. "What do you mean? Put me? Where *who* put me?"

Mary stretched one hand out and grabbed Jenna's for a quick squeeze. "Oh my God. You haven't been back down to the pit all day, have you?"

"No way," Jenna said on a sigh. "After my meeting, I came topside and I've been putting off going back down by hanging out on the Verandah Deck."

"So you don't know."

"Know what?" Jenna was beginning to think that maybe Mary had had a few margaritas too many. "What're you talking about?"

"It's the most incredible thing. I really can't believe it myself and I've seen it." She slapped one hand to her pale blue blouse and groaned like she was in the midst of an orgasm.

"Mary…what is going on?"

"Right, right." The blonde picked up her drink, took a big gulp and said, "It happened early this afternoon. Joe and I were up on the Promenade, you know, looking at all the shops. Well," she admitted, "I was looking, Joe was being dragged reluctantly along behind me. And when we came out of the Crystal Candle—which you should really check out, they have some amazing stuff in there—"

Jenna wondered if there was a way to get Mary to stay on track long enough to tell her what was happening. But probably not, so she took a sip of her drink and prepared to wait it out. She didn't have to wait long.

"When we came out," Mary was saying, "there was a ship steward waiting for us. He said, 'Mr. and Mrs. Curran?' all official-sounding and for a second I wondered what we'd done wrong, but we hadn't done anything and so Joe says, 'What's this about?' and the steward only told us to go with him."

"Mary…"

Her new friend grinned. "I'm getting to it. Really. It's just that it's all so incredible—right." She waved one hand to let Jenna know she was back on track, then she went right back to her story. "The steward takes us up to the owner's suite—you know, Nick Falco?"

"Yeah," Jenna murmured. "I know who he is."

"Who in the English-speaking world doesn't?" Mary said on a laugh, then continued. "So we're standing there in the middle of a suite that looks like a palace or something and Nick Falco himself comes up to us, introduces himself and *apologizes* about our cabin in the pit."

"What?" Jenna just stared at the other woman, not sure what to make of all this.

"I know! I was completely floored, let me tell you. I was almost speechless and Joe can tell you that that almost never happens." She paused for another gulp of her drink and when she finished, held up one hand for the waitress to bring another. "So there we are and Mr. Falco's being so nice and so sincere about how he feels so badly about the state of the rooms on the Riviera Deck—and can you believe how badly misnamed that deck is?—and he *insists* on upgrading us."

"Upgrading?"

"Seriously upgrading," Mary said as she thanked the waitress for her fresh margarita. She waited until the server had disappeared with her empty glass before continuing. "So I'm happy, because hey, that tiny cabin is just so hideous. And I'm expecting a middle-grade cabin with maybe a porthole, which would be *great*. But that's not what we got."

"It's not?" Jenna set her glass down onto the table and watched as Mary's eyes actually sparkled even harder than they had been.

"Oh, no. Mr. Falco said that most of the cabins were already full, which is how we got stuck in those tiny ones in the first place. So he moved us into a *luxury suite!*"

"He did?"

"It's on the Splendor Deck. The same level as Mr. Falco's himself. And Jenna, our suite is amazing! It's bigger than my *house*. Plus, he said our entire cruise is on him. He's refunding what we paid for that hideous cabin and insisting that we pay *nothing* on this trip."

"Wow." Nick had always taken great pride in keeping his passengers happy, but this was…well, to use Mary's word, *amazing*. Cruise passengers usually looked forward to a bill at the end of a cruise that could amount to several hundred dollars. Oh, the food and accommodations were taken care of when you rented your cabin. But incidentals could really pile up on a person if they weren't paying attention.

By doing this, Nick had given Mary and her husband a cruising experience that most people would never know. Maybe there was more heart to the man than she'd once believed.

"He's just so nice," Mary was saying, stirring her slender straw through the icy confection of her margarita. "Somehow, I thought a man that rich and that famous and that playboylike would be sort of…I don't know, snotty. But he wasn't at all. He was really thoughtful and kind, and I can't believe this is all really happening."

"It's terrific, Mary," Jenna said sincerely. Even if she and Nick had their problems, she could respect and admire him for what he'd done for these people.

"I'm really hoping your upgrade will have you somewhere near us, Jenna. Maybe you should go and see a steward about it, find out where they're moving you."

"Oh," Jenna said with a shake of her head, "I don't think I'll be moving." She couldn't see Nick doing her any favors. Not with the hostility that had been spilled between them only a few hours ago. And though she was happy for Mary and her husband, Jenna wasn't looking forward to being the only resident on the lowest deck of the ship. Now it would not only be small and dark, but small and dark and creepy.

"Of course you will," Mary countered. "They wouldn't move us and *not* you. That wouldn't make any sense at all."

Jenna just smiled. She wasn't about to go into her past history with Nick at the moment. So there was nothing she could really say to her new friend, other than, "I'll find out when I go downstairs to change. I've got a dinner appointment in about," she checked her wristwatch, "an hour and a half. So let's just have our drinks and you can tell me all about your new suite before I have to leave."

Mary frowned briefly, then shrugged. "Okay, but if you haven't been upgraded, I'm going to be really upset."

"Don't be." Jenna smiled and, to distract her, asked, "Do you have a balcony?"

"Two!" Mary crowed a little, grinned like a kid on Christmas morning and said, "Joe and I are going to have dinner on one of them tonight. Out under the stars…mmm. Time for a little romance now that we're out of the pit!"

Romance.

As Mary talked about the plans she and her husband had made for a night of seduction, Jenna smiled. She wished her friend well, but as for herself, she'd tried romance and had gotten bitten in the butt for her trouble. Nope, she was through with the hearts-and-flowers thing. All she wanted now was Nick's assurance that he would do the right thing and allow her to raise her sons the way she wanted to.

Her cabin was locked.

"What the—" Jenna slid her key card into the slot, whipped it out again and…nothing. The red light on the lock still shone as if it was taunting her. She knew it wouldn't do any good, but still, she grabbed the door handle and twisted it hard before shaking it, as if she could somehow convince the damn thing to open for her.

But nothing changed.

She glanced over her shoulder at what had been the Curran cabin, but no help would be found there. The happy couple were comfortably ensconced in their floating palace. "Which is all fine and good for *them*," Jenna muttered. "But what about *me?*"

Giving up, she turned around, leaned back against her closed door and looked up and down the narrow, dark corridor. This was just great. Alone in the pit. No way to call for help. She'd have to go back topside and find a ship phone.

"Perfect. Just perfect." Her head was a little swimmy from the margaritas and her stomach was twisted in knots of expectation over the upcoming dinner with Nick, and now she couldn't even take a shower and change clothes. "This is going so well."

She stabbed the elevator button and when the door opened instantly, she stepped inside. The Muzak pumping through the speakers was a simply hideous orchestral rendition of "Stairway to Heaven" and didn't do a thing to calm her down.

Jenna exited onto the Promenade Deck and was instantly swallowed by the crowd of passengers wandering around the shops. The lobby area was done in glass and wood with a skylight installed in the domed ceiling overhead that displayed a blue summer sky studded with white, puffy clouds.

But she wasn't exactly on a sightseeing mission. She plowed through the crowd to a booth where one of Nick's employees stood ready to help passengers with answers to their questions. The man in the red shirt and white slacks wearing a name tag that read Jeff gave Jenna a welcoming smile as he asked, "How can I help you?"

She tried not to take her frustration out on him. After all, he was trying to help. "Hi, I'm Jenna Baker, and I'm in cabin 2A on the Riviera deck and—"

"Jenna Baker?" he interrupted her quickly, frowned a little, then checked a clipboard on the desk in front of him.

"Yes," she said, attempting to draw his attention back to her. "I just came from my cabin and my key card didn't work, so—"

"Ms. Baker," he said, his attitude changing from flirtatious and friendly to crisp professionalism. "There's a notation here asking that you be escorted to the Splendor Deck."

Where Mary's new cabin was. So Nick had upgraded Jenna, as well? Unexpected and frankly, a relief. A suite would be much more comfortable than the closet she'd been assigned.

But... "All of my things are still in my cabin, so I really need to get in there to pack and—"

"No, ma'am," Jeff said quickly, smiling again. "Your cabin was packed up by the staff and your luggage has already been moved. If you'll just take that elevator—" he paused to point at a bank of elevators opposite them "—to the Splendor Deck, you'll be met and directed to your new cabin."

Strange. She didn't know how she felt about someone else rooting through her things, but if it meant she could get into a shower, change clothes and get ready for her meeting with Nick, then she'd go with it. "Okay then, and, um, thanks."

"It's a pleasure, Ms. Baker. I hope you enjoy your stay with Falcon Cruises."

"Uh-huh." She waved distractedly and headed for the elevators. Not much chance of her enjoying her cruise when she was here to do battle with the King of Cruise Lines. Nope, the most she could hope for was getting out of the pit and into a nicer cabin courtesy of one Mr. Nick Falco.

When the elevator stopped on the Splendor Deck, Jenna stepped out into a wide, lushly carpeted hallway. The ceiling was tinted glass, open to the skies but dark enough to keep people from frying in direct sunlight. The walls were the color of rich cream and dotted with paintings of tropical islands, ships at sea and even simple ocean scenes with whitecaps that looked real enough to wet your fingers if you reached out to touch them.

The one thing she didn't see was someone to tell her where to go now that she was here. But almost before that thought formed in her mind, Jenna heard the sound of footsteps hurrying toward her. She turned and buried her surprise when she recognized Teresa Hogan, Nick's assistant.

"Jenna. It's good to see you," the older woman said, striding to her with long, determined steps. Her smile looked real, her sharp green eyes were warm and when she reached out a hand in welcome, Jenna was happy to take it.

"Nice to see you, too, Teresa." They'd met during that magical week with Nick more than a year ago.

Ordinarily, as just an assistant to the cruise director, Jenna never would have come into contact with the big boss's righthand woman. But as the woman having an affair with Nick, Jenna'd met Teresa almost right away.

Teresa had been friendly enough, until the truth about Jenna being one of Nick's employees had come out. Then the coolly efficient Teresa had drawn a line in the sand, metaphorically speaking. She chose to defend Nick and make sure Jenna never had the chance to get near him again.

At the time, it had made Jenna furious, now she could understand that loyalty. And even appreciate it in a way.

"How've you been?" Jenna smiled as she asked, determined to keep the friendly tone that Teresa had begun.

"Busy." The older woman shrugged. "You know the boss. He keeps us hopping."

"Yes," Jenna mused. "He always did."

A long, uncomfortable moment passed before Teresa said, "So, you know about the cabins on the Riviera Deck being sealed."

"That's why I'm here," Jenna said, shooting a glance up and down the long, empty hallway. "I saw Mary Curran earlier, she told me she and her husband had been upgraded. And then I went to my cabin and couldn't get in. Jeff at information sent me here."

"Good." Teresa nodded and her short, dark hair didn't so much as dip with the movement. She pointed behind Jenna to the end of the wide, plush hall. "The Currans' suite is right along there. And now if you'll come with me, I'll take you to your new cabin. We can talk as we go."

They headed off in the opposite direction of the Currans'. Walking toward the bow of the great ship, Jenna casually glanced at the artwork as she passed it and tried to figure out what was going on. Being escorted by the owner's assistant seemed unusual. Shouldn't a steward have been put in charge of seeing her to her new accommodations? But did it really matter? Jenna followed along in Teresa's wake, hurrying to keep up with the woman who seemed always to be in high gear.

"You can imagine," Teresa said over her shoulder, "that Nick was appalled to find out the cabins on the lowest deck had been rented."

"Appalled, huh?" Jenna rolled her eyes. Clearly Teresa was still faithful to the boss. "Then why rent them at all?"

Teresa's steps hitched a little as she acknowledged, "It was a mistake. The cabins below were supposed to have been sealed before leaving port for this maiden voyage. The person responsible for going against the boss's orders was reprimanded."

"Shot at dawn? Or just fired without references?" Jenna asked in a low-pitched voice.

Teresa stopped dead and Jenna almost ran right into her.

"Nick doesn't fire indiscriminately and you know it." Teresa lifted her chin pointedly as she moved to protect her boss. "*You* lied to him. That's why you were fired, Jenna."

A flush stole through her. Yes, she'd lied. She hadn't meant to, but that's what had happened. And she hadn't been able to find a way out of the lie once it had begun. Still, he might have listened to her once the bag was open and the cat was out.

"He could have let me explain," Jenna argued and met that cool green stare steadily.

Just for an instant the harsh planes of Teresa's expression softened a bit. She shook her head and blew out a breath. "Look, Nick's not perfect—"

"Quite the admission coming from you."

Teresa smiled tightly. "True. I do defend him. I do what I can to help him. He's a good boss. And he's been good to me. I'm not saying that how he handled the… situation with you was right—"

Jenna stopped her, holding up both hands. "You know what? Never mind. It was more than a year ago. It's over and done. And whatever Nick and I had has ended, too."

Teresa cocked her head to one side and looked at her thoughtfully. "You really think so, hmm?"

"Trust me on this," Jenna said as they started walking again. "Nick is *so* over me."

"If you say so." Teresa stopped in front of a set of double doors. Waving one hand at them as if she were a game show hostess displaying a brand-new refrigerator, she said, "Here we are. Your new quarters. I hope you like them."

"I'm sure they'll be great. Way better than the Riviera Deck anyway."

"Oh," Teresa said with a smile, "that's certainly a fair

statement. You go on in, your things have been unpacked. I'm sure I'll be seeing you again."

"Okay." Jenna stood in the hall and watched as
Teresa strode briskly down the long hallway. There was
something going on here, she thought, she just couldn't
quite puzzle it out yet.

Then she glanced at her wristwatch, saw she had
less than an hour to get ready for her dinner with Nick
and opened the door with the key card Teresa had given
her.

She walked inside, took a deep breath and almost
genuflected.

The room was incredible—huge, and sprawlingly
spacious, with glass walls that displayed a view of the
ocean that stretched out into infinity. The wide blue sky
was splashed with white clouds and the roiling sea reflected that deep blue back up at it.

Pale wood floors shone with an old gold gleam and
the furniture scattered around the room looked designed
for comfort. There was a fireplace on one wall, a wet
bar in the corner and what looked to be priceless works
of art dotting the walls. There were vases filled with
glorious arrangements of fresh flowers that scented the
air until she felt as if she were walking in a garden.

"This can't be my cabin," Jenna whispered, whipping her head from side to side as she tried to take in
everything at once. "Okay, sure, upgraded to a suite. But
this is the Taj Mahal of suites. There has to be a mistake,
that's all."

"There's no mistake," Nick said as he walked easily into the room and gave her a smile that even from across the room was tempting enough to make her gasp. "This is my suite and it's where you'll be staying."

Four

"You can't be serious." Jenna took one instinctive step back, but couldn't go anywhere unless she turned, opened the door and sprinted down that long hallway.

"Damn serious," he said, and walked toward her like a man with all the time in the world.

He wore a dark blue, long-sleeved shirt, open at the collar, sleeves rolled back to his elbows. His black slacks had a knife-sharp crease in them, and his black shoes shone. But it was his eyes that held her. That pale blue gaze fixed on her as if he could see straight through her. As if he were looking for all of her secrets and wouldn't give up the quest until he had them.

"Nick, this is a bad idea," she said, and silently congratulated herself on keeping her tone even.

"Why's that?" He spread both hands out and shrugged. "You came to my boat. You tell me I'm the father of your children and insist we have to talk. So now you're here. We can talk."

Talk. Yeah.

In a floating palace that looked designed for seduction. Meeting Nick in her tiny cabin hadn't exactly been easy, but at least down there, there'd been no distractions. No easy opulence. No sensory overload of beauty.

This was a bad idea. Jenna knew it. Felt it. And didn't have a single clue how to get out of it.

"We shouldn't be staying together," she said finally, and winced because even to her she sounded like a prissy librarian or something.

"We'll be staying in the same cabin. Not together. There's a difference." He was so close now all he had to do was reach out and he could touch her.

If he did, she'd be a goner though, and she knew it.

"What's the matter, Jenna?" he asked. "Don't trust yourself alone with me?"

"Oh, please." She choked out a half laugh that she desperately hoped sounded convincing. "Could you get over yourself for a minute here?"

He gave her a slow smile that dug out the dimple in his left cheek and lit wicked lights in his eyes. Jenna's stomach flip-flopped and her mouth went dry.

"I'm not the one having a problem."

Did he have to smell so good?

"No problem," she said, lifting her chin and forcing

herself to look him dead in the eye. "Trust me when I say all I want from you is what your kids deserve."

The smile on Nick's face faded away as her words slammed home. Was he a father? Were those twin boys his? He had to know. To do that, he needed some time with Jenna. He needed to talk to her, figure out what she was after, make a decision about where to go from here.

Funny, Nick had been waiting all afternoon to enjoy that look of stunned disbelief on Jenna's face when she first walked into his suite and realized that she'd be staying with him. Payback for how he must have looked when he'd first seen the photo of the babies she claimed were his sons. But he hadn't enjoyed it as much as he'd thought. Because there were other considerations. Bigger considerations.

His sons. Nick's insides twisted into knots that were beginning to feel almost familiar. Countless times during the day, he'd looked at the photo of the babies he still carried in his shirt pocket. Countless times he'd asked himself if it was really possible that he was a father.

And though he wasn't prepared to take Jenna's word for his paternity, he had to admit that it wasn't likely she'd have come here to the ship, signing up for a cruise if it wasn't true. Not that he thought she'd have any qualms about lying—she'd lied to him when she first met him after all—but *this* lie was too easily found out.

So he was willing to accept the possibility. Which left him exactly where? *That* was the question that had been circling in his mind all afternoon, and he was no closer to an answer now than he had been earlier.

He looked her up and down and could admit at least to himself that she looked damn good to him. Her dark blond hair was a little windblown, stray tendrils pulling away from her braid to lay against her face. Her eyes were wide and gleaming with suspicion, and, strangely enough, that didn't do a damn thing to mitigate the attraction he felt as he drew in a breath that carried her scent deep into his lungs.

"I'll stay here, but I'm not sleeping with you," she announced suddenly.

Nick shook his head and smiled. "Don't flatter yourself. I said you're staying in my suite, not my bed. As it happens, there are three bedrooms here besides my own. Your things have been unpacked in one of them."

She frowned a little and the flush of color in her cheeks faded a bit. "Oh."

"Disappointed?" Nick asked, feeling a quick jolt of something hot and reckless punch through him.

"Please," she countered quickly. "You're not exactly irresistible, Nick."

He frowned at that, but since he didn't actually believe her, he let it go.

"I'm actually grateful to be out of that hole at the bottom of the ship," she added, glancing around at the suite before shifting her gaze back to his. "And if staying here is the price I have to pay for your attention, then I'll pay."

One dark eyebrow lifted. "How very brave of you to put up with such appalling conditions as these."

"Look," Jenna told him, "if you don't mind, it's been

a long day. So how about you just tell me which room is mine so I can take a shower. Then we'll talk."

"Fine. This way." He turned, pointed and said, "Down that hall. First door on the left."

"Thanks."

"My bedroom's at the end of the hall on the right."

She stopped, looked back at him over her shoulder and said, "I'll make a note."

"You do that," he whispered as she left the room, shoulders squared, chin lifted, steps long and slow, as if she were being marched to her death.

His gaze dropped to the curve of her behind and something inside him stirred into life. Something he hadn't felt since the last time he'd seen Jenna. Something he'd thought he was long past.

He still wanted her.

Spinning around, Nick stalked across the room to the wide bank of windows that displayed an awe-inspiring view of the sea. His gaze locked on the horizon as he fought to control the raging tide of lust rising inside him.

Jenna Baker.

She'd turned him inside out more than a year ago. Ever since, he'd been haunted by memories of their time together until he wasn't sure if what he was remembering was real or just fevered imaginings offered by a mind that couldn't seem to let go of the woman who'd lied to him. And Nick wasn't a man to forget something like that. Now she was back again. Here, trapped on his ship in the middle of the ocean with nowhere to go to escape him.

Yes, they had plenty to talk about—and if her children were indeed his sons, then there were a lot of decisions to be made. But, he told himself as he shoved both hands into his slacks pockets and smiled faintly at the sunlight glinting on the vast expanse of the sea, there would be enough time for him to have her again.

To feel her under him. To lay claim to her body once more. To drive her past the edge of reason. Then, when he was satisfied that he'd gotten her out from under his skin, he'd kick her loose and she'd be out of his life once and for all. He wouldn't even allow her to be a memory this time.

In Neptune's Garden, the elegant restaurant on the Splendor Deck, Jenna watched as Nick worked the room.

As the owner of the ship, he wasn't exactly expected to mingle with the passengers, but Nick was an executive like no other. He not only mingled, he seemed to enjoy himself. And with her arm tucked through his, Jenna felt like a queen moving through an adoring crowd.

Again and again, as they walked to their table, Nick stopped to chat with people sitting at the white linen–covered tables. Making sure they were enjoying the ship, asking if there was anything they needed and didn't have, if there was anything that the crew could do to make their stay more pleasurable.

Of course the single women on board were more than anxious to meet the gorgeous, wealthy, eligible Nick Falco. And the fact that Jenna was on his arm didn't dissuade them from flirting desperately.

"It's a beautiful ship, Mr. Falco," one woman said with a sigh as she shook his hand. She tossed her thick black hair back over her shoulder and licked her lips.

"Thank you," he said, smiling at her and the two other women seated with her. "I'm happy you're enjoying yourselves. If there's anything you need, please be sure to speak to a steward."

"Oh," the brunette cooed, "we will. I promise."

Jenna just managed to keep from rolling her eyes. All three women were looking at Nick as if he were the first steak they'd stumbled on after leaving a spa dinner of spinach leaves and lemon slices. And he was eating it up, of course.

When he turned to go, he led her on through the crowd and Jenna swore she could feel the death stare from those women boring into her back.

"Well, that was tacky," she murmured.

"Tacky?"

"The way she practically drooled on you."

"Ah," Nick said, flashing a quick grin at her as he opened his right hand—the hand the brunette had shaken and clung to. A cabin key card rested in the center of his palm and the number P230 was scrawled across the top in ink. "So I'm guessing this makes it even tackier."

"Oh, for God's sake," Jenna snapped, wanting to spin around and shoot a few daggers at the brunette with no class. "I was *with* you. For all she knew I was your girlfriend."

His pale blue eyes sparkled and his grin widened

enough that the dimple in his left cheek was a deep cleft. "Jealous?"

She tried to pull her hand free of the crook of his arm, but he held her tight. Frowning, she said, "No. Not jealous. Just irritated."

"By her? Or by me?"

"A little of both." She tipped her head back to look up at him. "Why didn't you give the key back to her?"

He looked genuinely surprised at the suggestion. "Why would I embarrass her in front of her friends?"

Jenna snorted indelicately. "I'm guessing it's next to impossible to embarrass a woman like *that*."

"This really bothers you."

It always had, she thought. When she first went to work for Falcon Cruise Lines, she'd heard all the stories. About how on every cruise there were women lining up to take their place in Nick's bed. He was a player, no doubt. But for some reason, Jenna had allowed herself to be swept up in the magic of the moment. She'd somehow convinced herself that what they'd had together was different from what he found with countless other women.

Apparently, she'd been wrong about a few things.

"One question," she said, keeping her voice low enough that no one they passed could possibly overhear.

"Okay."

"Are you planning on using that key?"

He only looked at her for a long moment or two, then sighing, he stopped a waiter, handed over the key card and whispered something Jenna didn't quite catch. Then he turned to her. "That answer your question?"

"Depends," she said. "What did you tell him?"

"To return the card to the brunette with my thanks and my regrets."

A small puddle of warmth settled in Jenna's chest and even though she knew it was foolish, she couldn't quite seem to quash it. "Thank you."

He dipped his head in a faint mockery of a bow. "I find there's only one woman I'm interested in talking to at the moment."

"Nick…"

"Here we are," he said, interrupting whatever she would have said as he seated her in the navy blue leather booth that was kept reserved for him. "Jenna, let's have some dinner and get started on that talk you wanted."

Jenna slid behind the linen-draped table and watched him as he moved around to take a seat beside her. "All right, Nick. First let me ask you something, though."

"What?"

"All the people you talked to as we came through the restaurant…all the women you flirted with…" Jenna shook her head as she looked at him. "You haven't changed a bit, have you?"

His features tightened as he looked at her, and in the flickering light of the single candle in the middle of their table, his eyes looked just a little dangerous. "Oh, I've changed some," he told her softly, and the tone of his voice rippled across her skin like someone had spilled a glass of ice water on her. "These days I'm a little more careful who I spend time with. I don't take a woman's word for it anymore when she tells me who she is. Now

I check her out. Don't want to run across another liar, after all."

Jenna flushed. She felt the heat of it stain her skin and she was grateful for the dim lighting in the restaurant. Folding her hands together in her lap, she looked at the snowy expanse of the table linen and said, "Okay, I'm going to say this again. I didn't set out to lie to you back then, Nick."

"So it just happened?"

"Well," she said, lifting her gaze reluctantly to his, "yes."

"Right." He nodded, gave her a smirk that came nowhere near being a real smile and added, "Couldn't figure out a way to tell me that you actually worked for me, so you just let it slide. Let me think you were a passenger."

Yes, she had. She'd been swept away by the moonlight and the most gorgeous man she'd ever seen in her life. "I never said I was. You assumed I was a passenger."

"And you said nothing to clear that up."

True. All true. If she'd simply told the truth, then their week together never would have happened. She never would have known what it was like to be in his arms. Never would have imagined a future of some kind between them. Never would have gotten pregnant. Never would have given birth to the two little boys she couldn't imagine living without.

Because of that, it was hard to feel guilty about what she'd done.

"Nick, let's not rehash the past, all right? I said I

was sorry at the time. I can't change anything. And you know, you didn't exactly act like Prince Charming at the time, either."

"You're blaming me?"

"You wouldn't even talk to me," she reminded him. "You found out the truth and shut me out and down so fast I was half surprised you didn't have me thrown overboard to swim home."

He shifted uncomfortably, worked his jaw as if words were clamoring to get out and he was fighting the impulse to shout them. "What did you expect me to do?"

"All I wanted was to explain myself."

"There was nothing you could have said."

"Well," she said softly, "we'll never know for sure, will we?" Then she sighed and said, "We're not solving anything here, so let's just let the past go, okay? What happened, happened. Now we need to talk about what *is.*"

"Right." He signaled to a waiter, then looked at her again. "So let's talk. Tell me about your sons."

"*Your* sons," she corrected, lifting her chin a little as if readying to fight.

"That's yet to be proved to me."

"Why would I lie?"

"Hmm. Interesting question," he said. "I could say you've lied before, but then we've already agreed not to talk about the past."

Jenna wasn't sure if she wanted to sigh in frustration or kick him hard under the table. This was so much more difficult than she'd thought it would be. Somehow,

Jenna had convinced herself that Nick would believe her. That he would look at the pictures of the babies and somehow *know* instinctively that these were his sons. She should have known better.

All around them the clink of fine crystal and the muted conversations of the other diners provided a background swell of sound that was more white noise than anything else. Through the windows lining one side of the restaurant, the night was black and the sea endless. The shimmer of colored lights hanging from the edges of the deck looked almost like a rainbow that only shone at night.

And beside her, the man who'd haunted her dreams and forged a new life for her sat waiting, watchful.

As she started to speak, a waiter approached with a bottle of champagne nestled inside a gleaming silver bucket. Jenna closed her mouth and bit her lip as the waiter poured a sip of the frothy wine into a flute and presented it to Nick for tasting. Approved, the wine was then poured first for her, then for Nick. Once the waiter had disappeared into the throng again, Jenna reached for her champagne and took a sip, hoping to ease the sudden dryness in her throat.

"So?" Nick prodded, his voice a low rumble of sound that seemed to slide inside her. "Tell me about the twins."

"What do you want to know?"

He shot her a look. "Everything."

Nodding, Jenna took a breath. Normally, she was more than happy to talk about her sons. She'd even been known to bore complete strangers in the grocery store with tales of their exploits. But tonight was different. Important. This was the father of her children. She had to make him understand that. Believe it. So choosing her words carefully, she started simply and said, "Their names are Jacob and Cooper."

He frowned a little and took a sip of his own champagne. "Family names?"

"My grandfathers," she said, just a touch defensively as if she was prepared to go toe to toe with him to guard her right to name her sons whatever she wanted.

"That was nice of you," he said after a second or two and took the wind out of her sails. "Go on."

While around them people laughed and talked and relaxed together, a tight knot of tension coiled about their table. Jenna's voice was soft, Nick leaned in closer to hear her and his nearness made her breath hitch in her chest.

"Jacob's sunny and happy all the time. He smiles from the minute he wakes up until the moment I put him down for the night." She smiled, too, just thinking of her babies. "Cooper's different. He's more…thoughtful, I guess. His smiles are rarer and all the more precious because of it. He's always watching. Studying. I'd love to know what he's thinking most of the time because even at four months, he seems almost a philosopher."

His gaze was locked on her and Jenna could see both of her sons in Nick's face. They looked so much like him, she couldn't understand how he could doubt even for a moment that they were his.

"Where are they now?"

"My sister Maxie's watching them." And was probably harried and exhausted. "The boys are crazy about her and she loves them both to death. They're fine."

"Then why did you get tense all of a sudden?"

She blew out a breath, slumped back against the booth and admitted, "It's the first time I've been away from them. It feels...wrong, somehow. And I miss them. A lot."

His eyes narrowed on her and he picked up his glass for a sip of wine. Watching her over the rim of the glass, he swallowed, then set the flute back onto the table. "Can't be easy, being a single mother."

"No, it's not," she admitted, thinking now about just how tired she was every night by the time she had the boys in bed. It had been so long since she'd been awake past eight o'clock at night that it was odd to her now, sitting here in a restaurant at nine. This was what it had been like before, though. When she'd only had herself to worry about. When she hadn't had two little boys depending on her.

God, how had she ever been able to stand the quiet? The emptiness in her little house? She couldn't even imagine being without her sons now.

"But," she added when he didn't say anything else, "along with all the work, a single mom gets all the perks to herself, too. I don't have to share the little moments. I'm the one to see them smile for the first time. To see them waking up to the world around them."

"So since you're not looking to share the good moments, that means you're not interested in having me involved in the twins' lives," he said thoughtfully. "All you really want is child support?"

She stiffened a little. Jenna hadn't even considered that Nick might want to be drawn into their sons' lives. He wasn't the hearth-and-home kind of guy. He was the party man. The guy you dated, but didn't bring home to mom.

"You and I both know you don't have any interest in being a father, Nick."

"Is that right? And how would you know that?"

"Well—"

He inclined his head at her speechlessness. "Exactly. You don't know me any more than I know you."

"You're wrong. I know that you're not the kind of man to tie himself down in one place. That week we were together you told me yourself you had no plans to ever get married and settle down."

"Who said anything about getting married?"

Jenna sucked in a breath and told herself to slow down. She was walking through a minefield here. "I didn't mean—"

"Forget it," he said.

Another waiter appeared, this time delivering a dinner that Nick had clearly ordered earlier. Surprised, Jenna looked down at the serving of breast of chicken and fettucine in mushroom sauce before lifting her gaze to his in question.

"I remembered you liked it," he said with a shrug.

What was she supposed to do with that? She wondered. He pretended to not care anything about her, yet he remembered more than a year later what her favorite foods were? Why? Why would he recall something so small?

Once the waiter was gone, Nick started talking again. "So answer me this. When you found out you were pregnant, why'd you go through with it?"

"Excuse me?"

He shrugged. "You were alone. A lot of women in that position wouldn't have done what you did. Giving birth, deciding to raise the babies on her own."

"They were mine," she said, as if that explained everything, and in her mind it did. Never for a moment had she considered ending her pregnancy. She'd tried to reach Nick of course, but when she couldn't, she'd hunkered down and started building a life for her and her children.

"No regrets?"

"Only the one about coming on this ship," she muttered.

He smiled faintly, laid his napkin across his lap and, picking up his knife and fork, sliced into his filet mignon. "I heard that."

"I meant you to." As Jenna used her fork to slide the fettucine noodles around her plate, she said, "Nick, my sons are the most important things in the world to me. I'll do whatever I have to to make sure they're safe."

"Good for you."

She took a bite of her dinner and, though she could tell it was cooked to perfection, the delicate sauce and chicken tasted like sawdust in her mouth.

"I'll want a DNA test."

"Of course," she said. "I've already had the boys' blood tests done at a local lab. You can send your sample in to them and they'll do the comparison testing."

"I'll take care of it tomorrow."

"What?" She shook her head, looked at him and said, "Don't you have to wait until we're back in San Pedro?"

"No, I'm not going to wait. I want this question settled as quickly as possible." He continued to eat, as though what they were discussing wasn't affecting him in the slightest. "We dock at Cabo in the morning. You and I will go ashore, find a lab and have them fax the findings to the lab in San Pedro."

"We will?" She hadn't planned on spending a lot of time with Nick, after all. She'd only come on board to tell him about the boys and frankly, she'd thought he wouldn't want anything more to do with her after that. Instead, he'd moved her into his suite and now was proposing that they spend even more time together.

"Until this is taken care of to my satisfaction," Nick told her softly, "I'm not letting you out of my sight. The two of us are going to be joined at the hip. So you might as well start getting used to it."

Five

Once the ship had docked and most of the passengers had disembarked for their day of shopping, sailing and exploring the city of Cabo San Lucas, Nick got busy. He'd already had Teresa make a few calls, and the lab at the local hospital was expecting them.

The sun was hot and bright and the scent of the sea greeted them the moment he and Jenna stepped out on deck. Ordinarily Nick would have been enjoying this. He loved this part of cruising. Docking in a port, exploring the city, revisiting favorite sites, discovering new ones.

But today was different. Today he was on a mission, so he wasn't going to notice the relaxed, party atmosphere of Cabo. Just as he wasn't going to notice the way Jenna's pale green sundress clung to her body or the way her legs looked in those high-heeled sandals. He had no interest in the fact that her dark blond hair looked like spilled honey as it flowed down over her shoulders and he really wasn't noticing her scent or the way it seemed to waft its way to him on the slightest breeze.

Having her stay in his suite had seemed like a good idea yesterday. But the knowledge that she was so close, that she was just down the hall from him, alone in her bed, had taunted him all night long. Now his eyes felt gritty, his temper was too close to the surface and his body was hard and achy.

Way to go, Falcon, he told himself.

"So where are we going?" she asked as he laid his hand at the small of her back to guide her down the gangplank to shore. Damn, just the tips of his fingers against her spine was enough to make him want to forget all about this appointment and drag her back to his cabin instead.

Gritting his teeth, he pushed that image out of his mind.

"Teresa called the hospital here," he muttered. "The lab's expecting us. They'll take a DNA sample, run it and fax the results to your lab. We should have an answer in a day or two."

She actually stumbled and he grabbed her arm in an instinctive move. "That fast?"

"Money talks," he said with a shrug. He'd learned long ago that with enough money, a man could accomplish anything. Way of the world. And for the first time, he was damned glad he was rich enough to demand fast action. Nick wanted this question of paternity settled.

Like now. He couldn't stop thinking about those babies. Couldn't seem to stop looking at the picture she'd given him of them.

Couldn't stop wondering how their very existence was going to affect—change—his life. So he needed to know if he was going to be a father or if he was simply going to be suing Jenna Baker for everything she had for lying to him. Again.

Her heels clicked against the gangway and sounded like a frantic heartbeat. He wondered if she was nervous. Wondered if she really was lying and was now worried about being found out. Had she thought he'd simply accept her word that her sons belonged to him? Surely not.

At the bottom of the gangway, a taxi was waiting. Silently blessing Teresa's efficiency, Nick opened the door for Jenna, and when she was inside, slid in after her. In short, sharp sentences spoken in nearly fluent Spanish, Nick told the driver where to go.

"I didn't know you spoke Spanish," she said as he settled onto the bench seat beside her.

"There's a lot about me you don't know," he said.

"I guess so."

Of course, the same could be said about what he knew of her. He remembered clearly their time together more than a year before. But in those stolen moments, he'd been more intent on burying himself inside her than discovering her thoughts, her hopes, her dreams. He'd told himself then that there would be plenty of time for them to discover each other. He couldn't have

guessed that in one short week he'd find her, want her
and then lose her.

Yet, even with the passion simmering between them,
Nick could recall brief conversations when she'd talked
about her home, her family. He'd thought at the time that
she was different from the other women he knew. That
she was more sincere. That she was more interested in
him, the man, than she was in what he was. How much
he had.

Of course, that little fantasy had been exploded
pretty quickly.

He dropped into silence again as the cab took off.
He didn't want to talk to her. Didn't want to think about
anything but what he was about to do. With a simple
check of his DNA, his life could be altered irrevocably
forever. His chest was tight and his mind was racing.
Cabo was no more than a colorful blur outside his window as they headed for the lab and a date with destiny.

In a few seconds the cab was swallowed by the
bustling port city. At the dock and on the main drive that
ran along the ocean, Cabo San Lucas was beautiful. The
hotels, the restaurants and bars, everything was new
and shone to perfection, the better to tempt the tourists
who streamed into the city every year.

But just a few short blocks from the port and Cabo
was a big city like any other. The streets were crowded
with cars, and pedestrians leaped off the sidewalks and
ran across the street with complete abandon, trusting
that the drivers would somehow keep from running
them down. Narrower, cobblestoned side streets spilled

off the bigger avenues and from there came the tantalizing scents of frying onions, spices and grilling meat.

Restaurants and bars crowded together, their chipped stucco facades looking a little tattered as tourists milled up and down the sidewalks, cameras clutched in sunburned fists. As the cab driver steered his car through the maze of traffic, Nick idly glanced out the window and noted the open-air markets gathered together under dark green awnings. Under that umbrella were at least thirty booths where you could buy everything from turquoise jewelry to painted ceramic burros.

Cabo was a tourist town and the locals did everything they could to keep those vacation dollars in the city.

"Strange, isn't it?" she mused, and Nick turned his head to look at her. She was staring out her window at the city and he half wondered if she was speaking to him or to herself. "All of the opulence on the beach and just a few blocks away…"

"It's a city, like any other," he said.

She turned her head to meet his gaze. "It's just a little disappointing to see the real world beneath the glitz."

"There's always a hidden side. To everything. And everyone," he said, staring into her eyes, wondering what she was feeling. Wondering why he even cared.

"What's hidden beneath your facade, then?" she asked.

Nick forced a smile. "I'm the exception to the rule," he told her. "What you see is what you get with me. There are no hidden depths. No mysteries to be solved. No secrets. No lies."

Her features tightened slightly. "I don't believe that," she said. "You're not as shallow as you pretend to be, Nick. I remember too much to buy into that."

"Then your memory is wrong. Don't look for something that isn't there, Jenna," he said softly, just in case their driver spoke English. "I'm not a lonely rich boy looking for love." He leaned in toward her, keeping his gaze locked with hers, and added, "I'm doing this DNA test for my own sake. If those babies are mine, then I need to know. But I'm not the white-picket-fence kind of guy. So don't go building castles in the air. You'll get trapped in the rubble when they collapse."

Jenna felt a chill as she looked into those icy blue eyes of his. All night she'd lain in her bed, thinking about him, wondering if she'd done the right thing by coming to Nick. By telling him about their sons. Now she was faced with the very real possibility that she'd made a huge mistake.

Once he was convinced that the boys were his, then what? Would he really be satisfied with writing out a child support check every month? Or would he demand time with his children? And if he did, how would she fit him into their lives?

Picturing Nick spending time in her tiny house in Seal Beach was almost impossible. His lifestyle was so far removed from hers they might as well be from different planets.

"Nick," she said, "I know there's a part of you that thinks I'm lying about all of this. But I'm not." She paused, watched his reaction and didn't see a thing that made her feel any better, so she continued. "So, before you take this DNA test, I want you to promise me something."

He laughed shortly, but there wasn't a single spark of humor lighting his eyes. "Why would I do that?"

"No reason I can think of, but I'm still asking."

"What?" he asked, sitting back, dropping one hand to rest on his knee. "What's this promise?"

She tried again to read his expression, but his features were shuttered, closing her out so completely it was as if she were alone in the cab. But he was listening and that was something, she supposed.

"I want you to promise me that whatever happens, you won't take out what you feel for me on our sons."

He tipped his head to one side, studied her for a long moment or two, then as she held her breath, waiting for his response, he finally nodded. "All right. I give you my word. What's between you and me won't affect how I treat your sons."

Jenna gave him a small smile. "Thank you."

"But if they *are* my sons," he added quietly, "you and I have a lot of talking to do."

The DNA test was done quickly, and before she knew it, Jenna and Nick were back in the cab, heading for the docks again. Her stomach was churning as her mind raced, and being locked inside a car hurtling down a crowded street wasn't helping. She needed to walk. Needed to breathe. Needed to escape the trapped feeling that held her in a tight grip.

Turning to Nick, she blurted suddenly, "Can we get out? Walk the rest of the way to the dock?"

He glanced at her, and whatever he saw in her face must have convinced him because he nodded, then spoke to the driver in Spanish. A moment later the cab pulled to the curb. Jenna jumped out of the car as if she were on springs and took a deep breath of cool, ocean air while Nick paid their fare.

Tourists and locals alike crowded the sidewalk and streamed past her as if she were a statue. She tucked her purse under her left arm and turned her face into the breeze sliding down the street from the sea.

"It's still several blocks to the ship," Nick said as he joined her on the sidewalk. "You going to be able to make it in those shoes?"

Jenna glanced down at the heeled sandals she wore then lifted her gaze back to his. "I'll make it. I just— needed to get out of that cab and move around a little."

"I don't remember you being so anxious," he said.

She laughed a little and sounded nervous even to herself. "Not anxious, really. It's just that since the boys were born, I'm not used to being still. They keep me running all day long, and sitting in the back of that cab, I felt like I was in a cage or something and it didn't help that neither one of us was talking and we'd just come from the lab, so my brain was in overdrive and—"

He interrupted the frantic flow of words by holding up one hand. "I get it. And I could use some air, too. So why don't we start walking?"

"Good. That'd be good." God, she hadn't meant to go on a stream of consciousness there. If he hadn't stopped her, heaven only knew what would have come out of her mouth. As it was, he was looking at her like she was a stick of dynamite with a burning fuse.

He took her arm to turn her around, and the sizzle of heat that sprang up from his touch was enough to boil her blood and make her gasp for air. So not a good sign.

Music spilled from the open doorway of a cantina and a couple of drunk, college-age tourists stumbled out onto the sidewalk. Nick pulled Jenna tight against him and steered her past them, but when they were in the clear, he didn't release her. Not that she minded.

"So what's a typical day for you now?" he asked as they moved along the sidewalk, a part of, yet separate from, the colorful crowd of locals and tourists.

"Typical?" Jenna laughed in spite of the fact that every nerve ending was on fire and lit from within due to Nick's arm wrapped tightly around her waist. "I learned pretty quickly that with babies in the house there's no such thing as typical."

She risked a glance at him, and his blue eyes connected with hers for a heart-stopping second. Then he nodded and said, "Okay, then describe one of your un-typical days for me."

"Well, for one thing, my days start a lot earlier than they used to," she said. "The twins sleep through the night now, thank God, but they're up and raring to go by six every morning."

"That can't be easy." His arm around her waist loosened a bit, but he didn't let her go and Jenna felt almost as if they were a real couple. Which was just dangerous thinking.

"No," she said quickly, to rein her imagination back in with cold, dry facts. Their lives were so different, he'd never be able to understand what her world was like. He woke up when he felt like it, had breakfast brought to his room and then spent the rest of his day wandering a plush cruise ship, making sure his guests were happy.

She, on the other hand…

"There are two diapers that need changing, two little bodies who need dressing and two mouths clamoring for their morning bottle. There are two cribs in the room they share and I go back and forth between them, sort of on autopilot." She smiled to herself as images of her sons filled her mind. Yes, it was a lot of work. Yes, she was tired a lot of the time. And no, she wouldn't change any of it.

"How do you manage taking care of two of them?"

"You get into a rhythm," she said with a shrug that belied just how difficult it had been to *find* that rhythm. "Cooper's more patient than his brother, but I try not to use that as an excuse to always take care of Jacob first. So, I trade off. One morning I deal with Cooper first thing and the next, it's Jacob's turn. I feed one, then the other and then get them into their playpen so I can start the first of the day's laundry loads."

"You leave them alone in a playpen?"

Instantly defensive, Jenna shot him a glare. "They're safe and happy and it's not as if I just toss them into a cage and go off to party. I'm right there with them. But I have to be able to get things done and I can't exactly leave them on the floor unattended, now, can I?"

"Hey, hey," he said, tightening his grip around her waist a little. "That wasn't a criticism…"

She gave him a hard look.

"Okay," he acknowledged, "maybe it was. But I didn't mean it to be. Can't be easy. A single mother with two babies."

"No, it's not," she admitted and her hackles slowly lowered. "But we manage. We have playtime and the two of them are so bright and so interested in everything…." She shook her head. "It's amazing, really, watching them wake up to the world a little more each day."

"Must be."

He was saying the right things, but his tone carried a diffidence she didn't much like. But then how could she blame him? He didn't believe yet that the boys were his sons. Of course, he would hold himself back, refusing to be drawn in until it had been proven to him that he was their father.

"When they take their naps, I work."

"Yeah," he said, guiding her around a pothole big enough to swallow them both, "you said you had your own business. What do you do?"

"Gift baskets," she said, lifting her chin a little. "I design and make specialty gift baskets. I have a few corporate clients, and I get a lot of business over the Internet."

"How'd you get into that?" he asked, and Jenna was almost sure he really was interested.

"I started out by making them up for friends. Birthdays, baby showers, housewarming, that sort of thing," she said. "It sort of took off from there. People started asking me to make them baskets, and after a while I realized I was running a business. It's great, though, because it lets me be home with the boys."

"And you like that."

Not a question, a statement. She stopped walking, looked up at him and said, "Yes, I like it. I couldn't bear the thought of the boys being in day care. I want to be the one to see all of their firsts. Crawling, walking, speaking. I want to hear their giggles and dry their tears. I want to be at the heart of their lives."

He studied her for a long minute or two, his gaze moving over her face as if he were trying to imprint her image on his mind. Or trying to read her thoughts to see if she had really meant everything she just said.

"Most women wouldn't want to be trapped in a house with two screaming babies all day," he finally said.

Instantly Jenna bristled. "*A*, the women you know aren't exactly the maternal type, now, are they? *B*, the boys don't scream all day and *C*, spending time with my kids isn't a trap. It's a gift. One I'm thankful for every single day. You don't know me, Nick. So don't pretend you do."

One dark eyebrow lifted, and an amused glint shone in those pale eyes of his. "I wasn't trying to insult you," he said softly. "I…admire what you're doing. What you feel for your sons. All I meant was, that what you said was nice to hear."

"Oh." Well, didn't she feel like an idiot? "I'm sorry. I guess I'm a little quick on the trigger."

"A little?" He laughed shortly, and started walking again, keeping his arm locked about her waist as if concerned she might wander off. "The words *Mother Grizzly* come to mind."

Even Jenna had to chuckle. "You're right, you know. I learned the moment the boys were born. I was so electrified just by looking at them…to know they'd come from me. It's an amazing feeling. Two tiny boys— one minute they're not there, and the next, they're breathing and crying and completely capturing my heart. I fell in love so completely, so desperately, that I knew instantly I would never allow anyone or anything to hurt them. *Nobody* criticizes my kids. Nobody."

"Yeah," he said, with a thoughtful look in his eyes. "I get it."

His hand at her waist flexed and his fingers began to rub gently, and through the thin fabric of her summery dress, Jenna swore she could feel his skin on hers. Her heartbeat jumped into high gear, and her breathing was labored. Meeting his gaze, she saw confusion written there and she had to ask, "What is it? What's wrong?"

Quickly he said, "Nothing. It's just…" He stopped, though, before he could explain. Then, shaking his head, he said, "Come on, we've still got a long walk ahead of us."

A half hour later Jenna's feet were aching and she was seriously regretting jumping out of that cab. But there were compensations, too. Such as walking beside Nick, his arm around her waist as if they were really a couple. She knew she should step out of his grasp, but truthfully, she was enjoying the feel of him pressed closely to her too much to do it.

It had been so long since their week together. And in the time since, she hadn't been with anyone else. Well, she'd been pregnant for a good part of that time, so not much chance of hooking up with someone new. But even if she hadn't been, she wouldn't have been looking. Nick had carved himself into her heart and soul in that one short week and had made it nearly impossible for her to think about being with anyone else.

Which was really too bad when she thought about it. Because he'd made it clear they weren't going to be getting together again. Not that she wanted that, or anything….

"Oh!" She stopped suddenly as they came abreast of the street market they'd passed on their way to the lab. An excellent way to clear her mind of any more disturbing thoughts of Nick. "Let's look in here."

Frowning some, like any man would when faced with a woman who wanted to shop, Nick said, "What could you possibly want to buy here? It's a tourist trap."

"That's what makes it fun," she told him, and slipped out of his grasp to walk beneath the awning and into the aisle that wound its way past at least thirty different booths.

She wandered through the crowd, sensing Nick's presence behind her. She glanced at tables set up with sterling silver rings and necklaces, leather coin purses and crocheted shawls that hung in colorful bunches from a rope stretched across the front of a booth. She smiled at the man selling tacos and ignored the rumbling of her stomach as she moved on to a booth selling T-shirts.

Nick came up behind her and looked over her head at the display of tacky shirts silk-screened with images of Cabo, sport fishing and the local cantinas. Shaking his head at the mystery that was women, he wondered why in the hell she'd chosen to shop here.

"Need a new wardrobe?" he asked, dipping his head so that his voice whispered directly into her ear.

She jumped a little, and he enjoyed the fact that he made her nervous. He'd felt it all day. That hum of tension simmering around her. When he touched her, he felt the heat and felt her response that fed the fires burning inside him. The moment he'd wrapped his arm around her waist, he'd known it was a mistake. But the feel of her body curved against his had felt good enough that he hadn't wanted to let her go.

Which irritated the hell out of him.

He'd learned his lesson with her a year ago. She'd lied to him about who she was. Who was to say she hadn't lied about her response to him? Wasn't lying still? But even as he thought that, he wondered if anyone could manufacture the kind of heat that spiraled up between them when their bodies brushed against each other.

"The shirts aren't for me," she was saying, and Nick pushed his thoughts aside to pay attention. "I thought maybe there'd be something small enough for the boys to—here!"

She pulled a shirt out from a stack and it was so

small, Nick could hardly believe that it could actually be worn. There was a grinning cartoon burro on the front and the words Baby Burros Need Love Too stenciled underneath it. "It's so cute! Don't you think so?"

Nick's breath caught hard in his chest as she turned her face up to his and smiled so brightly the shine in her eyes nearly blinded him. He'd given women diamonds and seen less of a display of joy. If this was an act, he thought, she should be getting an Oscar.

"Yeah," he said. "I guess it is." Then he looked past her to the woman who ran the booth and in Spanish told her they'd be needing two of the shirts.

Smiling, the woman found another matching shirt, dropped them both in a sack and held them out. Nick paid for the shirts before Jenna could dig in her purse. Then he took hold of her hand and, carrying the bag, led her back out onto the street.

"You didn't have to buy them," she told him once they were on their way to the dock again.

"Call it my first present to my sons."

She stumbled a little and he tightened his hold on her hand, steadying her even while he felt his own balance getting shaky.

"So you believe me?"

Nick felt a cold, hard knot settle into the pit of his stomach. He looked into Jenna's eyes and couldn't find the slightest sign of deception. Was she too good at hiding her secrets? Or were there no secrets to hide? Soon enough, he'd know for sure. But for now "I'm starting to."

Six

Three days later the ship docked in Acapulco.

"Oh, come on," Mary Curran urged, "come ashore with Joe and me. He's going scuba diving of all things, and I'd love some company while I spend all the money we saved by having this cruise comped."

Laughing, Jenna shook her head and sat back on the sofa in the living room of Nick's spectacular suite. "No, thanks. I think I'm going to stay aboard and relax."

Mary sighed in defeat. "How you can relax when you're staying in this suite with Nick Falco is beyond me. Heck, I've been married for twenty years and just looking at the guy gives me hot flashes."

Jenna knew just what her friend meant. For the past few days she and Nick had been practically in each other's pockets. They'd spent nearly every minute together, and when they were here in this suite, the spacious accommodations seemed to shrink to the size of a closet.

Jenna felt as if she were standing on a tight wire, uneasily balanced over a vat of lava. She was filled with heat constantly and knew that with the slightest wrong move, she could be immolated.

God, great imagery.

"Hello? Earth to Jenna?"

"Sorry." Jenna smiled, pushed one hand through her hair and blew out an unsteady breath. "Guess my mind was wandering."

"Uh-huh, and I've got a good idea where it wandered *to*."

"What?"

"Oh, honey, you've got it bad, don't you?" Mary leaned forward and squeezed Jenna's hand briefly.

Embarrassed and just a little concerned that Mary might be right, Jenna immediately argued. "I don't know what you mean."

"Sure you don't." Mary's smile broadened. "I say Nick's name and your eyes flash."

"Oh God…"

"Hey, what's the trouble? You're both single. And you're clearly attracted to each other. I mean, I saw Nick's face last night at dinner whenever he looked at you."

The four of them had had dinner together the night before, and though Jenna had been sure it would be an uncomfortable couple of hours—given the tension between her and Nick—they'd all had a good time. In fact, seeing Nick interacting with Joe Curran, hearing him laugh and tell stories about past cruises had really opened Jenna's eyes.

For so long, she'd thought of him only as a player. A man only interested in getting as many women as possible into his bed. A man who wasn't interested in anything that wasn't about momentary pleasure.

Now she'd seen glimpses of a different man. One who could enjoy himself with people who weren't members of the "celebrity crowd." A guy who could buy silly T-shirts for babies he wasn't even sure were his. A guy who could still turn her into a puddle of want with a glance.

"Do you want to talk about it?" Mary asked quietly.

Jenna took a long, deep breath and looked around the room to avoid meeting Mary's too-knowing gaze. Muted sunlight, diffused by the tinted glass, filled the room, creating shadows in the corners. It was quiet now, with Nick somewhere out on deck and the hum of the ship's powerful engines silenced while in port.

Shifting her gaze to Mary's, Jenna thought about spilling the whole story. Actually she could really use someone to talk to, and Mary had, in the past several days, already proven to be a good friend. But she couldn't get into it now. Didn't want to explain how she and Nick had come together, made two sons and then drifted apart. That was far too long a story.

"Thanks," she said, meaning it. "But I don't think so.

Anyway, you don't have time to listen. Joe will be waiting for you."

Mary frowned at her, but apparently realized that Jenna didn't feel like talking. Standing up, she said, "Okay, I'll go. But if you decide you need someone to talk to…"

"I'll remember. Thanks."

Then Mary left and Jenna was alone. Alone with her thoughts, racing frantically through her mind. Alone with the desire that was a carefully banked fire deep inside. Suddenly antsy, she jumped to her feet, crossed the room and left the suite. She'd just go up on deck. Sit in the sun. Try not to think. Try to relax.

The business of running a cruise line kept Nick moving from the time he got up until late at night. People on the outside looking in probably assumed that he led a life of leisure. And sure, there was still time for that. But the truth was he had to stay on top of everything. This cruise line was his life. The one thing he had. The most important thing in the world to him. He'd worked his ass off to get this far, to make his mark. And he wasn't about to start slowing down now.

"If the band isn't working, contact Luis Felipe here in town," he told Teresa, and wasn't surprised to see her make a note on her PDA. "He knows all the local bands in Acapulco. He could hook us up with someone who could take over for the rest of the cruise."

The band they'd hired in L.A. was proving to be more trouble than they were worth. With their rock star attitudes, they were demanding all sorts of perks that hadn't been agreed on in their contracts. Plus, they'd been cutting short their last show of the evening because they said there weren't enough people in attendance to make it worthwhile. Not their call, Nick thought. They'd been hired to do a job, and they'd do it or they'd get off the ship in Mexico and find their own way home.

"Got it," Teresa said. "Want me to tell the band their days are numbered?"

"Yeah. We'll be in port forty-eight hours. Give 'em twenty-four to clean up their act—if they don't, tell 'em to pack their bags."

"Will do." She paused, and Nick turned to look at her. They were standing at the bow of the ship on the Splendor Deck, mainly because Nick hadn't felt like being cooped up in his office. And he couldn't go to his suite because Jenna was there. Being in the same room with her without reacting to her presence was becoming more of a challenge.

The last few days had been hell. Being with her every day, sleeping down the hall from her at night, knowing she was there, stretched out on a king-size bed, probably wearing what she used to—a tank top and a pair of tiny, bikini panties—had practically killed him. He'd taken more cold showers in the last three days than he had in the past ten years.

His plan to seduce Jenna and then lose her was backfiring. He was the one getting seduced. He was the one nearly being strangled with throttled-back desire. And he was getting damned sick of it. It was time to make

a move. Time to take her to bed. Before they got the
results of that DNA test.

Tonight, he decided. Tonight he'd have Jenna Baker
back in his bed. Where he'd wanted her for the past year.

"Boss?"

He was almost surprised to hear Teresa's voice. Hell,
he'd forgotten where the hell he was and what he was
doing. Just thinking about Jenna had his body hard and
aching.

"What is it?" He half turned away from the woman
and hoped she wouldn't notice the very evident proof
of just how hungry for Jenna he really was.

"The lab in Cabo called. They faxed the results of the
DNA test to the lab in L.A."

"Good." His stomach fisted, but he willed it to
loosen. Nothing to do about it now but wait for the
results. Which would probably arrive by tomorrow. So,
yeah. Tonight was the night.

"Do you want me to tell Jenna?"

Nick frowned at his assistant, then let the expression
fade away. Wasn't her fault he felt like he was tied up
in knots. "No, thanks. I'll do it."

"Okay." Teresa took a deep breath, held it, then blew
it out. "Look, I know this is none of my business…"

"Never stopped you before," he muttered with a smile.

"No, I guess not," she admitted, swiping one hand
through her wind-tousled hair. "So let me just say, I
don't think Jenna's trying to play you."

He went perfectly still. From the shore came the
sounds of car horns honking and a swell of noise that

only a crowd of tourists released for the day could make. Waves slapped halfheartedly at the hull of the ship, and the wind whipped his hair into his eyes.

He pushed it aside as he looked at Teresa. "Is that right?"

She lifted her chin, squared her shoulders and looked him dead in the eye. "That's right. She's just not the type to do something like this. She never did give a damn about your money or who you were."

"Teresa—" He didn't want to talk about this and he didn't actually care what his assistant thought of Jenna. But knowing Teresa, there was just no way to stop her. An instant later, he was proved right.

"—still talking. And if I'm going to get fired for shooting my mouth off," she added quickly, "then I'm going to get it all said no matter what you think."

"Fine. Finish."

"I didn't say anything when you fired her, remember. I even agreed with you to a point—yes, Jenna should have told you she worked for you, but from her point of view I can see why she didn't."

"That's great, thanks."

She ignored his quips and kept talking. "I didn't even say anything when you were so miserable after she left that it was like working for a panther with one foot caught in a steel trap."

"Hey—"

"But I'm saying it now," she told him, and even wagged a finger at him as if he were a misbehaving ten-year-old. "You can fire me for it if you want to, but you'll never get another assistant as good as I am and you know it…."

Gritting his teeth because he knew she was right, Nick nodded and ordered, "Spit it out then."

"Jenna's not the kind to lie."

A bark of laughter shot from his throat.

"Okay, fine, she didn't tell you she was an employee. But that was one mistake. Remember, I knew her then, too, Nick. She's a nice kid with a good heart."

He shifted uncomfortably because he didn't want her to be right. It was much easier on him to think of Jenna as a liar and a manipulator. Those kind of women he knew how to deal with. A nice woman? What the hell was he supposed to do with one of those?

"And," Teresa added pointedly, "I saw the pictures of your sons—"

"That hasn't been confirmed yet," he said quickly.

"They look just like you," she countered.

"All babies look like Winston Churchill," Nick argued, despite the fact that he knew damn well she was right.

"Yeah?" She smiled and shook her head. "Winston never looked that good in his life, I guarantee it. They've got your eyes. Your hair. Your dimples." Teresa paused, reached out and laid one hand on his forearm. "She's not lying to you, Nick. You're a father. And you're going to have to figure out how you want to deal with that."

He turned his face toward the sea and let the wind slap at him. The wide stretch of openness laid out in front of him was usually balm enough to calm his soul and soothe whatever tensions were crowded inside him. But it wasn't working now. And maybe it never would again.

Because if he was a father…then his involvement with those kids wasn't going to be relegated to writing a check every month. He'd be damned if his children were going to grow up not knowing him. Whether Jenna wanted him around or not, he wasn't going anywhere. He was going to be a part of their lives, even if that meant he had to take them away from their mother to do it.

The ship felt deserted.

With most of the passengers still on shore exploring Acapulco, Jenna wandered decks that made her feel as if she were on board a ghost ship. That evening, she was back in Nick's suite and feeling on edge. She'd showered, changed into a simple, blue summer dress and was now fighting the fidgets as she waited for Nick to come back to the suite for dinner.

Funny, she'd spent nearly every waking moment with him over the past few days, feeling her inner tension mount incrementally. She'd convinced herself that what she needed was time to herself. Time away from Nick, to relax. Unwind a little, before the stress of being so close to him made her snap.

So she'd had that time to herself today and she was more tense than ever.

"Oh, you're in bad shape, Jenna," she whispered as she walked out onto Nick's balcony. She was a wreck when she was with him, and when she wasn't, she missed him. Her hair lifted off her neck in the wind, and the hem of her dress fluttered about her knees. Her sandals made a soft click of sound as she walked across the floor and she wrapped her arms around herself more for comfort than warmth.

From belowdecks, a soft sigh of music from the ballroom reached her, and the notes played on the cool ocean breeze, as if they'd searched her out deliberately. The plaintive instrumental seeped into her soul and made her feel wistful. What if coming on this trip had been a big mistake? What if telling Nick about their sons hadn't been the right thing to do? What if—she stopped her wildly careening thoughts and told herself it was too late to worry about any of that now. The deed was done. What would happen would happen and there wasn't a damn thing she could do about it now.

She sighed, leaned on the balcony railing and stared out at the sea. Moonlight danced on the surface of the water in a shimmer of pale silver. Clouds scuttled across a star-splashed sky, and the ever-present wind lifted her hair from her shoulders with a gentle touch.

"This reminds me of something."

Nick's deep voice rumbled along Jenna's spine, and she had to pull in a deep breath before she turned her head to look at him. He stood in the open doorway to the balcony. Hands in his pockets, he wore black slacks, a gleaming white shirt and a black jacket that looked as if it had been expertly tailored. His dark hair was wind ruffled, his pale eyes were intense, and his jaw was tight.

Her heart tumbled in her chest.

"What's that?" she whispered, amazed that she'd been able to squeeze out a few words.

He stepped out onto the balcony, and with slow, measured steps, walked toward her. "The night we met," he said, taking a place beside her at the railing. "Remember?"

How could she forget? She'd been standing on the Pavilion Deck of *Falcon's Treasure,* the ship she'd been working on at the time. That corner of the ship had been dark and deserted, since most of the passengers preferred spending time in the crowded dance club at the other end of the deck.

So Jenna had claimed that shadowy spot as her own and had gone there nearly every night to stand and watch the sea while the music from the club drifted around her. She'd never run into anyone else there, until the night Nick had stumbled across her.

"I remember," she said, risking a sidelong glance at him. She shouldn't have. He was too close. His eyes too sharp, his mouth too lickable. His scent too rich and too tempting. Her insides twisted and she dropped both hands to the cold, iron railing, holding tight.

"You were dancing, alone in the dark," he said, as if she hadn't spoken at all. As if he were prompting her memory. "You didn't notice me, so I watched you as you swayed to the music, tipping your head back, your hair sliding across your shoulders."

"Nick…"

"You had a smile on your face," he said, his voice

lower now, deeper, and she wouldn't have thought that was possible. "As if you were looking up into the eyes of your lover."

Jenna swallowed hard and shifted uneasily as her body blossomed with heat. With need. "Don't do this, Nick...."

"And I wanted to be the lover you smiled at. The lover you danced with in the dark." He ran the tip of one finger down the length of her arm, and Jenna shivered at the sizzle of something deliciously hot and wicked sliding through her system.

She sucked in a gulp of air, but it didn't help. Her mind was still spinning, her heart racing and her body lighting up like Times Square on New Year's Eve. "Why are you doing this?" she whispered, and heard the desperate plea in her own voice.

"Because I still want you," he said, moving even closer, dropping his hands onto her shoulders and turning her until she was facing him, until their bodies were so close only a single lick of flame separated them. "Because I watched you standing in the moonlight and knew that if I didn't touch you, I'd explode. I want you. Just as I did then. Maybe more."

Oh, she felt the same way. Everything in Jenna clamored at her to move into him. To lean her body against his. To feel the strength and warmth of him surrounding her. But she held back. Determined to fight. To hold on to the reins of the desire that had once steered her down a road that became more rocky the further along she went.

"It would be a mistake," she said, shaking her head, trying to ignore the swell of music, the slide of the trombone, the wail of the saxophone, that seemed to call to something raw and wild inside her. "You know it would."

"No," he said, sliding his hands up, along her shoulders, up the length of her throat, to cup her face between his palms. "This time would be different. This time, we know who we are. This time we know what we're getting into. It's just need, Jenna." His gaze moved over her features, and her breath caught and held in a strangled knot in her chest. "We both feel it. We both want this. Why deny ourselves?"

Why indeed?

Her mind fought with her traitorous body, and Jenna knew that rational thought was going to lose. The need was too great. The desire too hot. The temptation too strong. She did want him. She'd wanted him from the moment she first saw him more than a year ago. She'd missed him, dreamed of him, and now that he was here, touching her, was she really going to turn him down? Walk away? Go to her solitary bed and pray she dreamed of him again?

No.

Was she going to regret this?

Maybe. Eventually.

Was she going to do it?

Oh, yeah.

"There are probably plenty of reasons to deny ourselves," she finally whispered. "But I don't care about any of them." Then she went up on her toes as Nick smiled and flashes of hunger shone in his eyes.

"Atta girl," he murmured and took her mouth in a kiss that stole her breath and set her soul on fire.

His tongue slipped between her lips, stealing into her warmth, awakening feelings that had lain dormant for more than a year. His arms slid around her waist, pulling her in tight. Jenna lifted her own arms and linked them around his neck, holding him to her, silently demanding he deepen the kiss, take more from her.

He did.

His arms tightened until she could hardly draw breath. But who needed air? Jenna groaned, moved into him, pressing her body along his, and she felt the hard length of him jutting against her. That was enough to send even more spirals of heat dancing through her bloodstream.

Again and again, his tongue dipped into her mouth, tasting, exploring, divining her secrets. She gave as well as took, tangling her tongue with his, feeling the molten desire quickening within. He loosened his grip on her and she nearly moaned, but then his hands were moving, up and down her spine, defining every line, every curve. When his palms cupped her bottom and held her to him, she sighed into his mouth and gave herself up to the wonder of his touch.

"I need you," he whispered, dropping his mouth to the line of her jaw, nibbling at her throat.

She turned her head, allowing him easier access, and closed her eyes at the magic of the moment.

Around them, music swelled and the ocean breeze held the two of them in a cool embrace. Moonlight poured down on them from a black, starlit sky, and when Nick lifted his head and looked down at her, Jenna was trapped in his gaze. She read the fire in his eyes, sensed the tautly controlled tension vibrating through his body and felt his need as surely as she did her own.

"Now. Here." He lifted his hands high enough to take hold of the zipper, then slid it down, baring her back to the night wind. Then he pushed the thin straps of her dress down over her shoulders, and Jenna was suddenly glad she hadn't worn a bra beneath that thin, summer fabric.

Now there was nothing separating her from his touch. From the warmth of his hands. He cupped her breasts in his palms and rubbed her tender, aching nipples until she felt the tug and pull right down to the soles of her feet. She swayed into him, letting her head fall back and her eyes close as she concentrated solely on what he was doing to her.

It was everything. His touch, his scent filled her, overwhelming her with a desire that was so much more than she'd once felt for him. In the year since she'd seen him, she'd grown, changed, and now that she was with him again, *she* was more, so she was able to *feel* more.

"Beautiful," he said, his voice no more than a raw scrape of sound. His gaze locked on her breasts, he said, "Even more beautiful than I remembered."

"Nick," she whispered brokenly, "I want—"

"I know," he said, dipping his head, taking first one hardened nipple, then the other into his mouth. His lips and tongue worked that tender flesh, nibbling, licking, suckling, until Jenna's head was spinning and she knew that without his grip on her, she would have fallen into a heap of sensation at his feet.

He pushed her dress the rest of the way down, letting it fall onto the floor, and Jenna was standing in the moonlight, wearing only her high-heeled sandals and her white silk bikini panties. And she felt too covered. Felt as if the fragile lace of her underwear were chafing her skin. All she wanted on her now was Nick. She wanted to lie beneath him, feel his body cover hers, feel him push himself deeply inside her.

She loved him. Heaven help her, she still loved him. Why was it that only Nick could do this to her? Why was he the man her heart yearned for? And what was she going to do about it?

Then he touched her more deeply and those thoughts fled along with any others. All she could do was feel.

"Please," she said on a groan, "please, I need…"

"I need it, too," he told her, lifting her head, looking down into her eyes as he slid one hand down the length of her body, fingertips lightly dusting across her skin. He reached the elastic band of her panties and dipped his hand beneath it to cup her heat.

Jenna rocked into him, leaning hard against him, but Nick didn't let her rest. Instead, he turned her around until her back was pressed to his front and she was facing the wide emptiness of the moonlit sea.

He used one hand to tease and tweak her nipples while the other explored her damp heat. His fingers dipped lower, smoothing across her most tender, sensitive flesh with a feathery caress that only fed the flames threatening to devour her.

Jenna groaned again, lost for words. Her mind had splintered, no thoughts were gathering. She was empty but for the sensations he created. He dipped his head and whispered into her ear, "Watch the sea. See the moonlight. Lose yourself in them while I lose myself in you...."

She did what he asked, fighting to keep her eyes open, and focused on the shimmering sea as he dipped first one finger and then another into her heat. Jenna's breath hitched and she wanted to close her eyes, the better to focus on what he was doing, but she didn't. Instead, she stared unseeing at the broad expanse of sea and sky stretching out into infinity in front of her and fought to breathe as his magic fingers pushed her along a road of sensual pleasure.

He stroked, he delved, he rubbed. His fingers moved over her skin as a concert pianist would touch a grand piano. Her body was his instrument, and she felt his expert's touch with a grateful heart. Again and again, he pushed her, his fingers stroking her from the inside while his thumb tortured one particularly sensitive spot. And while Jenna moaned and twisted in his grasp, her eyes locked on the shimmering sea, she let herself go. She dropped any sense of embarrassment or worry. She pushed aside every stray thought of censure that leaped into her mind, and she devoted herself to the sensory overload she was experiencing.

"Come for me," Nick whispered, his voice no more

than a hush in her ear. His breath dusted her face, her neck, while his fingers continued the gentle, determined invasion. "Let me see you. Let me feel you go over."

His voice was a temptation. Because she was so close to a climax. Her knees trembled. Her body weakened even as it strove to reach the peak Nick was pushing her toward. Her breath came in ragged gasps, her heartbeat thundered in her ears and the tension coiling within was almost more than she could bear. And when she thought she wouldn't survive another moment, she cried out his name and splintered in his arms. Her body shattered, she rode the exquisite wave of completion until she fell at the end only to be caught and held in his strong arms.

Jenna dropped her head onto his shoulder, swallowed hard and fought to speak. "That was—"

"Only the beginning," Nick finished for her and picked her up, swinging her into his arms and stalking back into the suite. He was teetering on the edge of reason. Touching her, feeling her climax roar through her, sensing her surrender, had all come together to build a fire inside him like nothing he'd ever known before.

Seduction had been the plan.

But whose?

He'd thought to use her, feed the need that she'd caused, then be able to let her go. Get her out of his head, out of his blood. But those moments with her on the balcony only made him want more. He had to have her under him, writhing beneath him as he took her.

She lay curled against his chest, in a trusting manner that tore at him even as it touched something inside him he hadn't been aware of. She was trouble. He knew it. Felt it. And couldn't stop himself from wanting.

From having.

In his bedroom Nick strode to the bed, reached down with one hand and grabbed the heavy, black duvet in one fist. Then he tossed it to the foot of the mattress and forgot about it. He laid Jenna down on the white sheets and looked at her for a long moment. The moonlight caressed her here, as well, sliding in through the wide bank of glass that lined his bedroom suite. A silvery glow coated her skin as she stretched like a satisfied cat before smiling up at him.

"Come to me, Nick," she urged, lifting both arms in welcome.

He didn't need a second invitation. Tearing off his clothes, he joined her on the bed, covered her body with his and surrendered to the inevitable. More than a year ago, their first encounter had ended in his bed. Now, it seemed, they'd come full circle.

Nick ran his hands up and down her body and knew he'd never be able to touch her enough. He drew a breath and savored her scent. Dipped his head and tasted her skin at the base of her throat. Her pulse jolted beneath his mouth and he knew she was as eager as he, as needy as he.

He touched her core, delving his fingers into her heat again, and she lifted her hips from the bed, rocking into his hand, moaning and whispering to him.

His body ached and clamored for release. Every inch of him was humming, just touching her. Lying beside her. Jenna. Always Jenna who did this to him. Who turned him into a man possessed, a man who could think of nothing beyond claiming what he knew to be his.

With that thought, Nick tore away from her arms, ignoring the soft sound of disappointment that slipped from her throat. Tugging the drawer on the bedside table open, he reached in, grabbed a condom and, in a few quick seconds, sheathed himself. Then he turned back to her, levering himself over her, positioning himself between her thighs.

He gave her a quick smile. "Last time we forgot that part and look what happened."

"You're right," she said, reaching down to stroke his length, her fingers sliding over the thin layer of latex in a caress that had Nick gulping for air. "Now, will you come to me?"

He spread her thighs farther apart, leaned in close and locked his gaze with hers as his body entered hers. Inch by inch, he invaded her, torturing them both with his deliberately slow thrust.

Her hips moved beneath him, her eyes squeezed shut and she bit her bottom lip. Reaching up, her hands found his upper arms and held on, her short nails digging into his skin, and that was the last straw. The final touch that sent Nick over the edge of reason.

He pushed himself deep inside her and groaned at the tight, hot feel of her body holding his. His hips rocked, setting a rhythm that was both as old as time and new and exciting. She held on tighter, harder, her nails biting into his flesh with a stinging sensation that was counterpoint to the incredible delight of being within her.

Nick moved and she moved with him. Their rhythm set, they danced together, bodies joined, melded, becoming one as they reached for the same, shattering end that awaited them. He stared down into her eyes, losing himself in their depths. She met his gaze and held it until finally, as he felt her body begin to fist around his, she closed her eyes, shrieked his name and shuddered violently as her body exploded from the inside.

His own release came a scant moment later, and Nick heard himself shout as the tremendous relief spilled through him again and again, as if the pleasure would never end.

When he collapsed atop her, he still wasn't sure just who had seduced whom.

Seven

It was a long night.

As if they'd destroyed the invisible barrier keeping them separate, Jenna and Nick came together again and again during the night. Until finally, exhausted, they fell into sleep just before dawn.

When Jenna woke several hours later, she was alone in the big bed. Pushing her hair out of her eyes, she sat up, clutched the silky white sheet to her chest and stared around Nick's room as if half expecting him to appear from the shadows. But he didn't.

Carefully, since her muscles ached, she scooted off the bed, wandered down the hall to her own room and walked directly to the bathroom. As she took a long, hot shower, her mind drifted back to the night before and she wondered if things would be different between them now. But if she thought about that, hoped for it, how much more disappointed would she be if it didn't happen?

Nick had made no promises.

Just as he had made no promises last year during their one amazing week together.

So basically, Jenna told herself, she'd made the same mistake she had before. She'd fallen into bed with a man she loved—despite the fact that he didn't love her.

"Oh, man." She rested her forehead against the aqua and white tiles while the hot, pulsing streams of water pounded against her back. "Jenna, if you're going to make mistakes, and hey, everyone does…at least make *new* ones."

Out of the shower, she dried off and dressed in a pair of white shorts and a dark green tank top. Then she sat on her bed and tried to figure out her next move. The only problem was, she didn't have a clue what to do about what was happening in her world. This had all seemed like such a simple idea. Come to Nick. Tell him about the boys. Go home and slide back into her life.

But now, everything felt…complicated.

Muttering under her breath about stupid decisions and consequences, Jenna glanced at the clock on the bedside table and noticed the phone. Instantly her heart lifted. That's what she needed, she realized. She needed to touch base with the real world. To talk to her sister. To listen to her sons cooing.

Grabbing the receiver, she immediately got the ship's operator, gave them the number she wanted and waited while the phone on the other end of the line rang and rang. Finally, though, Maxie picked up and breathlessly said, "I don't have time for salesmen."

Laughing, Jenna eased back against the headboard of her bed and said, "Hello to you, too."

"Oh, Jenna, it's you." Maxie chuckled a little. "Sorry about that, but your babies are making me a little insane."

She jolted away from the headboard, frowning at the phone in her hand. "Are they okay?"

"*They're* fine," Maxie assured her. "I'm the one who's going to be dead soon. How do you do this every day? If I ever forget to tell you how amazing I think you are, remind me of this moment."

"Thanks, I will. So the boys are good?"

"Happy as clams," her sister said, then paused and idly asked, "although, how do we know clams are happy? It's not like they smile or whistle or something…."

"One of the great mysteries of the universe."

"Amen."

In the background, Jenna heard both the television set blaring and at least one baby crying. "Who is that crying?" she asked.

"Jacob," Maxie told her and her voice was muffled for a minute. "I'm holding Cooper and giving him a bottle and Jake wants his turn. Not exactly rating a ten on the patience scale, that boy."

"True, Jake is a little less easygoing than Cooper." Jenna was quiet then as Maxie brought her up to date on the twins' lives. She smiled as she listened, but her heart ached a little, too. She wanted to be there, holding her sons, soothing them, feeding them. And the fact that she wasn't literally tore at her.

"Bottom line, everything's good here," her sister said finally. "How about you? How did Nick take the news?"

"He doesn't believe me."

"Well, there's a shocker."

Jenna rolled her eyes. Maxie wasn't a big fan of Nick Falco. But then, her sister had been wined, dined and then dumped by a rich guy a couple of years before, and ever since then she didn't have a lot of faith in men in general—and rich men in particular.

"He took the DNA test, though, and was going to have the results faxed to our lab. He should have proof even he can't deny in the next day or two."

"Good. Then you're coming home, right?"

"Yeah." Jenna plucked at the hem of her shorts with her fingertips. She wouldn't stay on board ship for the whole cruise. She'd done what she'd come here to do, and staying around Nick any longer than was necessary was only going to make things even more complicated than they already were.

"I love my nephews," Maxie was saying, "but I think they're as ready to see you as I am."

"I miss them so much." Her heart pinged again as she listened to the angry sound of Jake's cry.

"Uh-huh, now tell me why you really called."

Jenna scowled. "I called to check on my sons."

"Oh, that was part of it. Now let's hear the rest," Maxie said.

"I don't know what you mean."

"Hold on, have to switch babies. Cooper's finished and it's Jake's turn."

Jenna waited and listened to her sister talking to both of the boys, obviously laying Cooper down and picking Jake up as the infant's cries were now louder and more demanding. She smiled to herself when his crying abruptly shut off and knew that he was occupied with his bottle.

"Okay, I'm back," Maxie said a moment later. "Now, tell me what happened between you and Nick."

"What do you mean?"

"You know exactly what I mean and the fact that you're avoiding the question tells me just what happened," her sister said. "You slept with him again, didn't you?"

Jenna's head dropped to the headboard behind her and she stared unseeing up at the ceiling.

"Jenna…"

"There wasn't a lot of sleeping, but yeah."

"Damn it, Jenna—"

She sat up. "I already know it was a mistake, so if you don't mind…"

"A mistake? Forgetting to buy bread at the market is a mistake. Sleeping with a guy who's already dumped you once is a disaster."

"Well, thanks so much," Jenna said drily. "That makes me feel so much better."

Maxie blew out a breath, whispered, "It's okay, Jake, I'm not yelling at you. I'm yelling at your mommy."

Then she said louder, "Fine. Sorry for yelling. But Jenna, you know nothing good can come of this."

"I know." Hadn't she awoken in an empty bed, with no sign of the tender lover she'd spent the night with? Nick couldn't have been more blatant in letting her know just how unimportant she was to him. "God, I know."

"Come home," Maxie urged.

"I will. Soon."

"Now."

"No," Jenna said, shaking her head as she swung her legs off the bed and sat up straight. "I have to talk to him."

"Haven't you said everything there is to say?"

Probably, Jenna thought. After all, it wasn't as if she was going to tell him she loved him. And wasn't that the only piece of information he was missing? Hadn't she done what she'd come here to do? Hadn't she accomplished her mission and more?

"Maxie…"

Her sister blew out a breath, and Jenna could almost see her rolling her eyes.

"I just don't want to see you destroyed again," Maxie finally said. "He's not the guy for you, Jenna, and somewhere deep inside, you know it. You're only asking to get kicked in the teeth again."

The fact that her sister was right didn't change anything. Jenna knew she couldn't leave until she'd seen Nick again. Found out what last night had meant to him, if anything. She had to prove to herself one way or the other that there was no future for them. It was the only way she'd ever be able to let go and make a life for herself and her children.

"If I get hurt again, I'll recover," she said, her voice firming as she continued. "I appreciate you worrying about me, Maxie, but I've got to see this through. So I'll call you when I'm on my way home. Are you sure you're okay to take care of the boys for another couple of days?"

There was a long moment of silence before her sister said, "Yeah. We're fine."

"What about work?" Maxie was a medical transcriber. She worked out of her home, which was a big bonus for those times when Jenna needed a babysitter fast. Like now.

"I work around the babies' nap schedules. I'm keeping up. Don't worry about it."

"Okay, thanks."

"Jenna? Just be careful, okay?"

The door to the suite opened and a maid stepped in. She spotted Jenna, made an apologetic gesture and started to back out again.

"No, wait. It's okay, you can come in now." Then to her sister, she said, "The maid's here, I've got to go. I'll call you soon. And kiss the boys for me, okay?"

When she hung up, Jenna didn't know if she felt better or worse. It was good to know her sons were fine, but Maxie's words kept rattling around in her brain. Yes, her sister was prejudiced against wealthy men, but she had a point, too. Jenna *had* been nearly destroyed after she and Nick had split apart a year ago.

This time, though, she had the distinct feeling that the pain of losing him was going to be much, much worse.

Nick had never thought of himself as a coward.

Hell, he'd fought his way to the top of the financial world. He'd carved out an empire with nothing more than his guts and a dream. He'd created a world that was everything he'd ever wanted.

And yet…a couple of hours ago, he'd slipped out of bed and left Jenna sleeping alone in his room because he hadn't wanted to talk to her.

"Women," he muttered, leaning on the railing at the bow of the Splendor Deck, letting his gaze slide over the shoreline of Acapulco, "always want to *talk* the morning after. Always have to analyze and pick apart everything you'd done and said the night before."

But there was nothing to analyze, he reminded himself. He'd had her, just as he'd planned, and now he was through—also as he'd planned.

Of course his body tightened and his stomach fisted at the thought, but that didn't matter. What mattered was that he'd had Jenna under him, over him, around him, and now he could let her go completely. No more haunted dreams. No more thinking about her at stray moments.

It was finished.

Scowling, he watched as surfers rode the waves into shore while tourists on towels baked themselves to a cherry-red color on the beach. Brightly striped umbrellas were unfurled at intervals along the sand, and waiters dressed in white moved among the crowd delivering tropical drinks.

So if it was finished, why the hell was he still thinking about her?

Because, he silently acknowledged, that night with her had been unlike anything he'd experienced since the last time they'd been together. Nick wasn't a monk. And since he was single, he saw no problem in indulging himself with as many women as he wanted. But no woman had ever gotten to him the way Jenna had.

She made him feel things he had no interest in. Made him want more than he should. That thought both intrigued and bothered him. He wasn't looking for anything more than casual sex with a willing woman. And nothing about Jenna was casual. He already knew that.

So the best thing he could do was stay the hell away from her.

Better for both of them. He pushed away from the railing in disgust. But damned if he'd hide out on his own blasted ship. He'd find Jenna, tell her that he wasn't interested in a replay of last night—and *now* who was lying? Turning, he was in time to see Jenna walking toward him, and everything in him tightened uncomfortably.

In the late-morning sunlight, she looked beautiful. Her blond hair hung loose about her shoulders. Her tank top clung to her breasts—no bra—and his mouth went dry. Her white shorts made her lightly tanned skin look the color of warmed honey. Her dark blue eyes were locked on him, and Nick had to force himself to stand still. To not go to her, pull her up close to him and taste that delectable mouth of hers again.

She hitched her purse a little higher on one bare shoulder and tightened her grip on the strap when she stopped directly in front of him. Whipping her hair back out of her eyes, she looked up at him and said, "I wondered where you disappeared to."

"I had some things to take care of," Nick told her and it was partially true. He'd already fired the band that had refused to clean up their act, hired another one and was expected at a meeting with the harbormaster in a half hour.

But he'd still been avoiding her.

"Look, Nick—"

"Jenna—" he said at the same time, wanting to cut off any attempt by her to romanticize the night before. Bad enough he'd done too much thinking about it already.

"Me first, okay?" she spoke up quickly, before he had a chance to continue. She gave him a half smile, and Nick braced himself for the whole what-do-I-mean-to-you, question-and-answer session. This was why he normally went only for the women who, like him, were looking for nothing more complex than one night of fun. Women like Jenna just weren't on his radar, usually. For good reason.

"I just want to say," she started, then paused for a quick look around to make sure they were alone. They were, since this end of the Splendor Deck was attached to his suite and not accessible to passengers. "Last night was a mistake."

"What?" Not what he'd been expecting.

"We shouldn't have," she said, shaking her head. "Sex with you was not why I came here. It wasn't part of my plan, and right now, I'm really regretting that it happened at all."

Instantly outrage pumped through him. She *regretted* being with him? How the hell was that possible? He'd been there. He'd heard her whimpers, moans and screams. He'd *felt* her surrender. He'd trembled with the force of her climaxes and knew damn well she'd had as good a time as he had. So how the hell could she be regretting it?

More, how could he dump her as per the plan if she was dumping him first?

"Is that right?" he managed to say through gritted teeth.

"Oh, come on, Nick," she said, frowning a bit. "You know as well as I do that it shouldn't have happened. You're only interested in relationships that last the length of a cruise, and I'm a single mom. I'm in no position to be anybody's babe of the month."

"Babe of the month?" He was insulted, and the fact that he'd been about to tell her almost exactly what she was saying to him wasn't lost on him.

She blew out a breath and tightened the already death grip she had on the strap of her purse. "I'm just saying that it won't happen again. I mean, what happened last night. With us. You and me. Not again."

"Yeah, I get it." And now that she'd said that, he wanted her more than ever. Wasn't that a bitch of a thing to admit? Not that he'd give her the satisfaction of knowing what he was thinking. "Probably best that way."

"It is," she said, but her voice sounded a little wistful. Or was he hearing what he wanted to hear?

Strange, a few minutes ago, he'd been thinking of ways to let her go. To tell her they were done. Now that she'd beaten him to the punch, he felt different. What the hell was happening to him, anyway?

Whatever it was, Nick told himself firmly, it was time to nip it in the bud. No way was he going to be tripping on his own heartstrings. Not over a woman he already knew to be an accomplished liar.

Besides, she hadn't come on this trip for him, he told himself sternly, but for what he could give her. She'd booked passage on his ship with the sole purpose of getting money out of him. Sure, it was for child support. But she still wanted money. So what made her different from any other woman he'd known?

"I'm attracted to you," she was saying, and it looked like admitting that was costing her, "but then I guess you already figured that out."

Was she blushing? Did women still do that?

"But I'm not going to let my hormones be in the driver's seat," she told him and met his gaze with a steely determination. "Pretty soon, you'll be back sailing the world with a brunette or a redhead on your arm and I'll be back in Seal Beach taking care of my sons."

The babies.

Hers? His?

He wasn't going there until he knew for sure. Instead,

he decided to turn the tables on her. Remind her just whose ship she was on. Remind her that he hadn't come to her, it had been the other way around.

"Don't get yourself tied up in knots over this, Jenna," he said, reaching out to chuck her under the chin with his fingertips. "It was one night. A blip on the radar screen."

She blinked at him.

"We had a good time," he said lightly, letting none of the tension he felt coiled inside show. "Now it's over. End of story."

He watched as his words slapped at her, and just for a minute he wished he could take them back. Yet as that feeling rushed over him, he wondered where it had come from.

"Okay, then," Jenna said, her voice nearly lost in the rush and swell of the sea below them, tumbling against the ship's hull. "So now we know where we stand."

"We do."

"Well, then," she said, forcing a smile that looked brittle, "maybe I should just fly home early. I can catch a flight out of Acapulco easily enough. I talked to my sister earlier and she's going a little nuts—"

He cut her off instantly. "Are the babies all right?"

She stopped, looked at him quizzically and said slowly, "Yes, of course. The boys are fine, but Maxie's not used to dealing with them twenty-four hours a day and they can be exhausting, so—"

"I'd rather you didn't leave yet," he blurted.

"Why not?"

Because he wasn't ready for her to be gone. But since admitting that even to himself was too lowering, he said, "I want you here until we get the results from the DNA test."

Her gaze dropped briefly, then lifted to meet his again. "You said we'd probably hear sometime today, anyway."

"Then there's no problem with you waiting."

"What's this really about, Nick?" she asked.

"Just what I said," he told her, taking her arm in a firm grip and turning her around. Heat bled up from the spot where his hand rested on her arm. He fought the urge to pull her into him, to dip his head and kiss the pulse beat at the base of her throat. To pull the hem of her shirt up so he could fill his hands with her breasts.

Damn, he was hard and hot and really irritated by that simple fact.

Leading her along the wide walkway, he started for his suite. "We've got unfinished business together, Jenna. And until it's done and over, you're staying."

"Maybe I should get another room."

"Worried you won't be able to control yourself?" he chided as he opened the door and allowed her to precede him into the suite.

"In your dreams," she said shortly, and tossed her purse onto the sofa.

"And yours," he said.

Jenna looked at him and felt herself weakening. It wasn't fair that this was so hard. Wasn't fair that her body wanted and her heart yearned even as her mind told her to back away. She had to leave the ship. Soon.

In the strained silence, a beep sounded from another room, and she glanced at Nick, a question in her eyes.

"Fax machine."

She nodded and as he walked off to get whatever had come in for him, Jenna headed for his bedroom. All she wanted to do was get the underwear she'd left in there the night before. And better to do it while he was occupied somewhere else.

Opening the door, she swung it wide just as Nick called out, "It's from the lab."

If he said anything else, she didn't hear him. Didn't even feel a spurt of pleasure, knowing that now he'd have no choice but to believe her about the fact that he was the father of her sons.

Instead Jenna's gaze was locked on his bed, and her brain short-circuited as she blankly stared at the very surprised, very *naked* redhead stretched out on top of Nick's bed.

Eight

"Jenna?" Nick's voice came from behind her, but she didn't turn.

"Hey!" The redhead's eyes were wide as she scrambled to cover herself—a little too late—with the black duvet. "I didn't know he already had company…."

Nick came up behind Jenna, and she actually felt him tense up. "Who the hell are you?" he demanded, pushing past Jenna to face the woman staring up at him through eyes shining with panic.

"Babe of the month?" Jenna asked curtly.

"Look," the redhead was saying from beneath the safety of the duvet, "I can see I made a mistake here and—"

"Oh," Jenna told her snidely, "don't leave on my

account," then she spun on her heel and marched down the long hall toward her own bedroom.

"Jenna, damn it, wait." Nick's voice was furious but she didn't care. Didn't want to hear his explanation. What could he possibly say? There was a naked woman in his bed. And he hadn't looked surprised, just angry. Which told Jenna everything she needed to know. This happened to him a *lot*.

That simple fact made one thing perfectly clear to Jenna.

It was so past time for her to leave.

God, she was an idiot. To even allow herself to *think* that she loved him. Was she a glutton for punishment?

She marched into her room on autopilot. Blindly she moved to the closet, grabbed her suitcase and tossed it onto the bed. Opening it up, she threw the lid back, then turned for the closet again. Scooping up an armful of her clothes, she carried them to the suitcase, dropped them in and was on her way back to the closet for a second load when Nick arrived.

He stalked right up to her, grabbed her arm and spun her around. "What the hell do you think you're doing?"

She wrenched herself free and gave him a glare that should have fried him on the spot. Jenna was furious and hurt and embarrassed. A dangerous combination. "That should be perfectly obvious, even to you. I'm leaving."

"Because of the redhead?"

"What's the matter, can't remember her name?"

"I've never even *met* her for God's sake," he shouted,

shoving one hand through his hair in obvious irritation, "how the hell should I know her damn name?"

"Stop swearing at me!" Jenna shouted right back. She felt as if every cell in her body was in a stranglehold. Her blood was racing, her mind was in a whirl of conflicting thoughts and emotions, and the only thing she knew for sure was she didn't belong here. Couldn't stay another minute. "I'm leaving and you can't stop me."

"Jenna, damn it, the results from the lab came in—"

Not exactly the way she'd imagined this conversation going, she told herself indignantly. Somehow she'd pictured her and Nick, reading the results together. In her mind, she'd watched as realization came over him. As he acknowledged that he was a father.

Of course, she hadn't pictured a naked redhead being part of the scene.

"Then you know I was telling you the truth. My work here is done." She grabbed up her sneakers, high heels and a pair of flats and tossed them into the suitcase on top of her clothes. Sure it was messy, but she was way past caring.

"We have to talk."

"Oh, we've said all we're going to say to each other," Jenna told him, skipping backward when he made a grab for her again. She didn't trust herself to keep her anger fired if he touched her. "Have your lawyers contact me," she snapped and marched into the connecting bathroom to gather up the toiletries she had scattered across the counter.

"Damn it," Nick said, his voice as tight as the tension coiled inside her. "I just found out I'm a *father,* for God's sake. I need a minute here. If you'll calm down, we can discuss this—"

"Shouldn't you be down the hall with Miss Ready-And-Willing?" Jenna inquired too sweetly as she pushed past him, her things in the crook of her arm.

He shook his head. "She's getting dressed and getting out," he said, grabbing Jenna's arm again to yank her around to face him.

God help her, her body still reacted to his hands on her. Despite everything, she felt the heat, the swell of passion rising inside to mingle with the fury swamping her, and Jenna was sure this wasn't a good thing. She had to get out.

But Nick only tightened his grip. "I didn't invite her. She bribed a maid."

She swallowed hard, lowered her gaze to his hands on her arms and said, "You're hurting me." He wasn't, but her statement was enough to make him release her.

"Jenna—"

"It's a wonder the woman had to bribe anyone. I'm sure the maids are used to letting naked women into your suite. Pretty much a revolving door around here, isn't it?"

"Nobody gets into my suite unless I approve it, which I didn't in this case," Nick added quickly. "And I hope for the maid's sake that it was a *good* bribe, because it just cost her her job."

"Oh, that's nice," Jenna said as she turned to zip her

suitcase closed. "Fire a maid because you're the horniest male on the face of the planet."

"Excuse me?"

Jenna straightened up, folded her arms across her chest and tapped the toe of her sandal against the floor as she glared up at him. "Everyone on this ship knows what a player you are, Nick. Probably wasn't a big surprise to the maid that a woman wanted into your suite and for all she knew, you *did* want her here."

He glared right back at her. "My life is my business."

"You're right it is." She grabbed the handle of her suitcase and slid it off the bed. Jenna didn't even care if she'd left something behind. She couldn't stay here a second longer. She had to get away from Nick, off this ship and back to the world that made sense. The world where she was wanted. Needed.

"And I don't owe you an explanation for anything," he pointed out unnecessarily.

"No, you don't. Just as you don't have to fire a maid because she assumed it was business as usual around here." Jenna shook her head, looked him up and down, then fixed her gaze on his. "But you do what you want to, Nick. You always do. Blame the maid. Someone who works hard for a living. Fire her. Make yourself feel better. Just don't expect me to hang around to watch."

"Damn it, Jenna, I'm not letting you walk out." He moved in closer and she felt the heat of his body reaching out for her. "I want to know about my sons. I want to talk about what we're going to do now."

Tightening her grip on the suitcase handle, Jenna

swung her hair back behind her shoulders and said softly, "What we're going to do now is go back to our lives. Contact your lawyer, set up child support. I'll send you pictures of the boys. I'll keep you informed of what's happening with them."

"It's not enough," he muttered, his voice low and deep and hard.

"It'll have to be, because it's all I can give you." Jenna walked past him, headed for the living room and the purse she'd left on a sofa. But she stopped in the doorway and turned for one last look at him.

Diffused sunlight speared through the bank of windows and made his dark hair shine. His eyes were shadowed and filled with emotions she couldn't read, and his tall, leanly muscled body was taut with a fury that was nearly tangible.

Everything in her ached for him.

But she'd just have to learn to live with disappointment. "Goodbye, Nick."

Jenna was gone.

So was the redhead.

And he didn't fire the maid.

Nick hated like hell that Jenna had been right about that, but how could he fire some woman when everyone on the damn ship knew he had women coming and going all the time? Instead, he'd had Teresa demote the maid to the lower decks and instructed her to make it clear that if the woman ever took another bribe from a guest, she'd be out on her ass.

Sitting at the desk in his office, he turned his chair so that he faced the sprawl of the sea. He wasn't seeing the last of the day's sunlight splashing on the water like fistfuls of diamonds spread across its surface. He didn't notice the wash of brilliant reds and violets as sunset painted a mural across the sky. Instead his mind continued to present him with that last look he'd had of Jenna. Standing in the open doorway of her bedroom, suitcase in her hand, wearing an expression that was a combination of regret and disappointment.

"What right does she have to be disappointed in me? And why the hell do I care what she thinks?" he muttered. He'd meant to have her and let her go. It had been a good plan and that's exactly what had happened. He ought to be pleased. Instead, his brain continued to ask him just why Jenna had been so pissed about the redhead.

Was she being territorial?

Did she really care for him?

Did it matter?

Then he glanced down at the single sheet of paper he still held in his hand. The fax from the lab in San Pedro was clear and easy to read.

His DNA matched that of Jenna's twins.

Nick Falco was a father.

He was both proud and horrified.

"I have two sons," he said, needing to hear the words said aloud. He shook his head at the wonder of it and felt something in his chest squeeze tightly until it was almost impossible to draw a breath.

He was a *father*.

He had *family*.

Two tiny boys who weren't even aware of his existence were only alive because of *him*. Pushing up from his chair, he walked to the wide bank of glass separating him from the ocean beyond and leaned one hand on the cool surface of the window. Sons. Twins. He felt that twist of suppressed emotion again and murmured, "The question is, how do I handle it? What's the best way to manage this situation?"

Jenna had left, assuming that he'd keep his distance. Deal with her through the comforting buffer of an attorney. He scowled at the sea and felt a small but undeniable surge of anger begin to rise within him, twisting with that sense of pride and confusion until he nearly shook with the rush of emotions he wasn't used to experiencing.

He was a man who deliberately kept himself at a distance from most people. He liked having that comfort zone that prevented anyone from getting too close. Now, though, that was going to change. It had to change.

Jenna thought she knew him. Thought he'd be content to remain a stranger to his sons. Thought he'd go on with his life, putting her and Jacob and Cooper aside. Knowing her, she thought he'd be satisfied to be nothing more than a fat wallet to his sons.

"She's wrong," he muttered thickly, and his hand on the glass fisted. "I may not know anything about being a father, but those boys are *mine*. And I'll be damned if I let *anyone* keep me from them."

Turning around, he hit a button on the intercom and
ground out, "Teresa?"

"Yes, boss?"

He folded the DNA report, tucked it into the breast
pocket of his shirt and said, "Call the airport. Hire a
private jet. I'm going back to California."

By the following morning, it was almost as if Jenna
had never been gone. She'd stopped on the way home
from the airport the night before to pick up the boys at
Maxie's house. She hadn't been able to bear the thought
of being away from them another minute. With the
twins safely in their rooms and her suitcase unpacked,
Jenna was almost able to convince herself that she'd
never left. That the short-lived cruise hadn't happened.
That she hadn't slept with Nick again. That she hadn't
left him with a naked redhead in his bedroom.

The pain of that slid down deep inside, where she
carefully buried it. After all, none of that had anything
to do with reality. The cruise—Nick—had been a short
jaunt to the other side of the fence. Now she was back
where she belonged.

She'd been awake for hours already. The twins didn't
take into consideration the fact that Mom hadn't gotten
much sleep last night. They still wanted breakfast at six
o'clock in the morning. Now she was sitting on the
floor in the middle of her small living room, working
while she watched her boys.

"I missed you guys," she said, looking over at her sons
as they each sat in a little jumper seat. The slightest

motion they made had the seat moving and shaking, which delighted them and brought on bright, toothless grins.

Jake waved one fist and bounced impatiently while Cooper stared at his mother as if half-afraid to take his eyes off her again for fear she might disappear.

"Your aunt Maxie said you were good boys," she said, talking to them as she always did. Folding the first load of laundry for the day, Jenna paused to inhale the soft, clean scent of their pajamas before stacking them one on top of the other. "So because I missed you so much and you were so good, how about we walk to the park this afternoon?"

This was what Jenna wanted out of her life, she thought. Routine. Her kids. Her small but cozy house. A world that was filled with, if not excitement, then lots of love. And if her heart hurt a little because Nick wasn't there and would never know what it was to be a part of his sons' lives, well, she figured she'd get over it. Eventually. Shouldn't take more than twenty or thirty years.

The doorbell had her looking up, frowning. Then she glanced at the twins. "You weren't expecting any-one, were you?"

Naturally, she didn't get an answer, so she grinned, pushed herself to her feet and stepped around them as she walked the short distance to her front door. Glancing over her shoulder, she gave the living room a quick look to make sure everything was in order.

The couch was old but comfortable, the two arm

chairs were flowered, with bright throw pillows tucked into their corners. The tables were small, and the rag rug on the scarred but polished wooden floors were handmade by her grandmother. Her home was just as she liked it. Cozy. Welcoming.

She was still smiling when she opened the front door to find Nick standing there. His dark hair was ruffled by the wind, his jeans were worn and faded, and the long-sleeved white shirt he wore tucked into those jeans was open at the throat. He looked way too good for her self-control. So she shifted her gaze briefly to the black SUV parked at the curb in front of her house. That explained *how* he'd gotten there. Now the only thing to figure out was *why* he was there.

Looking back up into his face, she watched as he pulled off his dark glasses, tucked an arm into the vee of his shirt and looked into her eyes. "Morning, Jenna."

Morning? "What?"

"Good to see you, too," he said, giving her a nod as he stepped past her into the house.

"Hey! You can't just—" Her gaze swept over him and landed on the black duffle bag he was carrying. "What are you doing here? Why're you here? How did you find me?"

He stopped just inside the living room, dropped his duffel bag to the floor and shoved both hands into the back pockets of his jeans. "I came to see my sons," he said tightly. "And trust me when I say it wasn't hard to find you."

"Nick…"

"And I brought you this." He pulled a small, sealed envelope out of his back pocket and handed it over. "It's from your friend Mary Curran. She was upset when she found out that you'd left the ship."

Jenna winced. She hadn't even thought of saying goodbye to the friend she'd made, and a twinge of guilt tugged at her.

"She said this is her telephone number and her e-mail address." He stared at her. "She wants you to keep in touch."

"I, uh, thanks." She took the envelope.

He looked at her, hard and cold. His pale eyes were icy and his jaw was clenched so tightly it was a wonder his teeth weren't powder. "Where are they?" he demanded.

Her mouth snapped closed, but she shot a look at the boys, jiggling in their bouncy seats. Nick followed her gaze and slowly turned. She watched as the expression on his face shifted, going from cool disinterest to uncertainty. Jenna couldn't remember ever seeing Nick Falco anything less than supremely confident.

Yet it appeared that meeting his children for the first time was enough to shake even his equilibrium.

Walking toward them slowly, he approached the twins as he would have a live grenade. Jenna held her breath as she watched him gingerly drop to his knees in front of the bouncy seats and let his gaze move from one baby boy to the other. His eyes held a world of emotions that she'd never thought to see. Usually he guarded what he was thinking as diligently as a pit bull on a short chain. But now…Jenna's heart ached a little in reaction to Nick's response to the babies.

"Which one is which?" he whispered, as if he didn't completely trust his voice.

"Um—" She walked a little closer, her sneakers squeaking a bit as she stepped off the rug onto the floor.

"No, wait," he said, never looking at her, never taking his gaze off the twins, "let me." Tentatively, Nick reached out one hand and gently cupped Jacob's face in his big palm. "This one's Jake, right?"

"Yes," she said, coming up beside him, looking down at the faces of her sons who were both looking at Nick in fascination. As usual, though, Jacob's mouth was open in a grin and Cooper had tipped his little head to one side as if he really needed to study the situation a bit longer before deciding how he felt about it.

"So then, you're Cooper," Nick said and with his free hand, stroked that baby's rounded cheek.

Jenna's breath hitched in her chest and tears gathered in her eyes. God, over the past several months, she'd imagined telling Nick about the boys, but she'd never allowed herself to think about him actually meeting them.

She'd never for a moment thought that he would be interested in seeing them. And now, watching his gentle care with her boys made her heart weep and every gentle emotion inside her come rushing to the surface. There was just something so tender, so poignant about this moment, that Jenna's throat felt too tight to let air pass. When she thought she could speak again without hearing her voice break, she said, "You really were listening when I told you about them."

"Of course," he acknowledged, still not looking at her, still not tearing his gaze from the two tiny boys who had him so enthralled. "They're just as you described them. They look so much alike, and yet, their personalities are so obvious when you're looking for the differences. And you were right about something else, too. They're beautiful."

"Yeah, they are," she said, her heart warming as it always did when someone complimented her children. "Nick," she asked a moment later, because this was definitely something she needed to know, "why have you come here?"

He stood up, faced her, then glanced again at his sons, a bemused expression on his face. "To see them. To talk to you. After you left, I did a lot of thinking. I was angry at you for leaving."

"I know. But I had to go."

He didn't address that. Instead he said, "I came here to tell you I'd come up with a plan for dealing with this situation. A way for each of us to win."

"Win?" she repeated. "What do you mean 'win'?"

Shifting his pale blue gaze back to hers, his features tightened, his mouth firming into a straight, grim line. A small thread of worry began to unspool inside of her, and Jenna had to fight to keep from grabbing up her kids and clutching them to her chest.

Only a moment ago she'd been touched by Nick's

first sight of his sons. Now the look on his face told her she wasn't going to be happy with his "plan."

"Look," he said, shaking his head, sparing another quick glance for the babies watching them through wide, interested eyes, "it came to me last night that there was an easy solution to all of this."

"I didn't come to you needing a solution. All I wanted from you is child support."

"Yeah, well, you'll get that." He waved one hand as if brushing aside something that didn't really matter. "But I want more."

That thread of worry thickened and became a ribbon that kept unwinding, spreading a dark chill through her bloodstream that nearly had her shivering as she asked, "How much more?"

"I'm getting to that," he said. "Like I said, I've been doing a lot of thinking since you left the ship. And finally, last night on the flight up here, it occurred to me that twins are a lot of work for any one parent."

What was he getting at? Why was he suddenly shifting his gaze from hers, avoiding looking at her directly? And why had she ever gone to him? "Yes, it is, but—"

"So my plan was simple," he said, interrupting her before she could really get going. "We split them up, each of us taking one of the twins."

"What?"

Nine

Nick couldn't blame her for the outrage.

She jumped in front of the babies and held her arms up and extended as if to fight him off should he try to grab the twins and run. "Are you insane? You can't split them up," she said, keeping her voice low and hard. "They aren't *puppies*. You don't get the pick of the litter. They're little boys, Nick. Twins. They need each other. They need *me*. And you can't take either of them away from me."

He'd already come to the same conclusion. All it had taken was one look at the boys, sitting in their little seats, so close that they could reach out and touch each other. But he hadn't known until he'd seen them.

"Relax," he said, lifting one hand to try to stop her

from taking off on another rant. "I said that's the plan I *did* have. Things have changed."

"You've been here ten seconds. What could have changed?" She was still defensive, standing in front of her sons like a knight of old. All she really needed was a battle-ax in her hands to complete the picture.

"I saw them," he said, and something in his voice must have reached her because her shoulders eased down from their rigid stance. "They're a unit. We can't split them up. I get that."

"Good." She blew out a breath. "That's good."

"I'm not finished," he told her, and watched as her back snapped straight as a board again. "I came here to see my sons, and now that I have, I'm not going anywhere."

She looked stunned, her mouth dropping open, her big, blue eyes going even wider than usual. "What do you mean?" Then, as she began to understand exactly what he meant, she shook her head fiercely. "You can't possibly think you're going to stay here."

This was turning out to be more fun than he'd thought it would be.

"Yeah, I am." Nick glanced around the small living room. You could have dropped two entire houses the size of hers into his suite on the ship, and yet there was something here that was lacking in his place, despite the luxury. Here, he told himself, she'd made a home. For her and their sons. A home he had no intention of leaving. At least not for a while. Not until he'd gotten to know his sons. Not until he'd come up with a way that he could be a part of their lives.

"That's crazy."

"Not at all," he said tightly, his gaze boring into hers. "They're my sons. I've already lost four months of their lives and I'm not going to lose any more."

"But Nick—"

He interrupted her quickly. "I won't be just a check to them, Jenna. And if that's what you were hoping for, sorry to disappoint."

She chewed at her bottom lip, folded her arms over her chest as if she were trying to hold herself together and finally said, "You can't stay here. There's no room. It's a two-bedroom cottage, Nick. One for the boys, one for me and you're *not* staying in my room, I guarantee that."

His body tightened and he thought he just might be able to change her mind on that front, eventually. But for now, "I'll bunk on the couch."

"But—"

"Look," Nick said. "It's simple. I stay here, get to know my kids. Or," he added, pulling out the big guns, "I sue you for sole custody. And which one of us do you think would win that battle? Your choice, Jenna. Which will it be?"

Her face paled, and just for a second Nick felt like a complete bastard. Then he remembered that he was fighting for the only family he had. His sons. And damned if he'd lose. Damned if he'd feel guilty for wanting to be a part of their lives however he had to manage it.

"You would do that?"

"In a heartbeat."

"You really are a callous jerk, aren't you?"

"I am whatever I have to be to get the job done," Nick told her.

"Congratulations, then. You win this round."

One of the babies began to cry, as if sensing the sudden tension in the room. Nick glanced down to see that it was Jacob, his tiny face scrunched up as fat tears ran down his little cheeks. An instant later, taking his cue from his brother, Cooper, too, let out a wail that was both heart wrenching and terrifying to Nick.

He threw a panicked look at Jenna, who only shook her head.

"You want a crash course in fatherhood, Nick?" She waved a hand at the boys, whose cries had now reached an ear-splitting range as they thrashed and kicked and waved their little arms furiously. "Here's lesson one. You made them cry. Now you make them stop."

"Jenna—"

Then, while he watched her dumbfounded, she scooped up the stack of freshly folded baby clothes and walked off down a short hallway to disappear into what he guessed was the boys' bedroom, leaving him alone with his frantic sons.

"Great," Nick muttered as he dropped to his knees in front of the twins. "This is just going great. Good job, Nick. Way to go."

As he dropped to his knees, jiggled the bouncy seats and pleaded with the boys to be quiet, he had the distinct feeling he was being watched. But if Jenna was standing in the shadows observing his performance, he didn't really want to know. So he concentrated on his sons and told himself that a man who could build a cruise ship line out of nothing should be able to soothe a couple of crying babies.

After all, how hard could it be?

By the end of the afternoon, Nick was on the ragged edge and Jenna was enjoying the show. He'd fed the boys, bathed them—which was entertainment enough that she wished she'd videotaped the whole thing—and now as he was trying to get them dressed. Jenna stood in the doorway to the nursery, silently watching with a delighted smile on her face.

"Come on, Cooper," Nick pleaded. "Just let me get this shirt on and then we'll—" He stopped, sniffed the air, then turned a horrified look on Jacob. "Did you?" He sniffed again. "You did, didn't you? And I just put that diaper on you."

Jenna slapped one hand over her mouth and watched Nick in a splash of sunlight slanting through the opened louvred blinds. The walls were a pale green and boasted a mural she'd painted herself while pregnant. There were trees and flowers and bunnies and puppies, painted in bright, primary colors, racing through the garden. A white dresser stood at one end of the room and an over-stuffed rocking chair was tucked into a corner.

And now there was Nick.

Staring down into the crib where he'd laid both boys for convenience sake, Nick shoved both hands through his hair—something he'd been doing a lot—and muttered something she didn't quite catch.

Still, she didn't offer to help.

He hadn't asked for any, and Jenna thought it was only fair that he get a real idea of what her days were like. If nothing else, it should convince him that he was *so* not ready to be a single parent to twin boys.

"Okay, Coop," he said with a tired sigh, "I'll get your shirt on in a minute. First, though, I've got to do something about your brother before we all asphyxiate."

Jenna chuckled, and Nick gave her a quick look. "Enjoying this, are you?"

"Is that wrong?" she asked, still grinning.

He scowled at her, then shook his head and wrinkled his nose. "Fine, fine. Big joke. But you have to admit, I'm not doing badly."

"I suppose," she conceded with a nod. "But smells to me as if you've got a little problem facing you at the moment."

"And I'll handle it," he said firmly, as though he was trying to convince himself, as well as her.

"Okay then, get to it."

He scrubbed one hand across his face, looked down into the crib and murmured, "How can someone so cute smell so bad?"

"Yet another universal mystery," she told him.

"Another?"

"Never mind," Jenna said, thinking back to her conversation with Maxie when Jenna was still on the ship. Before the redhead. Before she'd left in such a hurry.

Oh God. Jenna straightened up and closed her eyes. Maxie. Wait until *she* found out that Nick was here.

"You okay?" he asked.

Opening her eyes again, she looked at him, so out of place there in her sons' nursery, and told herself that this was just what he'd said their night together was. Nothing more than a blip on the radar. One small step outside the ordinary world. Once he'd made his point, got to know his sons a little, he'd be gone again and everything would go back to the way it was supposed to be.

Which was good, right?

"Jenna?"

"Huh? Oh. Yeah. I'm fine. Just…thinking."

He looked at her for a long second or two as if trying to figure out just what she'd been thinking. Thankfully, mind reading was *not* one of his skills.

"Right."

"So," Jenna said softly, "are you going to take care of Jake's little problem or do you need a rescue?"

He didn't look happy, but he also didn't look like he was going to beg off.

"No, I don't need a rescue. I said I could take care of them and I can." He took a breath, frowned again and reached into the crib.

Jenna heard the tear of the Velcro straps on the disposable diaper, then heard Nick groan out, "Oh my God."

Laughing, she turned around and left him to his sons.

Though it made her crazy, Jenna spent the rest of the day in her small garage, working on a gift basket that was to be delivered in two days. If Nick wanted to play at being a father, then she'd just let him see what it was like dealing with twin boys.

It felt strange to be right there at the house and still be so separate from the boys, but she had to make Nick see that he was in no way prepared to be a father. Had to make him see that taking her sons away from her would be a bad idea all the way around.

Just thinking about his threat sent cold chills up and down her spine, though. He was rich. He could afford the best lawyers in the country. He could hire nannies and bodyguards and buy whatever the court might think the boys would need.

"And where does that leave me?"

A single mom with a pitifully small bank account and an office in her garage. She'd have no chance at all if Nick really decided to fight her for their sons.

But why would he? That thought kept circling in her mind and she couldn't shake it. Was this all to punish her? Was it nothing more than a show of force? But why would he go to such lengths?

Shaking her head, she wrapped the completed basket with shrink-wrap cellophane, plugged in her travel-size hair dryer and focused the hot air on the clear plastic wrap. As she tucked and straightened and pulled, the gift basket began to take shape, and she smiled to herself despite the frantic racing in her mind.

When she was finished, she left the basket on her worktable where, in the morning, she'd affix a huge red bow to the top before packing it up to be delivered. For

now, though, she was tired, hungry and very curious to
see how Nick was doing with the boys.

She slipped into the kitchen through the connecting door and stopped for an appalled moment as she
let her gaze sweep the small and usually tidy room.
The red walls and white cabinets were pretty much
all she recognized. There was spilled powdered
formula strewn across the round tabletop, discarded
bottles that hadn't been rinsed and a *tower* of dirty receiving blankets that Nick had apparently used to
wipe up messes.

Shaking her head, she quietly walked into the living
room, half-afraid of what she would find. There wasn't
a sound in the house. No TV. No crying babies. Nothing.

Frowning, she moved farther into the room, noticing
more empty baby bottles, and a torn bag of diapers
spilled across a tabletop next to an open and drying-out
box of baby wipes. Then she rounded the sofa and
stopped dead. Nick was stretched out, fast asleep on her
grandmother's rag rug and on either side of him lay a
sleeping baby.

"Oh, my." Jenna simply stood there, transfixed by the
sight of Nick and their sons taking a nap together. A
single lamp threw a puddle of golden light across the
three of them even as the last of the sunlight came
through the front window. Nick's even breathing and the
soft sighs and coos issuing from the twins were the
only sounds in the room and Jenna etched this image
into her mind so that years from now she could call up
this mental picture and relive the moment.

There was just something so sweet, so *right* about the little scene. Nick and his sons. Together at last.

Her heart twisted painfully in her chest as love for all three of them swamped her. Oh, she was in so much trouble. Loving Nick was not a smart thing to do. She knew there was no future there for them. All he wanted was to be a part of her sons' lives—that didn't include getting close with their mother. So, what was she supposed to do? How could she love Nick when she knew that nothing good could come of it? And how could she keep her sons from him when she knew, deep down, that they would need a father as much as Nick would need them?

"Why does it have to be you who touches my heart?" she whispered, looking down at the man who'd invaded her life and changed her world.

And as she watched him, Nick's eyes slowly opened and his steady stare locked on her. "Do I?" he asked quietly.

Caught, there was no point in trying to deny what she'd already admitted aloud. She dropped to her knees. "You know you do."

Carefully, so as not to disturb the twins, Nick sat up, wincing a little at the stiffness in his back. But his gaze didn't waver. He continued to meet her eyes, and Jenna wished she could read what he was thinking. What he was feeling.

But as always, Nick's thoughts were his own, his emotions so completely controlled she didn't have a clue what was going on behind those pale blue eyes.

"Then why'd you leave the ship so fast?" Nick asked quietly.

"You know why." Just the memory of the naked redhead was enough to put a little steel back into her spine.

"I didn't even know her," he reminded her with just a touch of defensiveness in his voice.

"Doesn't matter," she said, lowering her voice quickly when Jacob began to stir. She hadn't meant to wake him up. Hadn't wanted to get into any of this right now. But since it had happened anyway, there was no point in trying to avoid it. "Nick, don't you see? The redhead was just a shining example of how different we are. She brought home to me how much out of my element I was on that ship. With you."

He reached out, skimmed his fingertips along her cheek and pushed her hair back behind her right ear. Jenna shivered at the contact, but took a breath and steadied herself. Want wasn't enough. A one-sided love wasn't enough. She needed more. Deserved more.

"I don't belong in the kind of life you lead, Nick. And neither do the boys."

"You could, though," he told her, his voice a hush of sound that seemed intimate, cajoling. "All three of you could. We could all live on the ship. You know there's plenty of room. The boys would have space to play. They'd see the world. Learn about different cultures, different languages."

Tempting, so tempting, just as he'd meant it to be. A reluctant smile curved her mouth, but she shook her head as she looked from him to the twins and back again. "They can't have a real life living on board a ship, Nick. They need a backyard. Parks. School. Friends—" She stopped, waved both hands and added, "A *dog*."

He tore his gaze from hers and looked at first one sleeping baby to the other before shifting his gaze back to hers. "We'll hire tutors. They can play with the passengers' kids. We could even have a dog if they want one. It could work, Jenna. We could make it work."

Though a part of her longed to believe him, she knew, deep down, that this wasn't about him wanting to be with her—finding a way to integrate her into his life—this was about him discovering his sons and wanting them with him.

"No, Nick," she whispered, shaking her head sadly. "It wouldn't be fair to them. Or us. You don't want me, you want your sons. And I understand that. Believe me I do."

He grabbed for her hand and smoothed the pad of his thumb across her knuckles. "It's not just the boys, Jenna. You and I…"

"Would never work out," she finished for him, despite the flash of heat sweeping from her hand, up her arm, to rocket around her chest like a pinball slapping against the tilt bar.

She wished it were different. Wished it were possible that he could love her as she did him. But Nick Falco simply wasn't the kind of man to commit to any one woman. Best that she remember that and keep her heart as safe as she could.

"You don't know that. We could try." His eyes were so filled with light, with hunger and the promise of something delicious that made Jenna wish with everything in her that she could take the risk.

But it wasn't only herself she had to worry about now. There were two other little hearts it was her job to protect. And she couldn't bring herself to take a chance that might bring her sons pain a few years down the road.

But instead of saying any of that, instead of arguing the point with him, she pulled her hand free of Nick's grasp and said softly, "Help me get the boys up to bed, okay?"

He drew up one leg and braced one arm across his knee. His gaze was locked on her, his features half in shadow, half in light. "This isn't over, Jenna."

As she bent over to scoop up Jacob, Jenna paused, looked into those pale blue eyes and said, "It has to be, Nick."

Ten

"Here?" Maxie repeated. "What do you mean he's here? Here in Seal Beach here?"

Jenna glanced back over her shoulder at her closed front door. She'd spotted Maxie pulling up out front and had made a beeline for the door to head her off at the pass, so to speak. "I mean he's *here* here. In the house here. With the boys here."

For three days now. She'd been able to avoid Maxie by putting her off with phone calls, claiming to be busy. But Jenna had known that sooner or later, her older sister would just drop by.

"Are you *nuts?*" Maxie asked. Her big, blue eyes went wide as saucers and her short, spiky, dark blond hair actually looked spikier somehow, as if it were actually standing on end more than usual. "What are you thinking, Jenna? Why would you invite him here?"

"I didn't invite him," Jenna argued, then shrugged. "He…came."

Maxie stopped, narrowed her eyes on Jenna and asked, "Are you sleeping with him?"

Disappointment and need tangled up together in the center of Jenna's chest. No, she wasn't sleeping with him, but she was dreaming of him every night, experiencing erotic mental imagery like she'd never known before. She was waking up every morning with her body aching and her soul empty.

But she was guessing her older sister didn't want to hear that, either, so instead, she just answered the question.

"No, Saint Maxie, defender of all morals," Jenna snapped, "I'm *not* sleeping with him. He's been on the couch the last couple of nights and—"

"Couple of nights?"

Jenna winced, then looked up and waved at her neighbor, who'd stopped dead-heading her roses to stare at Maxie in surprise. "Morning, Mrs. Logan."

The older woman nodded and went back to her gardening. Jenna shifted her gaze up and down the narrow street filled with forties-era bungalows. Trees lined the street, spreading thick shade across neatly cropped lawns. From down the street came the sound of a basketball being bounced, a dog barking maniacally and the muffled whir of skateboard wheels on asphalt. Just another summer day. And Jenna wondered just how many of her neighbors were enjoying Maxie's little rant. Shooting her sister a dark look, Jenna lifted both eyebrows and waited.

Maxie took the hint and lowered her voice. "Sorry, sorry. But I can't believe Nick Falco's been here for two nights and you didn't tell me."

Jenna smirked at her. "Gee, me, neither. Of course, I only kept it a secret because I thought you might not understand, but clearly I was wrong."

"Funny."

Jenna blew out a breath and hooked her arm through her sister's. No matter what else was going on in her life, Maxie and she were a team. They'd had only each other for the last five years, after their parents were killed in a car accident. And she wasn't going to lose her only sister in an argument over a man who didn't even *want* her.

"Max," she said, trying to keep her voice even and calm, despite the whirlwind of emotions she felt churning inside, "he's here to get to know the boys. His sons, remember? We're not together that way, and believe me when I say I'm being careful."

Maxie didn't look convinced, but then she wasn't exactly a trusting soul when it came to men. Not that Jenna could blame her or anything...not after she was so unceremoniously dumped by that jerk Darius Stone.

"This is a bad idea," Maxie said, as if she hadn't already made herself perfectly clear.

"He won't be here long."

"His kind don't need much time."

"Maxie..."

"You sure he's not staying?"

"Why would he?"

"I can think of at least three reasons off the top of my head," she countered. "Jacob, Cooper and oh, yeah, *you*. So I ask it again. Are you sure he's not staying for long?"

Hmm. No, she wasn't. In fact, Jenna would have thought that Nick would have had his baby fix by now and be all too glad to go back to his life. But so far he hadn't shown any signs of leaving.

Was it just the boys keeping him here?

Or did he feel something for her, too?

Oh God, she couldn't allow herself to start thinking that way. It was just setting herself up for more damage once he really did leave.

"Jenna—" Nick called to her from the front porch, then stopped when he saw Maxie and her talking and added, "Oh. Sorry."

No way to avoid this, Jenna thought dismally, already regretting putting her sister and her ex-lover in the same room together. But she forced a smile anyway. "It's okay, Nick. This is my sister, Maxie."

When neither of them spoke, Jenna gave Max a nudge with her elbow.

"Fine, fine," Max muttered, then raised her voice and said grudgingly, "Nice to meet you."

"Yeah. You, too."

"Well, isn't this special?" Jenna murmured, and wondered if she could get frostbite from the chill in the air between these two. "Come on in, Max," she urged, wanting her sister to see that she had nothing to worry about. That Nick wasn't interested in her and that she wasn't going to be pining away when he left. Surely, Jenna thought, she was a good enough actor to pull that off. "See the boys. Have some coffee."

Still looking at Nick, Maxie shook her head and said, "I don't know…"

"I went out for doughnuts earlier," Nick offered.

"Is he trying to bribe me?" Maxie whispered.

Jenna snorted a laugh. "For God's sake, Max, be nice." But as she followed her sister into the house, Jenna could only think that this must have been what it felt like to be dropped behind enemy lines with nothing more than a pocketknife.

Nick knew he should have left already.

Then he wouldn't have had to deal with Jenna's sister. Although, she'd finally come around enough that she hadn't looked as if she wanted to stab him to death with the spoon she used to stir her coffee.

The point was, though, with access to a private jet, he could catch up with the ship in Fort Lauderdale in time to enjoy the second half of the cruise to Italy. Then he wouldn't have to play nice with Jenna's sister—who clearly hated his guts. And he wouldn't be tormented by the desire he felt every waking moment around Jenna herself.

The last couple of nights he'd spent on her lumpy couch had been the longest of his life. He lay awake late into the night, imagining striding down the short hall to her bedroom, slipping into her bed and burying himself inside her. He woke up every morning so tight and hard he felt as if he might explode with the want and frustration riding him. And seeing her first thing in the morning, smelling the floral scent of her shampoo, watching her sigh over that first sip of coffee was another kind of torture.

She was here.

But she wasn't his.

Now Jenna was off to a packaging store, mailing out one of her gift baskets, and he was alone with his sons.

Nick walked into the boys' nursery to find them both wide awake, staring up at the mobiles hanging over their beds. The one over Jake's crib was made up of brightly colored animals, dancing now in the soft breeze coming in from the partially opened window. And over Cooper's bed hung a mobile made up of bright stars and smiling crescent moons.

He looked from one boy to the other, noting their similarities and their differences. Each of them had soft, wispy dark hair and each of them had a dimple—just like Nick's—in their left cheek. Both boys had pale blue eyes, though Cooper's were a little darker than his brother's.

And both of them had their tiny fists wrapped around his heart.

"How am I supposed to leave you?" he asked quietly. "How can I go back to my life, not knowing what you're doing? Not knowing if you've gotten a tooth or if you've started crawling. How can I not be here when you start to walk? Or when you fall down for the first time?"

Soft sunlight came through the louvered blinds on the

window and lay across the shining wood floor like gold bars. Outside somewhere on this cozy little street, a lawn-mower fired up and Jake jumped as though he'd been shot.

Instantly Nick moved to the crib, leaned over and laid one hand on his son's narrow chest. He felt the rapid-fire thud of a tiny heart beneath his palm, and a love so deep, so pure, so all encompassing, filled him to the point that he couldn't draw a breath.

He hadn't expected this. Hadn't thought to fall so helplessly in love with children he hadn't known existed two weeks ago. Hadn't thought that he'd enjoy getting up at the crack of dawn just so he could look down into wide eyes, eager to explore the morning. Hadn't thought that being here, with the boys, with their mother, could feel so…right.

Now that he knew the truth, though, the question was, what was he going to do about it?

Moving across the room to Cooper, he bent down, scooped his son up into his arms and cradled him against his chest. The warm, pliant weight of him and his thoughtful expression made Nick smile. He drew the tip of one finger along Cooper's cheek, and the infant boy turned his face into that now-familiar touch. Nick's heart twisted painfully in his chest as he stared down into those solemn blue eyes so much like his own.

"I promise you, I'll always be here when you need me." His voice was as quiet as a sigh, but Cooper seemed almost to understand as he gave his father one of his rare smiles. Nick swallowed hard, walked to where Jacob lay in his crib watching them and whispered, "I love you guys. Both of you. And I'm going to find a way to make this work.

When Jake kicked his little legs and swung his arms, it was almost a celebration. At least, that's what Nick told himself.

That night Jenna pulled on her nightshirt and made one last check on the twins before going to bed herself, as was her habit. Only, this time when she stepped into the room lit only by a bunny nightlight, she found Nick already there.

He wasn't wearing a shirt. Just a pair of jeans that lay low on his hips and clung to his legs like a lover's hands. He turned when she stepped into the room, and she felt the power of his gaze slam into her. In the dim light, even his pale eyes were shadowed, dark, but she didn't need to see those eyes to feel the power in them. Her skin started humming, her blood sizzling, but she made herself put one foot in front of the other, walking past Nick first to Cooper's crib, then Jacob's, smoothing each of the boys' hair, laying a gentle hand on their tummies as they slept.

And through it all, she felt Nick's gaze on her as surely as she would have a touch. Her breath came in shallow gasps and her stomach did a quick enough spin that she felt nearly dizzy. What was he doing in here? Why was he watching her as he was? What was he thinking?

Her hands were shaking as she turned to leave the

nursery with quiet steps. She got as far as the hallway when Nick's hand came down on her arm.

"Wait." His voice was hard and low, demanding.

She looked up at him, and here in the dark, where even the pale light from the plugged-in plastic bunny couldn't reach, Nick was no more than a tall, imposing figure moving in close to her.

"Nick—" Could he hear her heartbeat? Could he sense the fires he kindled inside her? Could he feel the heat pouring off her body in thick waves? "What are you doing?"

Heaven help her, she knew what he was doing. And more, she was glad of it. Just standing with him in the dark filled her with a sense of expectation that had her breath catching in her lungs.

"Don't talk," he whispered, moving in even closer, until their bodies were pressed together, until he'd edged her back, up against the wall. "Don't think." He lifted both hands and covered her breasts.

She sucked in air and let her head thunk back against the wall. Even through the thin cotton fabric of her nightgown, she felt the thrill of anticipation washing through her. His hands were hot and hard and strong. His thumbs moved across the tips of her nipples and the scrape of the fabric over her sensitive skin was another kind of sweet agony.

"Yes, Nick," she whispered, licking dry lips and huffing in breaths as if she'd just finished running a marathon. "No thinking. Only feeling. I want—"

"Me, too," he said, cutting her off so fast, she knew

instinctively that he was feeling the immediacy of the moment. "Have for days. Can't wait another minute. I need to be in you, Jenna. To feel your heat around me." He dropped his head to the curve of her neck and swept his tongue across the pulse point at the base of her throat.

She jerked in his arms, then lifted her hands until she could cup the back of his head and hold him there. While her fingers threaded through his thick, dark hair, he dropped one hand down the front of her body, skimming her curves, lifting the hem of her nightshirt. Then he was touching her bare skin and she arched into him as he slid his magical fingers beneath the elastic band of her panties.

He touched her core, slid his fingers into her heat and instantly, she exploded, rocking her hips with the force of an orgasm that crashed down on her with a splinter-ing fury. Whimpering his name, she clung to him with a desperate grip until the last of the tremors slid through her. Then she was limp against him until he picked her up and walked to her bedroom.

Holding on to him, Jenna smoothed her hands over his skin, his broad back, his sculpted chest, and when he sucked in a gulp of air, she smiled in the dark, pleased to know she affected him as deeply as he did her.

In moments she was on her bed, staring up at him as he tore his jeans off and came to her. In the next instant he'd pulled her nightshirt up and off, and slid her white lace panties down the length of her legs and tossed them onto the floor.

Since the second he'd walked, unannounced, into her home, Jenna had wanted this. She'd lain awake at night hungering for him, and now that he was here, she had no intention of denying either of them. Though, for all she knew, this was his way of saying goodbye. He might be getting ready to leave, to go back to his world.

And if that was the case, then she wanted this one last night with him. Wanted to feel him over and around her. Wanted to look up into those pale eyes and know that at least for this moment, she was the most important thing in the world to him.

Tomorrow could take care of itself.

He moved in between her legs and stroked her now all-too-sensitive center. She moaned softly, spread her legs farther and rocked her hips in silent invitation. All she wanted was to feel the hard, strong slide of his body into hers. To hold him within her.

Then he was there, plunging deep, stealing her breath with the hard thrusts of his body. He laid claim to her in the most ancient and intimate way. And Jenna gave him everything she had. Her hands stroked up and down his spine. Her short nails clawed at his skin. Her legs wrapped themselves around his hips and urged him deeper, higher.

When he bent his head to kiss her, she parted her lips and met his tongue with her own in a tangle of need and want that was so beyond passion, beyond desire, that she felt the incredible sense that *this* is where she'd always been meant to be.

He tore his mouth from hers, looked down into her eyes and said on a groan, "Jenna...I need you."

"You have me," she told him and then arched her spine as a soul-shattering climax hit them both hard. Holding him tight, Jenna called out his name as wave after wave of sensation crashed, receded and slammed down onto them again and again. She felt his release as well as her own. She held him as his body trembled and shook with a power that was mind numbing.

It seemed the pleasure would never end.

It seemed they were destined to be joined together for the rest of time.

But finally, inevitably, the tantalizing pressure and delight faded and they lay together in a silence so profound, neither of them knew how to end it.

Nick was gone when she woke up.

Not gone gone. His duffle bag was still in one corner of the living room, so he hadn't gone back to the ship. He was just nowhere to be found in the house. That shouldn't have surprised her. After all, he'd avoided her the morning after their night together on board ship, as well. But somehow, disappointment welled inside her, and she wondered if he was deliberately distancing himself from her. To make the inevitable leaving easier.

With the sting of unshed tears filling her eyes, she slipped into her normal routine of taking care of the boys, and tried not to remember how it had felt to have Nick there, sharing all of this with her.

Once the twins were fed and dressed, Jenna decided to get out of the house herself. Damned if she'd sit around the house moping, waiting for Nick to return so that he could break her heart by telling her he was leaving. She had a life of her own and she was determined to live it.

Buckling the boys into their car seats, she then grabbed up a stuffed diaper bag and her purse and fired up the engine on her car.

"Don't you worry, guys," she said, looking into the rearview mirror at the mirrors she had positioned in front of their car seats so that she could see their faces, "we're going to be fine. Daddy has to go away, but Mommy's here. And I'm never going to leave you."

Those blasted tears burned her eyes again and she blinked frantically to clear them away. She wasn't going to cry. She'd had an incredible night with the man she loved and she wasn't going to regret it. Whatever happened, happened.

When her cell phone rang, she assumed it was Maxie until she glanced at the screen and didn't recognize the number. "Hello?"

"Jenna."

"Nick," she said, and tried not to sigh at the sound of his deep, dark voice murmuring in her ear.

"You at home?"

"Actually," she said, lifting her chin as if that could help her keep her voice light and carefree, "I'm in the car. I'm taking the boys to the mall and—"

"Perfect," he said quickly. "Have you got a pen?"

"Yes, I have a pen, but what is this—"

"Write this down."

Both of her eyebrows lifted at the order. But she reached into her purse for a pen and a memo pad she always carried. Behind her Jacob was starting to fuss, and pretty soon, she knew, Cooper would be joining in. "Nick," she asked, pen poised, "what's this about?"

"Just...I want to show you something and I need you and the boys to come here."

"Here where?"

"Here in San Pedro."

She nearly groaned. "San Pedro?"

"Jenna, just do this for me, okay?" He paused, then added, "Please."

Surprise flickered through her. She couldn't remember Nick *ever* saying please before. So when he gave her directions, she dutifully wrote them down. When he was finished, she frowned and said, "Okay, we'll come. Should be there in about a half hour."

"I'll be waiting."

He hung up before she could ask any more questions, and Jenna scowled at her cell phone before she set it down on the seat beside her. "Well, guys, we're off to meet your father." Cooper cooed. "No, I don't know what this is about, either," she told her son. "But knowing your daddy, it could be anything."

It turned out to be a house.

Cape Cod style, it looked distinctly out of place in Southern California, but it was the most beautiful house Jenna had ever seen. It was huge, and she was willing to bet that five of her cottages would have fit comfortably inside. But for all its size, it looked like a family home. There was a wide front lawn, and when she stepped out of the car in the driveway, she heard the sound of the ocean and knew the big house must be right on the sea.

"What's going on here?" she wondered aloud. But then Jacob's short, sharp cry caught her attention and she turned to get her sons out of their seats.

"Jenna!"

She looked up and watched as Nick ran down the front lawn to her. He looked excited, his pale eyes shining, his mouth turned into a grin so wide, his dimple dug deeply into his left cheek. Naturally, Jenna felt an involuntary tug of emotion at first sight of him, and she wondered if it would always be that way.

God, she hoped not.

"Let me help with the boys," he said after giving her a quick, hard, unexpected kiss that left her reeling a little.

"Um, sure." She watched as he rounded the back of her car, opened the other back door and began undoing the straps on Cooper's car seat. "Nick, what's going on? Where are we? Whose house is this?"

He shot her another breath-stealing grin and scooped Cooper up into his arms. "I'll tell you everything as soon as we get inside."

"Inside?" Finished with Jacob's seat straps, she picked him up, cuddled him close and closed the car door with a loud smack of sound.

"Yep," Nick said. "Inside. Go on ahead. I'll get the diaper bag and your purse."

She took a step, stopped and looked at him. Dappled shade from the massive oak tree in the front yard fell across his features. He was wearing a tight black T-shirt and those faded jeans he'd been wearing the night before when they— *Okay, don't go there,* she told herself. "I can't just go inside. I don't know who lives here and—"

"Fine," he said, coming around the hood of the car, her purse under his arm and the diaper bag slung over that shoulder, while he jiggled Cooper on the other. "We'll go together. All of us. Better that way, anyway."

"What are you talking about?"

"You'll see." He started for the house and she had little choice but to follow.

The brick walkway from the drive to the front door was lined with primroses in vibrant, primary shades of color. More flowerbeds followed the line of the house, with roses and tall spires of pastel-colored stocks scenting the air with a heady perfume.

Jenna kept expecting the owner of the house to come to the front door to welcome them, but no one did. And when she crossed the threshold, she understood why.

The house was empty.

Their footsteps echoed in the cavernous rooms as Nick led her through the living room, past a wide staircase, down a hall and then through the kitchen. Her head turned from side to side, taking it all in, delighting in the space, the lines of the house. Whoever had designed it had known what they were doing. The walls were the color of rich, heavy cream, and dark wood framed doorways and windows. The floors were pale oak and polished to a high shine. The rooms bled one into the other in a flow that cried out for a family's presence.

This house was made for the sound of children's laughter. As Jenna followed Nick through room after room, she felt that there was a sense of ease in the house. As if the building itself were taking a deep breath and relishing the feel of people within its walls again.

"Nick…" The kitchen was amazing, but she hardly had time to glance at it as he led her straight through the big room and out the back door.

"Come on, I want you to see this," he said, stepping back so that she could move onto the stone patio in front of him.

A cold ocean wind slapped at her, and Jenna realized she'd been right, the house did sit on a knoll above the sea. The stone patio gave way to a rolling lawn edged with trees and flowers that looked as she imagined an English cottage garden would. Beyond the lawn was a low-lying fence with a gate that led to steps that would take the lucky people who lived here right down to the beach.

As Jenna held Jacob close, she did a slow turn, taking it all in, feeling overwhelmed with the beauty of the place as she finally circled back to look out at the sea, glittering with golden sunlight.

Shaking her head, she glanced at Nick. "I don't understand, Nick. What's going on? Why are we here?"

"Do you like it?" he asked, letting his gaze shift around the yard as he dropped the diaper bag and her purse to the patio. "The house, I mean," he said, hitching Cooper a little higher on his chest. "Do you like it?"

She laughed, uncertainty jangling her nerves. "What's not to like?"

"Good. That's good," he said, coming to her side. "Because I bought it."

"You—*what?*"

Nick nearly laughed at the stunned expression on her face. God, this had been worth all of the secretive phone calls to real estate agents he'd been making. Worth getting up and leaving her that morning so that he could finalize the deal with the house's former owners.

This was going to work.

It had to work.

"Why would you do that?"

"For us," he said, and had the pleasure of watching her features go completely slack as she staggered unsteadily for a second.

"*Us?*"

"Yes, Jenna. Us." He reached out, cupped her cheek in his palm and was only mildly disappointed when she stepped back and away from him. He would convince her. He *had* to convince her. "I found a solution to our situation," he said, locking his gaze with hers, wanting her to see everything he was thinking, feeling, written in his eyes.

"Our situation?" She blinked, shook her head as if to clear away cobwebs and then stared at him again.

The wind was cold, but the sun was warm. Shade from the trees didn't reach the patio, and the sunlight dancing in her hair made him want to grab her and hold her close. But first they had to settle this. Once and for all.

"The boys," he said, starting out slowly, as he'd planned. "We both love them. We both want them. So it occurred to me that the solution was for us to get married. Then we both have them."

She took another step back, and, irritated that she hadn't jumped on his plan wholeheartedly, Nick talked faster. "It's not like we don't get along. And the sex is great. You have to admit there's real chemistry between us, Jenna. It would work. You know it would."

"No," she shook her head again and when Jacob picked up on her tension and began to cry, Nick moved in closer to her.

He talked even faster, hurrying to change her mind. Make her see what their future could be. "Don't say no till you think about it, Jenna. When you do, you'll see that I'm right. This is perfect. For all of us."

"No, Nick," she said, soothing Jacob even as she smiled sadly up at him. "It's not perfect. I know you love your sons, I do. And I'm glad of that. They'll need you as much as you need them. But you don't love *me*."

"Jenna…"

"No." She laughed shortly, looked around the back-yard, at the sea, and then finally she turned her gaze on Nick again. "It doesn't matter if we get along, or if the sex and chemistry between us is great. I can't marry a man who doesn't love me."

Damn it. She was shutting him down, and he couldn't even find it in himself to blame her. Panic warred with desperation inside him and it was a feeling Nick wasn't used to. He was *never* the guy scrambling to make things work. People cowtowed to *him*. It didn't go the other way.

Yet here he stood, in front of this one woman, and knew deep down inside him that the only shot he'd have with her was if he played his last card.

"Oh, for—" Nick reached out with his free arm, snaked it around her shoulders and dragged her in close to him. So close that their bodies and the bodies of their sons all seemed to be melded together into a unit. "Fine. We'll do it the hard way, then. Damn it Jenna, I *do* love you."

"What?" Her eyes held a world of confusion and pain and something that looked an awful lot like hope.

She hadn't even looked that surprised when he'd shown up at her house a few days ago. That gave him hope. If he could keep her off balance, he could still win this. And suddenly Nick knew that he'd never wanted to win more; that nothing in his life had been this important. This huge. He had to say the right things now. Force her to listen. To really hear him. And to take a chance.

Staring down into her eyes, he took a breath, and then took the plunge. The leap that he'd never thought to make. "Of course I love you. What am I, an idiot?" He stopped, paused, and said, "Don't answer that."

"Nick, you don't have to—"

"Yeah, I do," he said quickly, feeling his moment sliding by. He hadn't wanted to have to admit to how he felt. He'd thought for sure that she'd go for the marriage-for-the-sake-of-the-boys thing and then he could have had all he wanted without mortgaging his soul. But maybe this was how it was supposed to work. Maybe you couldn't *get* love until you were willing to *give* it.

"Look, I'm not proud of this, but I've been trying to hide from what I feel for you since that first night we met more than a year ago." His gaze moved over her face and his voice dropped to a low rush of words that he hoped to hell convinced her that what he was saying was true. "I took one look at you and fell. Never meant to. Didn't want to. But I didn't have a choice. You were there, in the moonlight and it was as if I'd been waiting for you my whole damn life."

"But you—"

"Yeah," he said, knowing what she was going to say. "I pulled away. I let you go. Hell, I told myself I *wanted* you to go. But that was a lie." Laughing harshly, he said, "All this time, I've been calling you a liar, when the truth is, I'm the liar here. I lied to you. I lied to myself. Because I didn't want to let myself be vulnerable to you."

"Nick—" She swallowed hard and a single tear rolled down her cheek. He caught it with the pad of his thumb.

"It would have been much easier on me," he admitted, "if you'd accepted that half-assed, marriage-of-convenience proposal. Then I wouldn't have had to acknowledge what I feel for you. Wouldn't have to take the chance that you'll throw this back in my face."

"I wouldn't do that—"

"Wouldn't blame you if you did," he told her. "But since you didn't go along with my original plan, then I have to tell you everything. I love you, Jenna. Madly. Completely. Desperately."

Fresh tears welled, making her eyes shine, and everything in him began to melt. What power she had over him. Over his heart. And yet he didn't care anymore about protecting himself.

All that mattered was her.

"You walk into a room and everything else fades away," he said softly. "You gave me my sons. You gave me a glimpse into a world that I want to be a part of."

Another tear joined the first and then another and another. In her arms, Jacob hiccuped, screwed up his little face and started to cry in earnest. Quickly, Nick took the boy from her and cradled him in his free arm. Looking down at his boys, then to her, he said, "Just so you know, I'm not prepared to lose, here. Nick Falco doesn't quit when he wants something as badly as I want you. I won't let you go. Not any of you."

He glanced behind him at the sprawling house, then shifted his gaze back to her again as he outlined his master plan. "We'll live here. You can do your gift baskets in the house instead of the garage. There's a great room upstairs that looks over the ocean. Lots of space. Lots of direct light. It'd be perfect for you and all of your supplies."

She opened her mouth to speak, but Nick kept going before she could.

"I figure until the boys are in school, we can live half the year here, half on board ship. It'll be good for 'em. And if they like the dog I bought them, we'll take her along on the ship, too."

"You bought a d—"

"Golden retriever puppy," Nick said. "She's little now, but she'll grow."

"I can't believe—"

The words kept coming, tumbling one after the other from his mouth as he fought to convince her, battled to show her how their lives could be if she'd only take a chance on him.

"Once they're in school, we can cruise during the summers. I can run the line from here and I have Teresa. I'll promote her," he said fiercely. "She can do the on-board stuff and stay in touch via fax."

"But Nick—"

"And I want more kids," he said, and had the pleasure of seeing her mouth snap shut. "I want to be there from the beginning. I want to see our child growing within you. I want to be in the delivery room to watch him— or her—take that first breath. I want in on all of it, Jenna. I want to be with you. With them," he said, glancing at the twins he held cradled against him.

The boys were starting to squirm and he knew how they felt. Nick's world was balanced on a razor's edge, and he figured that he had only one more thing to say. "I'm not going to let you say no, Jenna. We belong together, you and me. I know you love me. And damn it, I love you, too. If you don't believe me, I'll find a way to convince you. But you're not getting away from me. Not again. I won't be without you, Jenna. I can't do it. I won't go back to that empty life."

The only sound then was the snuffling noises the twins were making and the roar of the sea rushing into the cliffs behind them. Nick waited what felt like a lifetime as he watched her eyes.

Then finally she smiled, moved in close to him and wrapped both arms around him and their sons. "You really are an idiot if you think I'd ever let you get away from me again."

Nick laughed, loud and long, and felt a thousand pounds of dread and worry slide from his shoulders. "You'll marry me."

"I will."

"And have more babies."

"Yes." She smiled up at him, and her eyes shone with a happiness so rich, so full, it stole Nick's breath. "A dozen if you want."

"And sail the world with me," he said, dipping his head to claim a kiss.

"Always," she said, still smiling, still shining with an inner light that warmed Nick through. "I love you, Nick. I always have. We'll be happy here, in this wonderful house."

"We will," he assured her, stealing another kiss.

"But you're going to be housetraining that puppy," she teased.

"For you, my love," Nick whispered, feeling his heart become whole for the first time in his life, *"anything."*

* * * * *

FOR BLACKMAIL...
OR PLEASURE

by
Robyn Grady

Dear Reader,

Everyone makes mistakes. Forgetting to lock the door. Leaving the roast on too long. Oh, and hands up to those who have fallen in love with the wrong man. In the aftermath, we dust ourselves off and confirm that some valuable lessons have been learned. But what if we fall for him again? And harder the second time.

My heroine in *For Blackmail...or Pleasure* prides herself on her integrity. When the going gets tough, Donna Wilks doesn't make the easy choice – she makes the only choice. However, Donna has two weaknesses, and the most dangerous by far is her charming but arrogant ex.

Tate Bridges knows about mistakes – big mistakes that can never be undone or forgiven. He is determined to save what remains of his family from life's biggest knocks, and he will succeed using any means available... including blackmail.

For Blackmail...or Pleasure explores the grey area between social boundaries and staunch personal commitment. The very nature of moral dilemmas means that issues and judgements are rarely black or white, particularly when love – and last chances – are at stake.

Hope you enjoy!

Best,

Robyn

ROBYN GRADY

left a fifteen-year career in television production knowing the time was right to pursue her dream of writing romance. She is thrilled to be an author for the Desire™ line. She has degrees in English literature and psychology, loves the theatre and the beach, and lives on Australia's glorious Sunshine Coast with her wonderful husband and three adorable daughters. Robyn loves to hear from her readers! You can contact her at www.robyngrady.com.

This book is dedicated to my husband,
a gorgeous alpha male – with a conscience. With
thanks to my editor-in-a-million,
Melissa Jeglinski.

One

"What a coincidence. Just the person I needed to see."

Donna Wilks recognized the deep, deceptively pleasant voice at her back and choked on a mouthful of champagne. The surrounding black-tie hype vanished from conscious thought. She forgot that tonight was the most important of her career and its success could help so many. As she slowly turned, only one thing registered. Soon she would come face-to-face with her past.

Tate Bridges, Australian broadcasting mogul—the man who had shattered her heart.

Gathering herself, Donna met his eyes and lifted her chin. "I don't believe in coincidence. What are *you* doing here?" She paused to smile at a passing senator then snapped at Tate. "And what the hell do you want with me?"

His darkly handsome face creased in pretended offense. "After five long years? Perhaps a kiss hello is too much to expect—"

She cut him off. "Sorry. I don't have time for this right now."

Tate's casual charm was not only entrancing, it could also be deadly. Whatever lay behind this convenient meeting, it ended now.

As she spun away, her stiletto snagged on the carpet. Gasping, she tipped sideways at the same instant strong arms shot out to catch and reinstate her, front and center. So close, Tate's sensual mouth grinned. His ocean-blue eyes did not.

"If I were you, Donna, I'd make time."

Senator Michaels, a slight and eager man, had circled back.

"Sorry to interrupt." The senator gave Tate a wary glance, pushed silver-framed spectacles up the bump on his nose and spoke to Donna. "Just want to say—fabulous turnout. The ballroom looks spectacular. Tonight's benefit will not only raise Sydney's awareness of your cause, but hopefully plenty of support—" he tapped his back pocket "—precisely where it counts."

As the senator melted back into the animated crowd, Tate glanced indolently around the room. "The senator's right. An impressive turnout for a very worthy cause." He thanked a waiter, accepted his trademark martini and swirled the green olive back and forth. "You always were a crusader. Guess this kind of goal comes with the territory."

Recovered from her near spill, Donna smoothed back a strand of blond hair fallen loose from her chignon. "If you're interested in my efforts to supply more crisis accommodations for abused women, see my assistant." She indicated a bright-eyed brunette who sat with an attentive group by a white baby grand. "April will be more than happy to note your donation."

"Oh, plenty of time for that."

His mouth closed around the olive. Lidded eyes fused to hers, he slowly withdrew the toothpick and leisurely chewed.

A bevy of sparks chased up her legs. Shivering, she ran a damp palm down her black satin sheath and tore her gaze away. He transformed a simple gesture into a deliberate, sensual act so easily. Confident. Sexy.

Way too dangerous.

Only one thing terrified her more than falling for her ex-lover again, and that was defying him.

After his father had passed away, Tate had claimed the title chief executive officer of TCAU16—and it wasn't long before enemies both inside and outside the television network had learned that Tate Bridges was a man neither to refuse nor ignore. After almost a decade winning every big business battle he'd instigated, he'd become known as Australia's Corporate King, though she doubted the title itself impressed him. Tate thought in terms of tangibles, like building, and cementing power in every aspect of his life.

Once she'd been in awe of him. Tonight, for more reasons than one, she wished only to escape.

Skimming a glance over the dazzling evening gowns and crisp dinner suits adorning the ballroom, she stifled a worn-down sigh. "Okay. You have my attention. Can we please just cut to the chase?"

This fund-raiser evening had been organized by the same philanthropic organization that had donated to her project's establishment costs. Every valuable contact she'd ever made was here. She could not afford to waste one moment of networking time.

"I want you to help prevent an injustice."

The muscles in her midsection knotted.

His request was intended to convey a noble slant

as well as a dash of flattery. She might not be able to will away the physical attraction crackling between them, but if he thought she was still that gullible twenty-three-year-old who had hung on his every word, he could guess again.

Her voice was low and laced with indignation. "You think you know me. Appeal to my sense of valor and I'll bow to your bidding."

He raised a brow and sipped his martini.

That same air of entitlement had drawn her to him all those years ago. Nothing attracted her more than a man who was self-possessed—unless it was a man who was self-possessed, built like a power athlete, and made love with a finesse that left her breathless.

The knot in her stomach pulled tighter and Donna dropped her eyes. It hurt to even look at him, let alone remember.

Over the hum of conversation and tinkle of piano keys, the rich timbre of his voice reached out. "My brother appeared in court yesterday."

Understanding dawned, bright and clear. She slowly shook her head. "I should have known your family was behind this. No, I take that back. Libby is a sweetheart. Blade was the one who made bad decisions, and you were always the one to dive in and pull him out."

His eyes narrowed to warning slits. The message was clear: Don't go there.

"Blade's facing assault charges."

The news hit her with the force of a physical blow, but she hid her reaction by setting her glass on a passing waiter's tray. "And what would you like me to do about that?" She shrugged. "Bribe a judge?"

A lock of coal-black hair fell over his brow when he cocked his head, interested to hear more.

Soft fingers of panic closed around her throat. "That was a joke, Tate."

"From the crowd I've seen here tonight, you make some impressive connections. I'm not above a bribe for something this important."

No kidding.

Exasperated, she set off, weaving through the crowd, headed for French doors that opened onto a city-view balcony. She needed air, but more she needed to end this conversation. The sexual sparks were perilous enough; she didn't want government, legal or corporate VIPs overhearing a conversation concerning kickbacks.

Opening the balcony door, she silently cursed. Why tonight, of all nights?

But she knew why. He'd specifically chosen this time and place to put her off balance—to make it easier for him to take control.

Outside, muggy summer heat hit her like a wall, but she persevered and crossed the sandstone tiles to reach a stone pillar entwined with bloodred bougainvillea. Knowing her nemesis would be directly behind, she crossed her arms and turned on her heel.

"I honestly believe you'd stoop to any level to shield your family, no matter what they were guilty of," she told him.

Coming to a stop, Tate braced his long legs shoulder width apart. Sliding one hand into a trouser pocket, he said in all sincerity, "I'm not ashamed to admit it."

Donna told herself not to stare at that broad chest, which looked more than magnificent in a starched dress shirt visible beneath the jacket, or breathe too deeply his masculine sandalwood scent that somehow seemed stronger now they were alone. Instead she thought of how Tate's parents had died nine years ago, leaving him responsible for a rebellious teen and a desperately sad little girl.

She understood his need to protect his siblings, and admired his dedication on a purely emotional level. But she didn't need her psychology degree to see that Tate refused to acknowledge the truth: by constantly bailing Blade out, he was not only condoning bad behavior, in a sense, he was promoting it.

Sometimes tough love was the best love.

Donna rested her shoulder against the cool hard pillar. "The jury came in long ago. You and I aren't on the same page as far as Blade is concerned. But I won't argue now." She needed to get back to her guests.

Not that Tate would care about the project she'd put her heart and soul into these past years. As far as he was concerned, Tate Bridges's priorities were everyone's priorities. Dedication and pride were the very qualities that made him great, as well as so damn arrogant.

Tate placed his glass on a nearby ledge. "As soon as we settle a point, I'll let you get back to appeasing your conscience."

Her blood turned to ice. Brows knitted, she searched his eyes. "Just what is that supposed to mean?"

A flicker of emotion—cynicism perhaps, surely not concern—passed across his eyes. "Let's stay on track. We were discussing my brother's predicament."

He set one palm high on the pillar and, leaning, penned her in. As his gaze traveled to her lips, her breasts tingled beneath her soft cowl neckline and a flood of warmth washed up her neck. He leaned closer and the heat swept south. When she shifted to press her bare back farther away and against the stone, the gleam in his eyes told her he'd noticed and approved.

"I'll ask a question," he said, his breath warm against her lips, "you'll say yes and we'll both be on our way."

As unease warred with mutinous desire, movement beyond Tate's shoulder caught her eye. April, her assistant, appeared at the balcony doors and looked around. Donna slumped with relief. Rescued...for the moment.

Aware of company, Tate reluctantly straightened and eased aside.

Spotting Donna, April waved and approached. She sent a quick curious nod Tate's way before addressing her boss. "Mrs. deWalters is searching for you. You probably shouldn't keep her waiting. I heard her say she has a late dinner appointment and needs to leave soon."

Donna's knees turned to rubber. Oh, Lord. Mrs. deWalters was the one person she promised herself she'd speak with tonight.

She tried her best to smile. "I'll be right in."

As April left, Tate crossed his arms and growled. "Maeve deWalters. I'd have given you more credit than to get tangled up with that old battle-axe."

A history of antagonism and resentment ran wide and deep between the Bridgeses and deWalterses families. Donna knew little about the feud, other than how it had affected Blade and the woman he'd once loved, Kristen deWalters. But that had nothing to do with her.

"Mrs. deWalters has indicated she may be interested in providing significant financial support toward maintenance costs." The Sydney doyen of society might be pretentious and haughty, but Donna wouldn't let that interfere with getting her housing project up and running. "I do not intend to let this opportunity slide."

Tate lowered his arms. "That's your business. Mine is helping Blade. The judge requested a psychological assessment. First thing Monday our barrister will send correspondence requesting your services."

The air left her lungs as the trapdoor swung open. Lord in heaven, she should have seen something like this coming.

She focused on his implacable expression. "Let me get this straight. You want to bribe me into giving your brother a positive assessment in exchange for a donation tonight?"

He hitched up one shoulder then let it drop. "Works for me."

Her hands balled into fists as a scream built in her throat, but training and reason pushed the frustration down. "When will you get it through your head, the world isn't yours to dominate and command? I won't fudge a report. If your brother is innocent of those assault charges, he should have nothing to fear. But if he acted criminally, he needs to acknowledge that and, perhaps, suffer some consequences."

Tate's blue eyes lit with an emotion too cold to be amusement. "So you believe in consequences?"

What a question! "If someone won't admit they have a problem, they're likely to continue to make the same mistakes." Blade was a prime example. Seemed he was still a hothead, in part because he'd been allowed to be.

Tate stood very still. His dominating presence amplified to fill and consume every inch of dimly lit space. "I take it you don't want to help."

Despite it all, her heart went out to him. Tate loved his brother fiercely. She hated to think what he might do to protect Blade, or Libby. But she would not—*could not*—get involved. Much more than professional ethics demanded it.

She tried one last time. "I don't like to see anyone in trouble, but at twenty-eight it's time Blade took responsibility for himself." Last month she'd turned the same age and heaven knows she'd had to work on some issues, half of them stemming back to Tate. But she'd survived. So would Blade. "I will not go against my ethics and act improperly for anyone for any reason." She took a breath then moved to leave. "Now, if you'll excuse me." She'd kept Maeve de-Walters waiting long enough. She was getting back in there *now*.

His voice lowered—dark velvet spilling over rock. "The state board seems to think you already have."

Her blood stopped pumping. He knew about the complaint to the Psychologists Registration Board?

Shifting her feet, she blinked and found her voice. "If you're talking about that ridiculous allegation—"

"Charges of professional misconduct are hardly ridiculous."

The fine hairs on her arms rose at his patronizing tone. The situation was so absurd she shouldn't bother to argue. Surely Tate knew her principles better than most.

"I can't speak in specifics," she began, "but clients with deep issues sometimes experience transference in their therapy."

"Transference...the redirection of a client's feelings from a significant person to their therapist. Often manifested as an erotic attraction."

Something dark shifting behind his eyes told her to tread carefully. She angled her head. "Been studying up on Freud lately?"

"Some psychobabble is bound to rub off when you date a dedicated shrink for a year."

The happiest and most torturous twelve months of her life. After their breakup, she'd felt gutted and hung out to dry for what seemed like forever. Still, she couldn't bring herself to regret her time with Tate. No man compared. But that didn't mean she wanted to travel down that bittersweet road a second time. Not that rekindling of any flames would be an issue.

She got back on topic. "The unfortunate reality is a percentage of clients may believe their therapist returns their intimate feelings then feel betrayed when their affections aren't reciprocated."

"You needn't speak in generalities," Tate informed her. "I've met the man. He's quite convinced of his claim against you."

Donna's mouth went dry. She could barely form a word. "You—you've met?"

"Jack Hennessy showed up on the station's doorstep, demanding to talk to the head man. Said he had a big story and would sell it to the highest bidder, be that my network or one of my rivals. When my subordinate said your name had been mentioned I spoke to Hennessy in person."

Her gut pitched in a sickening roll. "What did you say?"

"I bought the sole rights to his story for an undisclosed amount. My company lawyer confirms that we can present a version that shouldn't result in any subsequent lawsuits. The exclusive is mine to do with as I wish."

"To air to the public?" A cheap shot at the ratings couldn't be Tate's aim. Despite the blinders he'd worn during their relationship, he had never purposely set out to hurt her. In fact, he did his best to protect those he loved.

Of course, *their* love had died long ago.

Tate rubbed his forehead. "My initial objective was to give the guy some sense of power by handing over a big check, then bury the whole ugly mess."

The pressure eased between her shoulders. The relief was so great she could have fainted...but for a single word in Tate's explanation.

She narrowed her eyes. "*Initial* objective."

"Now I'm thinking one hand should wash the other."

A giant alarm bell rattled inside her brain. She assessed his granite expression. So that was his game. Her suspicion had been more than sparked when Tate had mentioned the allegation lodged against her with the Psychologists Registration Board. Now with deadly clarity she realized his earlier remark had been strategic in leading up to this point.

"I would like to propose an exchange," he continued, straightening to his full imposing height. "If you take this assignment and my brother gets the leg up I know he deserves, the story will remain buried." He held up a hand. "And before you spout off about putting faith in the legal system, perhaps we should discuss statistics relating to innocent people sharing cells with criminals who kill to get change for breakfast. Wrongly accused who languish in jail because lawyers and judges and so-called expert witnesses set off domino effects that ruin people's lives. This cock-and-bull charge could result in a twelve-month prison term. Justice will prevail is a great ideal, but I won't take that chance with my own flesh and blood. I intend to stop this side-show before it has a chance to spiral any more out of control."

Her heart squeezed at the loyalty and stony conviction of his words even as another self-righteous side said nothing justified what he asked.

She set her teeth and shook her head. "No matter how you paint it, this is blackmail." *Give me what I want or face the consequences.*

His blue eyes shone in the moonlight. "A person can only be blackmailed if they have something to hide. If I were you, I'd thank my lucky stars I was the one who bought that exclusive." His tone dropped, low and lethal. "Give Blade a positive assessment, Donna, and get on with your life."

The same chill she'd felt earlier spread like a shroud over her skin. She swallowed against the acrid taste rising in her throat.

"I know how much you love your brother and sister," she ground out. "I took that into consideration whenever you did crazy things in their names. But don't do this. You can't save your family from every fall, Tate, even potentially fatal ones."

The dark slashes of his eyebrows drew together as if he might actually be considering her advice. His eyes probed hers for a long, heartening moment before he rolled back one big shoulder and raised his cleft chin. "I have my priorities."

She glared at him. "And you've let me know once again exactly what they are." As raindrops fell to darken the tiles, she hugged herself and pushed out a breath. "I won't agree to falsify your brother's report. But I will promise to give him a fair assessment."

His lip curled. "I'm not interested in what you think is fair. Given our history, I doubt you'd lose sleep if Blade spent a few months behind bars."

Her back went up. Did he know anything about her? "My job is to help people. I don't want to see anyone go to jail."

"I'm here to make certain that you don't."

He leaned in till his body heat radiated through the thin fabric of her gown and her head swam with the blinding force of his will.

"You won't file a positive report unless you can stand by your words?" He grinned. "So be it. You will spend time enough with Blade to be convinced this was an isolated incident, whether that takes one hour or two hundred."

An isolated incident in a decade full of continuing bad-boy behavior—not likely. Not that she based professional assessments on personal knowledge or background. She was ethical to the core, even when faced with highly unethical situations.

Still, for the moment Tate appeared to have her by the throat. And valuable networking time was slipping by. She needed to get back inside. Mrs. de-Walters wouldn't wait forever and Donna would never get another chance like this to pin her down. Best appease Tate…at least for now.

Reluctantly she nodded. "When's the trial?"

The tension tacking back his broad shoulders appeared to relax a notch. "In two months."

If she couldn't think of a way out of this, Tate would expect her to spend every available moment with his brother until she buckled, which was impossible. Best set some boundaries now.

"I'll see if I have any time free next week."

"Look very hard, Donna, or Maeve deWalters might view a series of stories on sexual misconduct in the therapist world. Of course, if you're innocent, you should have nothing to fear."

How dare he twist her words. Blade's and her situations weren't the same. Even when she was cleared, the scandal invoked by such a story would create such a furore, she'd have a hard time getting anyone to fund her project. Grants could freeze and everything she'd worked for could go up in the smoking ruins of her reputation.

To think she'd almost married this man.

Years of responsible self-healing suddenly came to naught. Her words were a shaky threadbare growl. "I hate you."

His jaw flinched. "Then I'm no worse off."

She despised giving in. She'd much rather tell him to go straight to hell. But that had never been an option. "Where and when?"

Tate's chest inflated. Battle won.

"At my television studios. Monday at ten. Don't be late." So indelible and debonair in that tux, he turned then surprised her by wheeling back. "One more thing."

Before she had time to think, the steel band of his arm gripped her waist.

His kiss was swift, overwhelming, deep—the

same superb rhythm and skill she remembered, yet strangely so much more. With his palm holding her head, memories hurtled back and the years slipped away. In this indefinable surreal moment, she was Tate's again and, incredibly, nothing else mattered. Despite their problems, she'd always felt extraordinarily complete whenever he held her.

Loved her…

Brutal reality—where they were, what she'd done—finally kicked in. Shoving at his rock-hard chest, she squirmed and, lost for breath, managed to break free.

Down his left cheek, the dimple she'd once adored appeared as he genuinely smiled. He was so damn superior.

He turned and crossed to the doors with that casual king-of-all stride. "Just wanted to let you know how sexy you are when you're mad."

Shaking with indignation and insufferable desire, she longed to shout out how arrogant he was. But as Tate disappeared into the ballroom, leaving the doors ajar, the words withered on her tongue. Through the crack, she saw Mrs. deWalters's lime-green velveteen dress headed for the main exit.

Sorting her scrambled brain, Donna pulled herself together. She had to focus and get in there fast.

She darted across the tiles, but thoughts of

Tate—his taste, scent and skill—lingered. Somehow she needed to figure out a way to placate him without jeopardizing her professional integrity. And when this ordeal was over, she would never need to see or, heaven forbid, kiss him again, because that was the last thing she wanted.

Even if her traitorous body whispered otherwise.

Two

Late Monday morning, Tate swept like a hurricane into his spacious top-floor office. Spotting Donna Wilks sitting in the second of three guest chairs, he hesitated before closing the door.

He didn't quite meet her eyes as he loosened his tie and thundered toward his desk. "I was held up."

"Only for an hour and sixteen minutes."

At her unimpressed expression and the light shadows beneath her eyes, Tate's conscience twinged but he pushed the guilt aside. Despite what she thought, he understood everyone's time was precious, including hers. She might look like a break would do her good, but he could bet Donna hadn't had his dog of a day.

Circumstances had changed.

She checked her watch—not the slim gold-bracelet piece he'd given on her twenty-third birthday but a large practical face with a black leather band. He noted her slender arm as he passed. The bracelet suited her mocha-cream complexion far better.

Ignoring the winter-sport sponsorship agreement that needed a signature by noon, he hitched a hip over a desk corner. At the same time, she crossed long shapely legs and laced her hands in the lap of a stylish navy and white-trim dress. He breathed in deep. Damn, she smelled good—like the roses he used to buy her.

"I have an appointment at one," she told him, "so let's get down to business. Will Blade and I speak here?"

Back to reality.

"Blade's not in."

She stared for a long, awkward moment before her face hardened with a humorless grin.

"Now I see how this arrangement will work. You jerk me around from breakfast to dinnertime, and my clients suffer because I can't keep their appointments." She stood, large turquoise-colored eyes more wounded than angry. "I know your priorities are supposed to come before anyone else's, but couldn't you at least have phoned to let me know?"

Despite her plea, and his full-length view of her lithe body, Tate remained cool. "Things were out of control here this morning."

She swept up her slim leather briefcase. "I'd like to sympathize, but your blowout has nothing to do with me."

"Guess again." He slid off the desk and crossed his arms. "A film of Blade's alleged assault has been shown by a rival network as a promo for their six-o'clock news."

Donna dropped back into the chair. "Oh, no."

Needing to work off more energy, Tate crossed to the wall-to-wall window and stared at commuter ferries zigzagging white wash across Sydney Harbor's wide blue bite. "The footage shows Blade lunging at the cameraman to stop him from filming, which, by the way, was pretty much the extent of this so-called assault."

Still, having those images televised up and down the east coast was hardly good for Blade's state of mind, or this network.

He'd appointed Blade hands-on executive producer of the new current affairs program due to launch in a few weeks. The opposition saw their opportunity to discredit and had slogged a double whammy. Hell, if he'd been them, he might have done the same.

Rotating, he leaned back and braced an arm on either side of the window ledge. "My attorney had the footage pulled off the air. He's uncertain about our chances of having it excluded from court."

Her fine wing-tip eyebrows slanted. "I'm sorry, Tate."

As he took in her flawless even features, framed by a fall of honey-blond hair, an invisible band squeezed his rib cage. That's what got him about Donna every time—what had had him hooked for so long. While she didn't always agree with his methods or opinion, she had a good heart.

But a good heart wasn't enough to convince him that she was capable of giving his brother an impartial assessment. To the contrary, he was almost certain she'd be influenced by the past—one night in particular—and condemn Blade before he'd opened his mouth.

But he possessed the key to turn that negative into a surefire positive. If Donna refused to see Blade and, ultimately, refused to provide a positive assessment, she risked Tate airing Hennessy's potentially damaging story.

Blackmail was an ugly word, but no matter what

it took, he wouldn't let Blade spend even one trumped-up day in jail. After their discussion Saturday night, he held all the cards. Donna wouldn't defy him. Few people did.

She unfolded from the chair again. "You'll let me know when I can meet with Blade."

"Absolutely—let's say this Friday at noon." A nice kickoff to the weekend.

She gave him a weary look that said his audacity in organizing her life appalled her. Then she surprised him by saying, "As it so happens, I'm free all afternoon Friday."

His expression opened up as his arms unraveled. "That's a turnaround."

"This might work better if I give Blade chunks of time, rather than bits and pieces."

"I'm thinking that your choice here relates to the fact that giving Blade bits and pieces is less convenient to your schedule and practice than blocking off an entire afternoon when you can spare one." She'd always been a smart lady. "I can live with that."

She had her own opinion of Blade, but surely if she spent enough time with his brother she would realize this assault charge was an isolated incident, that Blade had been provoked beyond any man's endurance. Once that happened, Tate could come clean. He had no real intention of carrying out his threats. He'd simply played his highest card.

He wished he had a choice—something that didn't flood him with guilt when his guard was down. One day, when Donna had a family, she'd appreciate how strong the impulse to protect one's own could be. God knows it had taken a tragic lesson nine years ago for him to appreciate it.

As she headed for the oak door, he focused on the natural sway of her hips and endless legs that tapered to professional yet exceptionally sexy high heels. His groin flexed as he remembered their recent kiss, the way she'd melted for a full five seconds before self-control dragged her away.

He pressed his thumb to the side of his wistful grin.

He could still smell her fragrance as his mouth had possessed hers for the first time in too long. What he wouldn't give to taste her just once more.

Filing that thought away, he straightened his necktie and crossed to see her out. Moving into his private reception lounge, he witnessed a woman bouncing up on tiptoe, her T-shirt-clad arms flung around Donna's neck.

"What are you doing here?" his sister cried out, finally stepping back. "I haven't seen you in ages!"

Past Donna's shoulder, Libby spotted her rather amused, always indulgent, brother. She marched up and set her fists on her designer-jean hips. "I'm ashamed of you." She whacked his arm. "Why didn't you tell me Donna was visiting?"

As Libby skipped back to the guest of honor, Tate wondered if he'd ever owned such a youthful spring, even at the tender age of twenty-two. Hard to believe this was the same shell of a girl he'd become guardian of after their parents' unexpected deaths. Much of Libby's metamorphosis he attributed to Donna. She'd been best friend, confidante and supportive big sister when Libby had needed it most.

"Are you here on business?" Libby went on, holding both Donna's hands. "Or is this a social call?" Her unusual violet-colored gaze sparkled as it lobbed from Donna to Tate. Shoulders slowly hunching up, she bit her lip. "And maybe I should shut up now."

Enjoying the reunion scene, Tate stepped forward, his face set with a mock-stern look. "Maybe you're right."

Donna didn't seem as prepared to overlook the they-might-be-getting-back-together misunderstanding. Her smile was thin but forgiving. "We're not dating, Libby."

His sister's bottom lip dropped. "You're seeing someone else?"

Tate stopped himself from telling her to pull back; he wanted to hear the answer.

Donna's mouth opened, but words took a moment to flow. "Work takes up pretty much all my time."

Libby scrutinized her. "You don't date at all?"

Donna hesitated. "Not...recently."

Tate's mouth hooked at one side. *Interesting.*

Libby's eyes grew big and bright. "Well, you're not leaving till I get the complete lowdown. What you're up to. Where you're living now." She found Donna's hands again and squeezed. "I've wondered about you so often."

Linking their arms, Libby prepared to lead Donna away, presumably to her office in children's production for one of her famous chocolate-sprinkle lattes that were more ground chocolate than anything else.

But Donna held back. After flicking a considering glance Tate's way, she smiled at Libby. "Can I take a rain check? I'll be back Friday noon. We can catch up then, if you're around."

"Sure, I'll be around." Libby shared a curious look with Tate. "But, Tate, when I asked Blade about our usual end of week meeting, he said you were both locked in for a location shoot in Queensland Friday. Or that's what I thought he rumbled, right before he fumed out of here a couple hours ago."

Tate cursed under his breath—firstly because he didn't want Donna hearing the words *fume* and

Blade in the same sentence, and secondly because he'd completely forgotten the location job when he'd arranged Friday's meeting.

He couldn't defer the location shoot. The deadline to get the show up and running by the start of the new season was already tight. Staff to hire, the show's opening vision to shoot. He couldn't afford any delay.

Donna turned to Tate, the expression on her beautiful face smug. "Guess we'll make it another time."

Tate wondered about the shoot, about Blade, then Donna—those smudges under her eyes—and made a snap decision.

He spoke to Libby. "Isn't your show recording today, sweetheart?"

"Nope. Talent's sick."

"I think I just heard a page for you," he lied, swinging his sister around and patting her on her way.

Over a shoulder, Libby grinned. "I get it. You want a private word before she goes." She stage-whispered to Donna, "One day he'll treat me like a grown-up."

Donna rolled her eyes and laughed. "We can only hope."

As Libby and Donna said their goodbyes, Tate raked a hand through his hair. He hadn't realized quite how much he'd missed the sound of Donna's laughter. Hadn't quite understood how much he'd missed *her,* full stop. He thought he'd gotten over her. Thought she must have gotten over him, too.

When Libby disappeared around the corner, Donna met his eyes. "What did you want to say?"

Her level tone said, *I've wasted enough time.* But her eyes were shuttered as if trying to hide the fact she was affected, too—by Libby's reaction on seeing her again, to a surge of memories the encounter had evoked. So many good times. Admittedly, there'd been some bad ones, too.

As he studied her face, his heart rate sped up.

He'd gotten on with life and put the demise of their year-long love affair down to experience. But now something more than instinct said he should pursue this sexual buzz. Wasn't time supposed to be a great healer?

He cleared his throat and took the plunge. "I want you to come to Queensland on Friday. You can meet with Blade there."

Her face contorted then she almost laughed. "Saturday you came close to ruining my night, today you had me sit and wait for over an hour. Now you're suggesting I jump on a jet and fly away with you to some palm-lined beach." She tapped her temple. "You have rocks in your head."

But perhaps then she recalled the unforgettable vacation they'd shared up north, because she hesitated and provided a flimsy footnote. "Besides, I have a stack of appointments that morning."

"Reschedule."

Her eyes went wide. "You're not serious?"

He turned the tables. "You were the one who suggested giving Blade chunks of time rather than pieces."

Her lips compressed, the same moist rims his tongue had run along two nights ago when he'd insisted she give in to him, then had taken that memorable bonus.

She must have read his mind. "Know your problem, Tate? You push too hard and expect too much."

He rationalized. "You did a paper once on the benefits of assertive behavior."

The magnet that was her body drew him nearer. As he invaded her personal space, her eyes grew glassy. She obviously wanted to leave, but he believed some reckless part of her wanted to stay just as much.

Her lower lip quivered. "I know what you're thinking. You're planning some time management of your own."

That made him think of her watch and whether she'd kept the gold bracelet. She used to take it off and leave it on the bedside table the moment he lowered the lights and slipped his hand over her waist to draw her near.

Edging closer, he shrugged and played dumb. "I'm not sure what you mean."

"While you've got me on your books, you're considering wrangling in a little added value."

He merely smiled. He wouldn't confirm or deny.

She swallowed, but stood her ground. "I'm giving you fair warning…you took me by surprise the other night. I won't let it happen again. Whatever was between us years ago is over, Tate. It's dead."

He nodded sagely then, giving in to his most basic animal need, set a hand on either side of that small waist and pulled her close.

As his mouth slanted over hers, her neck rocked back, she mewled in her throat and her briefcase hit the ground. He scooped his other palm upward to brace her back and took full advantage.

Her parted lips tasted sweeter than any he'd known. The brush of her breasts as he arched over her made his blood race and sizzle. Whether she could help it or not, she had surrendered. He felt it to his bones. Knew it in his heart.

She might hate him, but she wanted him, too.

Their mouths gradually drew apart. Still caressing her, he murmured against her lips, "Okay. We're clear. You won't let it happen again."

Her dreamy, lidded look evaporated like a flash of steam. Her body trembled before she wrenched away. Running both hands down the seams of her dress, she glanced anxiously about her feet and collected her briefcase. When she looked up, she was still short of breath and her voice was tellingly deep.

"You don't play fair. You've *never* played fair. This doesn't change a thing."

He kept a straight face. "If you say so."

Half turned to leave, she pinned him with a look. "Don't patronize me, Tate. I'm a woman, not a child."

He watched her glistening lips move and his insides tugged. His reply was half tease, half apology. "Let me make it up to you." Surely a day in paradise was a good place to start.

Her heart, and cynicism, showed in her eyes. "You can't ever make it up. Not with a trip, not with seduction and certainly not with blackmail."

Tate stared at the empty doorway, which led to and from his personal reception lounge, long after Donna had left—until his secretary, Molly, strolled in, scores of production-cost reports bundled in her arms. Trance broken, he headed toward his office but, needing to make arrangements, made a detour to Molly's desk. Both sets of knuckles resting on the timber, he thought it through.

Fair or unfair didn't come into it. The only rules

he played by were his own. And he always played to win, whether at work, with family, or a woman. Yet five years ago he'd let Donna go....

"Molly," he began, certain of his plan, "I need another return flight booked to Queensland."

Molly removed a pen from her salt-and-pepper bun and scribbled a note. "Anything else?"

"Three nights' accommodation." He rapped the timber once and headed for his office. "I'm returning Monday morning."

So was Ms. Wilks.

Three

Four days later, Donna jumped as she heard two familiar male voices drifting up the resort's slate path. Shifting, she set her lime and soda on the sun lounger tray and quickly arranged the sarong over her bright yellow one-piece.

Feeling trapped and, yes, a little intrigued, she'd finally buckled to Tate's "suggestion" that she accompany him to Queensland. She'd even succumbed to temptation and packed a small bag with essentials—sun lotion, bathing suit and matching sarong. However, irrespective of the informal setting, she was here as a professional; she might be lolling by a sparkling palm-fringed pool, but limits applied, and covering up was obviously one of them.

As she flicked the sarong again, making certain to conceal both sun-kissed shins, the men sauntered into sight. In knee-length black shorts and an ocher jersey knit shirt, Blade sat on the lower end of an adjacent sun lounger and chuckled at her state of repose. "Hard life?"

Dressed in tailored chinos and a white dress shirt, sleeves rolled to the forearms, Tate looked slightly more of the part of broadcasting executive on location. Pulling up a deck chair, he trailed a hand through his hair and eyed what he could see of her outfit.

"I take it you've had a relaxing time while we were gone."

Flushing, she looked away. "It's been...pleasant."

While rules didn't strictly apply with regard to client-interview locations, her ethical Richter scale was noticeably shaking. The sooner this getaway was over the better, for personal as much as professional reasons.

The longer she stayed in this relaxed south-seas atmosphere, the more memories taunted her and the more her defenses fell. The less control she had over her rebellious emotions, the more unacceptable physical urges would grip her whenever Tate was near.

A waiter arrived to take drink orders—a dry martini for Tate, a juice for Blade.

Donna sat up taller. Now that the men had their location business out the way, for what it was worth, she and Blade might as well get down to business. But she'd need to be dressed appropriately. Time to collect her clothes and a few belongings from the day locker the concierge had provided.

Somewhere close by, a cell phone peeled out the *Mission: Impossible* tune. Blade reached into his back pocket. His face, similar in complexion and structure to Tate's, pinched as he read the text message. "It's from our baby sister."

The sinews along Tate's bronzed forearms tensed on the chair arms as he shunted forward. "She in trouble?"

"No. But my car is." Blade tossed his phone onto the tray. "I buckled when Libby asked this morning if she could borrow it. That text let me know someone in a parking lot swiped the left side—and not just the paint."

Tate explained to Donna, "Blade has a new Lexus convertible." His eyebrow flexed. "Very smart."

"But now very scratched," Blade ended.

Donna expected Blade to roar. Instead he grinned, raked a hand through his collar-length dark hair and fell back against the length of his lounger.

"Libby is such a little minx," he said. "On Monday she asked for the keys just as I was heading out. I put on my sternest face, said a definite no, and still she came back." The hand resting on his forehead dropped to the sandy ground. "It's my fault. I'm a sucker. We all are where Libby is concerned."

Something clicked and Donna focused more on what he'd said. "Monday morning Libby asked for the keys?"

Blade sat up. "I did my best to make her think I was livid she'd even suggested it. The company provides her with a very nice mid-range BMW. Certainly not as expensive as the Lexus, but you'd think she'd be happy given she rear-ended and darn near totaled her brand-new Merc three months ago. My insurance will go through the roof."

Donna chewed her lip. So that's why Libby had mentioned Blade had been "fuming" that morning. Not because he'd seen that footage, but because he'd manufactured a hard-hearted act when his sister had put on the screws to borrow his new convertible.

She preferred to think of Libby as a minx rather than the introverted teen she'd once known. And, despite everything, she was relieved to witness Blade's sense of humor; they'd barely spoken on the flight up, he'd been so engrossed in paperwork.

45

But a snapsho ROBYN GRADY
enough. If Blade harbe ghter side wasn't nearly
gression, as the assault charal problem with ag-
capades attested to, time with hined and past es-
                                    ild reveal it.
The waiter reappeared, tray in han   nd Tate
accepted his drink. Blade was reaching whe. the
waiter fumbled and juice splashed and drenched
his shirt. Blade jumped up and flicked his wet hand
while the waiter bowed and apologized.

Blade patted down the air. "Honestly, it's fine,"
he told the waiter, who was dabbing the mess with
a napkin and muttering in a Latino accent. To stop
the fuss, Blade grabbed the hem and yanked the
soiled shirt over his head. He shrugged at all three.
"I was looking forward to a dip anyway."

The waiter finally backed away, but before Blade
moved off toward the pool, he sent her and Tate a
lopsided grin. "It's good to see you two finally over
your gripes. You always looked great together."

As Blade slipped off his loafers then jogged off
to dive in the pool, fire consumed Donna's cheeks
and neck. She and Tate were not *together.* Never
would be again.

Thankfully, Tate didn't comment except to say,
"He's grown into a brother to be proud of."

From what she'd seen just now, a part of her
might agree. But her profession required an inquir-

... as discrete data. She ing, analytical mind ... ibility that either the phone couldn't dismiss drink, perhaps both, had been call or the s... light his amicable character. She staged to ... would ... nothing past Tate. Which was precisely why, despite her doubts, she couldn't afford *not* to take his blackmail threat seriously.

As they watched Blade swim the length of the pool, flip, then freestyle back with a relaxed, powerful stroke, Donna's thoughts deepened. "He was such a troubled young man when we knew each other."

Her tummy fluttered. She shouldn't have spoken aloud and for more reasons than one. The past five years had seemed to drag, yet now Tate was here, sitting so close that "when we knew each other" could have been yesterday.

Tate crossed an ankle over the opposite knee. "Blade had good reason to be troubled. He was in love with a girl he wanted to marry. Then her meddling witch of a mother announced Blade wasn't good enough and pushed Kristin to accept another man's proposal." He raised his chin as if only now realizing that of course she already knew the background. "I defy anyone to handle that situation without falling in a heap once or twice."

"Flying completely off the rails" was more like it. "And this assault incident has some connection to

Kristin, I believe." She'd received her official court request and had read the notes on the encounter.

Tate nodded. "Last month, Kristin's husband, a big-shot property dealer in the States, dumped her like yesterday's laundry. For sensationalism's sake, the gossipmongers decided the reason was because Kristin and Blade were having a raging affair. Of course, the media needed a statement. When a reporter and cameraman cornered Blade that day, bombarding him with allegations and questions, Blade swore, shoved the camera out of his face then strode away."

Work had been so intense lately, she hadn't watched the news in weeks. "It must be horrible to worry about stories circulating that simply aren't true."

From his focused expression, Tate didn't make the connection between Blade's situation and her own. Typical.

"Blade handled it well until that jerk of a reporter wanted to know if it was true that Kristin was pregnant with his child and ill because he refused to see her."

The sick ache of disgust formed in Donna's stomach and she groaned. "Where and why do they come up with such things?"

"They take a seed and make it into an oak tree, all for the sake of audience share. In many cases, the media don't report the news—they create it."

She raised an eyebrow. *Tell me about it.*

Donna watched Blade push up out the water. As he swiped a fresh towel from a chair and ruffled his dark hair, a pair of young women in bikinis passed, giggling as they eyed him. Blade didn't appear to notice, but rather moved to stretch out on a lounger, stomach down.

"He seems to have matured," Donna found herself admitting.

Tate's foot dropped from his knee to the ground. "That sounded like a positive assessment."

"Do you ever quit?" The answer, of course, was no.

Another, not so easily answered question came to her mind. "I thought he might be irritated, even angry, when you set this meeting up today." The Blade she remembered hadn't wanted anyone's help.

With an almost sheepish air, Tate rubbed the back of his neck. "I said you asked to see him in a relaxed atmosphere rather than the sterile environment of an office."

The air left her lungs. "You didn't! Blade thinks this was my idea?"

Tate's confidence was back with a vengeance. "He was uncertain when I said you were my choice to do his assessment. But today broke the ice. You've seen him in his true light. He's seen you. Everything's good."

She tried to tamp down the flush of annoyance. "I have a strong feeling he won't be happy when he finds out the truth. No one likes being manipulated, Tate."

Herself included.

"When this is all over, I'll tell him the truth."

Although Donna was miffed, on another level she understood his mind-set. Many parents and guardians were overprotective—some even qualified as controlling. But that kind of dominant behavior could turn around and bite. Case in point, Mrs. deWalters.

She might have believed she acted in her daughter's best interests when she'd forbidden Kristin to marry the man she so obviously loved. But Maeve had mentioned last Saturday evening that she hadn't heard from her only child in years. Which brought to mind another young woman.

"If you're still steering Blade's life, I shudder to think what poor Libby has to put up with." Donna sent him a querulous look. "You let her go on dates, don't you?"

"Only if her homework is done." His poker face dissolved. "Of course I let her date. She's over twenty-one. I couldn't stop her if I wanted to."

"From what I saw Monday, you treat her like a teen in junior high more than a woman in her twenties."

He blinked twice, obviously offended. "She

holds a responsible position at the station. So responsible, in fact, I need to check up regularly to make certain it's not too much."

Donna had to grin.

Her attention drifted to his large hands loosely threaded in his lap and a lick of desire curled in her stomach. She'd loved his hands—the way they looked, the way they had touched her. The way they'd once held her with an intoxicating blend of innate strength and tenderness.

"I know what you're thinking," he said.

Guilty, Donna's wide eyes snapped up.

"But I'm not a dictator," he explained, carrying on their conversation. "I'm their..."

When he paused to find an appropriate word—protector, defender?—Donna supplied one that put the whole conversation in context. "You're their big brother."

The building's afternoon shadow had crept over her. At the contrast in temperature, a shiver danced across her skin. Time to move and change clothes.

Standing, she secured the sarong under her arms then twisted the ends to tie at her nape. She felt Tate's focus upon her the entire time, watching and no doubt wondering about the power surge arcing between them. She couldn't afford to let him know she was wondering, too. If he saw any lapse, any weakening in her resolve, he would show no mercy. The thought of a merciless Tate both worried and, quite frankly, excited her.

After smoothing down the silk batik fabric, she removed her hat and smiled innocently. "So, when's our flight back again?" She assumed it would be sometime early evening, not that a late flight was a problem. Tomorrow was the weekend and because she always kept Mondays free for administrative tasks, she had no appointments until Tuesday. "I'd like to know our time frame before I sit down to speak with Blade."

His eyes were dark and hooded, as if, while she'd been covering up, in his mind he'd been easing the swimsuit off.

Slowly, he got to his feet. "Plenty of time. We'll go for a walk. Not every day you get to stroll through paradise. I spend too much time stuck behind a desk. I'm sure you do, too."

A sexy grin bracketed one corner of his mouth as he held out one large neat hand.

Donna's heart thudded in her chest. She was afraid—scared witless, in fact—that if she accepted, he would take that as a sign she wanted to be kissed again. She was even more afraid that some demented part of her actually wanted him to. Tate Bridges was like a drug—he'd taken an age to cleanse from her system and after another tiny taste, she found herself edgy, craving him all over again.

They'd parted not because he'd cared so much about Blade and Libby, but because he refused to acknowledge how deeply his ambivalence toward her feelings continued to wound her. The night of their engagement party, Tate hadn't arrived because he'd been busy rescuing Blade from a scrap similar to the one he currently faced. It had been the final blow in a series of similar incidents. She could understand that his siblings and network were important to him. But where had their importance as a couple stood, or her individual feelings as his girlfriend and, later, fiancée? Their relationship would never have worked then, just as a repeat performance wouldn't work now—*particularly* now. But clearly Tate had his own ideas.

He didn't merely want to kiss her.

Still, she did need to stretch her legs. Surely she could handle a short stroll. Manufacturing a smile, she nodded. "Sure. A quick walk might be nice." But when she ignored his hand, he took hers anyway.

Her body buzzed and slipped up a gear as his grip, both strong and sensual, conjured up a profound sense of nostalgia. Tate was unique in every sense—a man born to lead and hold his course, no matter the cost. But she didn't need a legend. She needed a partner who truly cared. A man who knew the value of compromise. Unfortunately, Tate could never be that man.

When she tried to tug from his hold, he appeared not to notice and began to walk. Unwilling to cause a scene among the other guests by the pool, there seemed little choice but to go along.

They meandered down a path bordered by rustling bangalow palms. The air was warm but fresh, fragrant with the crush of grevillea, pine and sea salt. Eventually they stopped on the crest of a sandy knoll. Donna gazed out over the cerulean-blue water.

Nothing had changed. The view, the clean ocean scent, the incontestable sense of kismet…all a picture-perfect copy of their last visit to the coast.

Tate's sultry voice didn't break the atmosphere so much as blend with it. "We never talked about that night."

As the deep strum of his words took meaning, she surfaced from her haze and bit down against a sharp stab of regret. She didn't want to talk about that. She knew it was weak, but for just one moment longer she wanted to hold on to the illusion that reflected happier, more naive times.

His thumb circled the back of her hand. "Donna?"

Concentrating on the horizon, she tried to push the question aside. "What night?"

"You know what night."

Despite the humidity, an ice-cold shaft whistled down her spine. Grudgingly she nodded. Yes, she knew—the night of their engagement party. She'd spent every day since trying to obliterate the memories.

"The past is past." Her voice was firm, but she wouldn't look at him. She couldn't handle the complicated soul-to-soul connection they seemed to share even now.

"My delay," he went on, "couldn't be avoided."

Fighting memories, she tried to free her hand again, but he turned, capturing her other hand.

Dropping her chin, she clamped her eyes shut and garnered all the moral strength she felt draining from her limbs. If she tried hard enough, she could hold the vision back. To see that night—to remember—hurt too much.

"I got your messages. I know what happened."

"You didn't return my calls."

Don't look at him. Don't fall into those ocean-blue eyes.

"I returned one." The next morning, when the guests had gone home—her family and their friends who had all been so disappointed for her. Their well-intentioned support had only made it harder.

Donna cringed. Damn it, now she could see their

pitying faces. Could feel the shame eating at her heart. And she remembered, too, when she'd gotten home, that she'd cried till well after dawn. She couldn't bear the crush of those memories. She wanted them gone, buried forever.

She'd loved him so much.

Tate let go one hand to tilt up her chin. His intense gaze searched hers as a pulse beat at the side of his neck. "I needed to speak with you…explain."

This was killing her—all over again.

"We spoke, Tate. There was nothing more to say." A brave smile thinned her lips. "And, it's okay, *really*."

He'd said he was sorry. She'd said that wasn't enough. How many times had he left her waiting—in restaurants, at her apartment or his, and then later at appointments organized around what was to be their forthcoming wedding? Yes, he was a busy man, but as far as feelings were concerned, he could also be an inconsiderate one. If that was life as his girl-friend and fiancée, she'd made up her mind she didn't want to stick around for life as his wife. After the en-gagement party, he'd left messages, knocked on her door, pounded once or twice, but she'd remained strong…except for that one heart-wrenching slip.

She stomped on the image.

Until a week ago, she thought she'd successfully wiped her conscience clean of Tate Bridges. She should never have walked with him. Should never have come here today.

She tried again. "There's no need to dredge it up again."

His voice deepened. "What if I want to?"

His persistence should have rankled but, instead, she felt the inappropriate urge to laugh.

"You truly are the most arrogant man I've ever met. You blatantly coerce me into helping your brother. Kiss me when you know you have no right. Now you want to—" exasperated, she threw up her free hand "—I don't know what."

His eyes glistened out from the encroaching shadows. "You know perfectly well what."

He lifted her hand till his mouth pressed upon the back of her wrist. A tingling pleasure spiraled up her arm. Mouth lingering, his tongue looped the sensitive flesh, channeling the raw hunger directly to her core.

His scent enveloped her. As his mouth trailed up her arm, his other hand found the small of her back and urged her in against his hips.

He was hard.

Liking the glorious feel of him way too much, she squirmed. "Tate…don't."

"Because you don't want me to hold you? Don't like the push of me against you?" He pressed more firmly and she bit her lip against a soft cry of need. "I think you do, Donna. I think you like it very much."

She closed her eyes but refused to slant her head and offer her neck as he kissed her shoulder. No one else would ever make her feel like this, as if nothing else existed but grasping passion and the aching need to fill it.

But she had to remember…she had to let him know. "I wanted you to stay out of my life."

His smile brushed her jaw. "That must be why you keep kissing me back."

To prove a point, he claimed her lips again, languidly, as if he could take all the time in the world and still she wouldn't refuse him. With each stroke, the thrill went lower, deeper, till everything she was belonged only to him. She should have felt imprisoned by his power. Instead, Lord help her, she felt released.

As his kiss broke into moist meaningful snatches, lucidity peeped through. They were in the open, making love and building to more dangerous, irreversible things. Yet she couldn't bear to tear away from him. He felt too good.

Her palms fanned his hot, hard chest. She sighed and burned with longing. "I must be mad."

"Yep. Completely gone."

His hand slid in between the folds of her sarong

and she lost her good judgment beneath a twirling blanket of desire. But a remnant of common sense still nagged.

Eyes drifting open, she summoned a frown. "I won't sleep with you, Tate. We're going to fly home and that will be the end of kissing and touching and…"

His fingertip drew a circle above the apex of her thighs. When his touch slid down between, Donna moaned and forgot what she was saying.

How did he do it? With little effort, in so short a time, he made her forget everything and want only him.

He nuzzled that sweet spot just below her earlobe and a luscious gloss of abandon cascaded to her toes.

"I've reserved a bungalow with a spa bath overlooking the waves, just like before."

A delicious throb kicked off at her hub and she dug her fingers into his biceps. All comprehension past the hum of his voice and magic of his touch melted away. What had he said? Something important. She forced her brain to work.

"You're staying the night?"

"*We're* staying *three* nights."

She heard and, at some level, understood. She should object…definitely would.

Through her swimsuit, he rubbed her *there* and

she leaned toward him. "I'm not. I can't. I…I don't have any clothes."

As his lips grazed hers, she felt his smile. "That won't be a problem."

Four

By the time they returned to the pool area, Donna's face was hot with shame. What a deplorable lack of control. Such an obvious miscalculation of power.

How dim-witted to expect she could show Tate she no longer desired him. The simple truth was, she *did* desire him—ferociously. Another moment and they might have shed their clothes and satisfied each other then and there on the sand.

It wouldn't have been the first time.

But as they walked together side by side now, Tate's hand flexing and squeezing hers while they navigated the shifting crystal-blue pool water,

Donna's stomach somersaulted. Her throat felt thick, and she couldn't stop swallowing. He expected her to succumb, completely and tonight. He wouldn't be pleased to learn that since the last explosive kiss she'd had a change, not so much of heart as of reason.

The bungalow and spa bath were now off-limits, no matter how much her raging hormones begged or Tate and his sizzling caresses tried to persuade her. And she had a foolproof way to achieve her aim.

If she couldn't trust herself or Tate, she would have to put her faith in Blade. Heaven knows what excuse Tate intended to give his brother when they met back here. Or perhaps Blade already knew about Tate's cozy three-day plan.

However, irrespective of what left Tate's mouth she would stick to her guns and, more importantly, stick to Blade's side until they were safely back in Sydney. She would handle tomorrow when tomorrow came. Today she had to escape and Blade's company was her only sure ticket out.

Strange. Five years ago she'd secretly, perhaps selfishly, wished Blade Bridges out of her life; Tate was always rushing off to save his hothead brother from one ill-fated escapade or another. But right now she only wanted to keep Blade close. With him near, she could hardly forget the past and why three days in paradise could only end in misery.

Stopping by the lounger where they'd last seen Blade, Tate glanced around the bobbing palm fronds and massive navy-blue and white sun umbrellas. A few people dotted the sandy perimeter of the pool, one couple chatted at the Balinese-style bar near a trickling rock waterfall, but Blade was nowhere to be seen.

Tate pulled up the waiter who had spilled the juice earlier. "Have you seen my brother?"

Donna tried to see past the main building's floor-to-ceiling tinted windows. Blade, too, had left some belongings in a private locker earlier. Perhaps he'd gone to collect a change of clothes. Or maybe he'd dried off and was enjoying the tinkling chords of the piano she heard wafting out from inside. He had to be here somewhere.

The waiter nodded. "The gentleman left in a hurry. He said I should give you this when you returned." He dug into his pocket and handed over a message written on resort paper.

Donna read over Tate's arm.

Received urgent phone call. Must catch earlier flight. Sorry. Blade.

Donna's world shuddered on its axis. Blade had left.

But as Tate scrunched the note in his fist, her mind jolted back into gear. She had to follow Blade, catch a cab to the airport. And she had to do it now before Tate took her in his arms again.

She spoke to the waiter. "Can you arrange a cab to the airport?"

Before the waiter could reply, Tate, cell phone already to his ear, gripped her wrist.

"No need to jump to conclusions and follow just yet." He cursed and stabbed a button with his thumb. "Blade's not answering." He punched in another number. "I'll get Libby on the phone and—" He focused on his call. "Libby? What's wrong?" He frowned. "Did you call Blade?" He shook his head. "No, not about the scratch on the car."

As the waiter edged away, Donna sighed with relief. Whatever urgent matter had spurred Blade away had nothing to do with Libby. At least she could travel to the airport free from worry over the young woman she'd once thought of as her own sister, and who had come close to being just that through marriage. Some weeks after their breakup, she'd left messages with the Bridges's housekeeper. Apparently Libby had been away overseas on an extended vacation with friends, but she never returned those calls. Donna had assumed Libby had decided not to keep in touch, but after the wonderful reception she'd received at Tate's office the other day, she wondered whether those messages had ever made it into Libby's hands.

Setting her thoughts back on track, Donna tugged to release her arm, but Tate, focused on a third call now, bound her to him, his strong fingers cuffing her wrist with just the right amount of pressure—not tight, but firm. Trying to ignore his heated touch, Donna studied the path leading into the main building...and freedom.

She would simply tell Tate quietly, clearly, that she wanted to catch the next flight home. She glanced up at him—larger than life, exuding magnetism and confidence in any situation—and a convulsive shiver ran through her. How very close she'd come to disaster.

His mouth tight with concern, Tate disconnected and slipped the cell into his trouser pocket. "Nothing's wrong at the station, either. Must be something personal."

If Donna could spare the brain power, she might be concerned, too. But she had her own problems. Best get it over with. "Tate, I know what happened back on the beach must have led you to believe..."

The line etched between Tate's eyebrows eased. He redirected his attention to her and he slowly smiled.

"Ah, yes, our...conversation. I recall something about clothes, or lack thereof." The simmering line of his gaze traveled down her throat, across her tingling breasts. "Right now I'm thinking you're overdressed. We both are."

"If I need to apologize for giving you the wrong impression, I will. But then you should apologize for leading me into this ambush."

He held her gaze for a moment then exhaled, slow and patient. "We need to talk."

"No, we do not." There'd been enough talk. Talk that led to lover's whispers in her ear and forbidden sensations spilling through her body. "We need to leave all this behind, once and for all."

He spoke close to her lips. "What are you so afraid of?"

"I'm afraid of getting tangled up with you again! Falling for your charm, then being relegated to the back of the line." *Constantly telling myself I can change you if only I try harder.* "You have your life exactly as you shaped it. But I don't want to *fit* in with your life, Tate. I want to be part of—"

She bit the rest off before she said things she didn't mean.

Needing to create some semblance of distance between them, she locked her arms over her chest. "Read my lips. We're past tense, Tate."

The dimple in his cheek appeared as he chuckled. "Donna, that kiss was definitely present tense."

"I won't deny we still share a sexual chemistry..."

"Let's work from that point." He came closer.

Trembling inside and out, she stepped back. "It took time to get over you. I have my own life. I'm well respected." Hell, she respected herself and didn't intend for that to change.

"You work too hard." His curled knuckle stroked her cheek. "You need a break."

"You're right. I do need a break, Tate. From you and your manipulations. I'm taking a cab to the airport, with or without you."

The wide ledge of his shoulders went back, then he shrugged. "Fine."

She held her breath, waiting for more.

Sliding both hands into his trouser pockets, he tucked in his chin. "I'm not the type to force a lady, Donna, you know that."

As if he would ever need to use force. An encouraging touch here, an enticing stroke there... She wouldn't be the only woman to have liquefied beneath his skills in the bedroom.

Pushing aside the image of his bed—with them in it—she gathered her wits. The often seductive slant of his mouth appeared resigned. In fact, he looked at ease with her decision. As if...he were now as eager as she was to leave.

Her crossed arms fell to her sides and she sent

him a grudging smile. "Well, all I can say is I'm glad you're taking this so well."

"I don't continue to waste time on lost causes."

She flinched at the twinge beneath her ribs. Yes, she knew that from old. And that was exactly how she wanted it. Over and done with. For good.

Retracting his hands from his pockets, he started down the path—not the one they'd walked down earlier. This path was marked by a waist-high wooden sign that read, Private Poinsettia Accommodation.

"I'll grab my stuff," he tossed over one shoulder, "and we'll leave."

Next minute, she was alone. Music started up behind her, evening shadows crept in, and her poor brain seized up more. Grab his stuff… He meant go to his reserved bungalow where some of his belongings must already be stashed.

Like a cymbal clap, another thought struck. She narrowed her eyes and slowly grinned. Of course! This was a sham, a trick to leave her here, off balance, wondering, so she would eventually follow and end up smack-dab in his lair and he could—

Down the path, Tate reappeared from behind an evergreen spray of pigmy date palms. Black briefcase in hand, along with a bag she now recognized as a small overnighter, he was moving toward her quickly. Her throat constricted.

Heck...he really was eager to go.

Tate didn't so much join her as stride right past. While her foolish heart teetered then dropped to the ground, he stopped, turned and jerked his head at her. "You coming?"

She was about to mumble something half intelligent when he swore and strode back past again. "Left my phone on the table."

She blinked after him. Left alone again...with a night bird calling, poolside music playing and her self-conscious thoughts going wild. She'd never felt less attractive, not even as a gangly teenager with an embarrassing overbite.

How conceited to think the indomitable Tate Bridges would put up a fight for her. He'd thought he had a good chance, but clearly he wasn't overly concerned one way or the other. How ludicrous to believe he still cared enough.

Kicking herself, she shook her head. He had never cared for her the way she'd cared for him. Still cared, to be painfully honest.

Endless minutes ticked by. Finally she spied movement down the path, then glimpsed him, phone to ear, as he paced out from behind the pigmy palms, then back, out of sight once more.

Her sandaled foot grated up the sand then took one hesitant step forward. If he was stuck on some business call or had finally tracked down a troubled Blade, who knew how long the call would last.

Time rolled on. Her pulse started to pound and palms began to sweat. Counting the seconds, she laced her hands and squeezed.

Her heart leapt when she saw Tate pace into view. And out of sight again.

That does it.

She huffed and started off. This was absurd. She knew all about Tate and his phone calls. He'd shown up over an hour late at a restaurant once when he'd got "stuck." She would simply tell him she was leaving.

She glimpsed just a bit of him before he ducked into the private bungalow. Arriving at the door to the humble-looking hideaway, her step faltered. The thatched roof cottage gave the impression of complete isolation; the pool music was a distant percussive thump, the surrounding trees a picturesque natural screen. Tate's briefcase sat unattended on one of two rattan chairs on the open verandah.

Senses prickling, she listened to Tate's conversation traveling from inside—something to do with a news editor walking out. How much longer? Damn the man, had he completely forgotten about her? She would not be shoved aside again.

As she mounted the three stairs, the spa bath at the far end of the verandah caught her eye. Her center contracted as a wistful ribbon wound around her heart. An invisible string tugged her closer until she was bending, her hand drifting through the soft bubbling water.

Mango and lime underpinned by jasmine…

She knew the scent, would never forget it. It took her back to the best week of her life. To a time when she and Tate had been happy, with only themselves to worry about and no outside cares demanding his time. With all her heart she had believed in them.

Believed in their future.

Her concentration shifted and she frowned. It was quiet. No one-sided conversation filtering out. Tate had finished his call and, clearly, she was finished here.

She didn't hear but rather felt him behind her. Holding herself taut, she gradually turned.

His eyes roamed first her face then the full length of her still body. His eyebrows slowly pinched before his gaze eased up to pierce hers.

As he started toward her, each step measured and filled with unadorned purpose, her own legs lost strength. Halfway to her, he undid the first button on his shirt, then the next.

Her breathing shallowed out before falling to uneven snatches of air when, still walking, he pulled the shirttails from his pants.

Her voice came out a squeak. "Tate…I don't… this isn't…"

Every sip of oxygen left her lungs as he lifted her off the ground. She found herself slung in the steely hammock of his arms, his bare chest hot and inviting.

"Please…"

How to end that sentence? *Please don't?* If that were true, why did it seem her entire life was reduced to this moment?

After kicking off his loafers, he ascended the steps to the spa's wooden platform then down into the swirling frothing pool. As the water lapped her bottom, he focused on her lips and murmured in a deep level voice, "I won't kiss you."

The unbearable expectation at her center coiled higher, tighter. She swallowed against the nerves fluttering in her throat.

"You won't?"

His smile confirmed it. "You're going to kiss me."

She swallowed again. "I am?"

"And you'll keep on kissing—" his mouth dropped closer "—and kissing—" closer "—and then…"

Drowning in him, she threaded a weak arm around his neck and brought him down to her parted lips.

"Then—" Lord help her "—I'll kiss you again."

Five

The fact that they were fully clothed didn't matter. Donna clung to Tate's neck, her mouth fused to his, knowing soon everything would be shed—clothes, inhibitions, doubt.

As he brought her higher into his arms, deepening the kiss, she understood that at this moment history played no part in her desire for him. If aching for his embrace was wrong, so be it. If longing for the pleasure only his body gave was bad, she didn't care. She was so tired of being "strong" and "good."

She found great satisfaction in her profession,

but helping clients to cope with life's problems took its toll. Instead of easing others' pain, tonight she only wished to salve her own. And Tate's hard-muscled ministrations were just the balm.

Gradually his mouth released hers and she found herself being lowered to stand in the churning scented pool. As warm water massaged and tickled her thighs, she drank in the vision of Tate's solid bronzed chest. The shirt, which he'd finished unbuttoning, hung on his shoulders. Her fingers itched to remove it and savor the full intoxicating effects of his bared torso and arms.

As if reading her mind, he cocked one dark eyebrow. "Do it."

A tremor of guilty pleasure ripped through her veins. Heart racing, she exhaled slowly and slipped the fabric off his back. The shirt fell and swirled off through the suds. She couldn't keep her eyes from the captivating sight before her.

Tate's physique was even more masculine than she remembered…big biceps, strained and dangerous…perfectly honed pectorals pleading for her touch. His abdomen, defined by rungs of tanned muscle, naturally drew her attention down to a dark leather belt resting on his lean hips.

He said, "My turn."

Her breath burned in her lungs as he came

forward to kiss her temple at the same time his fingers delved behind her neck. Effortlessly he released the knot then, holding one corner, dragged the batik fabric from her body. Bending, he swept the sarong through the water, caught his shirt along the way and tossed both garments toward the vacant rattan chair.

While she stood before him—exposed, vulnerable, alive—he frowned playfully. "Nope. Still not even."

His large hands first circled her throat then traveled down the receptive curves where her neck met her collarbone. Shaky with anticipation, she let her eyes drift shut. She was a trembling, desperate, mindless mass, and he'd barely touched her.

"Donna, open your eyes."

A command? This minute he could say anything, do anything, and she would gladly obey.

Satisfied once she'd fixed her gaze on his, his line of vision scanned south, sizzling along her throat and across to where his left hand rested lightly on her swimsuit strap. Afraid her legs might dissolve beneath her, she watched the thick fringes of his lashes blink once before his hand slid meticulously down. One side of her swimsuit went, too.

His chest inflated as his lidded gaze soaked up the view. His fingers measured the lower arc of her breast, tested the weight then sculpted a stroke that ended with his thumb and forefinger gently pinching the tip. Overcome by exquisite weakness, she gripped his hips to stop from toppling forward.

With the same degree of skill, he drew the other strap down. Hands bracing her upper arms, he brought her closer, till his lowered mouth covered one aching nipple. His tongue worked around the peak, flicking, sucking, before, teeth skimming, he drew away.

Donna moaned. She was near frantic with longing to have him do it again.

When he released her arms, she slunk down, sighing as the water lapped her tummy, chest, throat. Acutely aware of Tate releasing his belt, unzipping his trousers, her anticipation wound ever higher until he finally let them fall.

Her throat swelled at the sight of him.

Pure male perfection.

After tossing out the last of his clothes, he lowered into the water and moved over to her. Kissing her, he maneuvered the rest of the swimsuit down over her hips and from her pliant legs. Her sandals slipped off along with the yellow Lycra. At last they were naked…natural and meant to be.

Growling his satisfaction, he twirled her over onto his lap. With his back propped against the spa wall, his mouth descended to sample her other breast. Lost in rapture, Donna arched back until her hair floated and trailed in the water behind her.

Conscious of the swell of his arousal resting between her legs, she sighed as he caressed her where her body needed it most. When his touch lightly circled, she shuddered against the almost violent push of pleasure. Afraid he might be sidetracked, she held his hand there and pulled herself back up toward him till her chest lay sloped against his. With her other hand she found him—hard as stone, hotter than a brand.

His throat hummed as he rubbed his bristled chin against her jaw. "You feel so good."

She nipped his lower lip in reply.

His magic had whisked her past the point of no return, and yet she knew this went against everything she'd vowed to avoid. The man had left her heart in tatters. Five years on he'd blatantly disregarded her feelings and worth again.

Still, here she was...helpless in his arms. She wouldn't consider words like *careful,* or *conscience,* or *guilt.* Not a night passed where she didn't lay her head on the pillow and wish for the comfort of his physical heat.

Now she had him—Tate Bridges rippling with vitality, lulling her toward a precipice that tonight she would willingly fling herself from. Some time away from duty, sweet memories to hold on to and smile back on. Especially when he stroked there.

"We need protection."

His announcement jolted her back. They felt so close, it was torture to agree. She'd had no lovers since Tate, but other considerations shouldn't be ignored, no matter how desperately she wanted him.

He moved first. Standing thigh-deep in the bubbles, he took her hand and drew her up. He led her from the spa, dripping and deliciously warm, over the timber boards, through the bungalow entrance, then into the dusk-filled bedroom.

He shook out one of two large white towels, which lay on the gold brocade quilt, and patted her—hair, throat, shoulders, ribs. He gave every inch his full attention until she was dry all over. When he was satisfied, and she was biting her inside cheek against the urge to push him back onto the spread, he scrubbed his chest with the towel then dropped it at their feet. He moved to fling back the quilt then returned. With the barest of smiles, he circled her, edging her around till she was forced to sit then crawl backward over the sheets.

With her in position, he rummaged around his overnighter and retrieved one small square wrap. His husky voice carried in the looming darkness.

"Don't worry, I have more."

She flinched at the admission but smothered the hurt. Of course, he was prepared. And a part of her was flattered by his forethought. He still wanted her, after all these years. The glaring truth was she wanted him, too.

Foil wrap in hand, he prowled up over the embroidered silk. As if too much time had been wasted, he pinned her beneath him, hands above her head, and captured her mouth with his. Fireworks exploded throughout her hypersensitive body. Soon he would take her. The anticipation was blissful agony.

His hand sailed down the curve of her waist, over her hip and across to find her feverishly ready. After securing the condom, he eased inside her. She sighed and moved to meet him as his lips brushed her brow.

Within moments, the hypnotic grind and rhythm built to near self-combustion.

She found her breath and whispered against his ear, "Don't hold back."

Six

Hands cupping her head, Tate smiled at Donna's words. As he moved he murmured close to her lips, "Five years without you. This kind of pleasure is a crime."

His mouth dropped to cover her parted lips. When his tongue found hers, hot and hungry, the intensity leapt from high to clearing-the-stratosphere. Already he anticipated the next time, and the next.

The slim column of her neck arced. The lock of her thighs squeezed before her legs twined over his to help drive him in. Sweet heaven, he'd like this to last, but neither of them were superhuman.

Donna made that long, purring sound in her throat he'd once been so familiar with. She was close. His eyes closed as the urge to succumb challenged every switched-on cell in his body.

She whispered his name, then sucked her lips in and rolled her head first to one side then the next. He concentrated only on tangibles—position, sensation—and held her tighter.

It was time.

The release shot through his veins. Beneath him, Donna writhed and clung on as if the world had fallen away and he was her only anchor. The pulsing echoed in his head, compounded low in his belly.

Yes, paradise had never felt so good.

The peak lasted a lifetime...and not nearly long enough. As the throbbing eased his face lifted from her hair. Filling his lungs, he saw she was smiling, too, but her sparkling eyes already hinted at doubts.

Biting down against the jolt in his gut, he traced a path with his fingertip from her temple down her cheek. He kissed her nose.

"Welcome back."

But as her gaze held his, the smile slipped. Long lashes fluttered when she blinked several times. "I don't know what just happened."

He twined a lock of her fair hair around his finger. "I'd be happy to explain in greater detail."

Her frown verged on playful. "Sex was always good between us. That was never the issue."

He kissed the curve of her shoulder. "It's one hell of an issue now."

Her voice was almost firm. "This can't happen again, Tate. For so many reasons. If anyone finds out we're romantically involved while I'm assigned to your brother's case…" Shuddering, she wriggled out from under him. "I couldn't face my peers, or myself, again."

When she tried to leave his bed, he tugged her back, his arm locking her in place beside him. He gave her a squeeze. "No one will find out."

"That's not the point. What we've done crosses the line." Her fist clenched low on her stomach. "I should never have let you push me into seeing Blade in the first place."

Tate frowned. His blackmail threat had been empty. That story about her would never air, but now more than ever he couldn't let her know. She would remove herself from the case and there was always the chance his brother might be stuck with a negative report from another psychologist. Equally disturbing—he would lose whatever personal hold he had on Donna.

Getting her back in his bed hadn't been his initial objective, no matter what she might believe. Although it still needled that she'd cut him off after their engagement party without so much as a decent conversation, he'd come to accept—even welcome in a way—that they would never be husband and wife.

Clearly he wasn't made for marriage and the lifetime of obligations that followed. He had more than enough responsibility already. But renewing their lovers relationship? That was a different story.

Sure, he had regrets, but enjoying Donna's body again, feeling how she wanted him, too, wasn't one of them. She must realize he would never go ahead and crucify her with a report that would destroy her reputation.

This week, his private investigator had confirmed she'd had no lover since him. He might have tempted her with stolen kisses, but she'd willingly surrendered to the bait. Actions spoke louder than words.

She wanted to be here—naked, together—as much as he.

He moved onto his side and gathered her closer. Her silken curves fired up his blood once more. He didn't want to talk, unless it was about making love.

"Let's keep the world outside for now." He gently cradled her head and circled her temple with his thumb. "We have three days together. And I want them just to be about us."

Before he could seal that declaration with a kiss,

she pushed against him and eased out of bed. He regretted losing her warmth, but the view of her naked body made up for it.

Her full breasts rose and fell with each uneven breath. In the muted light filtering through a break in the bedroom curtains, her cheeks looked flushed—from residual pleasure or fresh angst?

"You're not listening, Tate. I *can't* get involved, and not only for professional reasons. You haven't changed. If anything, you're more stubborn than ever."

Her back slowly straightened. "I'm going to catch that flight." She found a towel and wrapped it around herself.

Adrenaline spiked through his system. But he controlled the rev and sat up slowly, deliberately. "You'll stay with me."

"I might have just done the dumbest thing in my life, but I'm not completely stupid."

He felt a muscle tick in his cheek. "We had problems in the past but tonight we can take the first step in moving forward."

"Nice try, but you're a stone, and stone doesn't change."

"Have you seen the Grand Canyon?"

"We don't have ten million years."

Irritation prickled the back of his neck. "You

really ought to cut yourself some slack. Carrying all that guilt around must be tiring."

She stopped fiddling with her slipping towel and simply glared at him. "Besides accommodating you today, what do I have to feel guilty about?"

Tate groaned. Both he and Donna had taken on heavy personal loads; at times he felt the weight so intensely he thought his back might break. In that way they were very similar but for one vital difference.

No matter how hard he tried to make up for his part in his parents' deaths, he would never feel fully redeemed. But at least he acknowledged that torment for what it was—personal blame.

His haunted sense of loyalty had contributed to their relationship's breakdown, but so had hers. When he'd known her last, he'd held his tongue when perhaps he should have pressed her.

He lowered his voice. "We both know why you're desperate to get these extra safe houses off the ground."

Her gaze held before darting to the left. "There's a shortage of accommodation, which means fewer options for women in trouble who need a place to stay."

A well-rehearsed response.

"And?"

Her mouth opened and closed before she manufactured a casual tone. "A friend...a close friend was also an inspiration."

"You and Judith lived together in your last foster home."

Abandoned as a baby, Donna had become a ward of the state. She'd spoken to him about it only once. Given the tight line of her mouth now, she'd still rather not discuss it. She'd appreciate his next point even less.

"The year we were together," he continued, "Judith died, a victim of domestic homicide." He hesitated, but pushed on. "You couldn't save her, Donna."

She closed her eyes and winced. "I told her to move into my apartment, but she said she didn't want to put me in any kind of danger."

"But there *was* a shelter she could have gone to?"

She frowned, irritated. "You know all this."

He was certain he *didn't* know it all. More to the point, he suspected Donna needed to face it now before they could move on.

She looked at him hard before shifting her weight and pushing out the words.

"Judith's father had also been abusive. Before being placed in foster care, she spent a lot of time with her mother in shelters. She had horrible memories of living with groups of strangers whenever her home life erupted. So she wanted to wait for an individual house or duplex where she could have some privacy. But whenever one eventually freed up, she'd talk herself out of leaving."

Not looking at Tate, but rather through him, Donna held her towel tight at her breast. "Judith hadn't gone to college. She didn't have any job at that stage, and she refused to take money from me." Her eyes blazed and watered then she growled, "How I wish she'd never met that man."

Seemed he'd turned on a tap. Those last months they'd been together, she'd refused to talk about Judith's death. She'd grown more and more sullen because, as far as he could fathom, she couldn't save her friend and therefore deserved to be punished. Like a self-fulfilling prophesy, eight weeks after the funeral, he and Donna were no longer a couple.

She pushed some drying hair behind her ear. "Rehashing this is pointless."

He raised his brows. She was the one doing the talking. And the message was loud and clear: Donna Wilks helped people. Donna couldn't help her friend. Therefore, Donna didn't deserve happiness.

She'd brought down the final ax on their relationship and in hindsight perhaps that had been best. Each had their responsibilities, and ghosts, to serve. But now that the dust had settled, one force linked them still: he wanted her and she wanted him. Weddings were no longer the issue. But they could comfort each other, every night if they wished, and wasn't that a good thing?

He smiled softly and patted the sheet. "You're tired. Forget about planes. Come back here and relax."

Let me hold you and you can hold me.

"Relax? That's real cute coming from an extortionist."

He frowned at her jaded look.

Enough talk.

He reached over and caught her waist. As she looked at him with anger, mistrust and desire in her eyes, he wanted to say, *I won't let anything hurt you.* But, given her last comment and his current inability to refute it, he bit those words off. Two others came to mind. His throat ached as he said them.

"Come back."

Her mouth trembled before an impassive look hardened her face and her frame tensed. "I have enough to regret. All I want is to stand under a long hot shower, get dressed and go."

After a drawn-out moment, he nodded. Tomorrow morning he'd be in there with her, sponging her back. She might have won this battle, but he would win the war.

As she moved into the attached bathroom, the

bedside extension caught his eye. The message light was blinking red. His mind flew in a circle. Blade or anyone at the station would use his cell number.

He stabbed the message button and listened. As the shower water began to hiss, Tate sank down onto the mattress. Given who had left that message for Donna, and the tone of that voice, guess their secret was out.

Seven

Donna left the bathroom in an oversized guest robe, fluffing one side of her shampooed hair with a fresh towel. She stopped in her tracks at the sight greeting her.

Tate was pouring champagne. And he hadn't dressed.

Her already warm skin began to sizzle as her respiratory picked up pace. He was playing a scintillating game of seduction and this was full-throttle, second-half kickoff.

Drawn but also determined, she dropped the

towel inside the bathroom and knotted her arms over her chest. "*That's* a waste of time."

She'd made one doozy of a slip, but all was not lost. No one need know she'd fallen into bed with her blackmailer, her ex-lover. Now she merely had to keep her head and make it out of here intact.

Tate peered over his big bare shoulder as if he'd forgotten she'd been in the next room. "I've only poured one glass." He took a sip. "Not French but still very fine."

As he turned to stopper the bottle, she glared. He knew she loved champagne, but she was in no mood for celebrating. For all intents and purposes, he'd cross-examined her, and only minutes after making love. He was merciless. Worse, she would never admit it, but he had made a valid and insightful point.

She felt responsible for Judith's death, even though she knew she shouldn't. As a friend or therapist she could listen and make suggestions for change, but she couldn't make problems disappear, or force others to make smart choices. It was frustrating, painful, but true. No human being could make another end a self-destructive relationship.

Tate lifted a chrome lid to reveal a colorful fruit and cheese platter, causing her taste buds to tingle. But her mouth watered more at the sight of Tate's toned back, the way his muscles rippled across the polished flesh. His presence dominated the room, despite wearing nothing but a towel lashed around his lean hips.

As he turned, her midsection contracted at his crooked smile. No one had a right to look that gorgeous.

"This is an appetizer," he said. "Room service is twenty-four hours so we don't need to think about dinner yet."

Garnering every molecule of strength, she waved her hands. "I'll eat something on the plane."

Declining to comment, he strolled over with a cracker and cheese. He bit off half. Before she could object, he slipped the other half past her lips. Grunting, she pushed his hand away.

His eyes crinkled. "It's not blue vein. Don't worry."

She wasn't worried about mold. She worried about itching to touch his hard, smooth body now and paying with her heart later.

As he crossed back to the platter, she slowly chewed and remembered how as teens living with the same foster family, she and Judith had studied through the day and giggled through the night, dreaming about the more sophisticated breed of bad boy—irresistible enigmas with jet-black hair, piercing blue eyes and untamable hearts. After her friend's funeral, those memories had clawed at

Donna's gut and eaten at her brain until she'd come to her senses and ended a relationship that could only continue to bring her pain.

She hadn't been able to save her friend but she had saved herself. Not from physical harm—Tate would *never* physically hurt her—but rather from emotional grief. Her series of safe houses would help others in Judith's situation restore their confidence, their identities, maybe even save their lives.

She tightened the tie of her robe.

Nothing and no one would keep her from fulfilling that goal, the promise she'd made to herself.

Tate cut the fruit. "I had your belongings sent for."

Donna frowned.

He edged over a seductive look. "Did you really expect me to keep you here tied up and naked?"

Her tummy fluttered. She shoved that evocative thought aside and replaced it with another, more sensible one. Having her clothes sent over simply saved her organizing it herself. If she were in a more generous mood, she might thank him.

He waved a slice of mango. "Want some?"

As she shook her head, his mouth closed over the fruit. She could taste the sweetness and licked her lips. She remembered the last time they'd been at this resort, how she'd rubbed mango-scented oil on his chest and he'd rubbed her—

With a start, she pulled herself back from the past. A little light-headed, she spied her bag and walked toward the bed.

In a hurry, she tore her wrinkle-proof dress from the tote bag. A piece of jewelry came with it and fell on the rug at her feet. Her heart sprang to her throat.

She swooped down to grab it, but Tate, there in a blink, beat her to it.

He dangled the gold links before her. "Well, well…I wondered if you'd kept this."

Snatching the watch from his fingers, she down-played the significance of his discovery. "It's an expensive and beautiful watch. Why wouldn't I still have it?"

His sizzling gaze moved over her lips down to her neck, heating her skin. His smile grew broader.

"You weren't wearing it this morning. I'd have noticed." He lightly touched her left wrist.

Although her flesh responded, she refused the blatant come-on and turned away. Begging her heart to quit thumping, she shucked back one shoulder with a haughty air. "I couldn't find my other watch and grabbed this in a hurry on the way out. I forgot to put it on."

That was her story and she'd stick to it. She wouldn't admit that after seeing him again, she'd had a crushing desire to drag the watch from the bottom of her jewelry box to wear for the first time in years.

Feeling Tate behind her—his mesmerizing heat—she held herself tight. Her breath caught in her chest as his gravelly voice rumbled and tickled her ear.

"Nice try," he teased, "but you're a lousy liar."

"Yet others do it so well." She gave him a pointed glare.

The phone buzzed. Rather than answer it, Tate sauntered back to the platter and champagne bucket.

He raised a second chilled glass, tracing a finger down its running condensation. "Sure you won't have one? It's your favorite."

All the more reason to decline. Champagne slid down easier than water but the bubbles went straight to her head. She needed her wits about her, these next few moments more than ever.

The phone kept ringing.

She glanced between the extension and Tate. On her way to the bathroom to change, her dress and underwear in hand, she jerked her chin. "Are you going to get that?"

Shoulders holding up the wall, he crossed one ankle over the other and raised his glass. "I'm off duty."

A thread of disquiet wove through her. Tate was never off duty.

Her pace eased up. "Did I hear it ring while I was in the shower?"

"Nope." He tipped the glass to his mouth, ready to sip. "Probably just housekeeping."

A chill scuttled up her spine. Tate couldn't resist answering a call, no matter the time of day, no matter where they were. When they'd dated, it had driven her nuts. The only time he refused to pick up was if they were making love. Something was wrong and from his overly nonchalant mood, she couldn't help but believe she was involved.

She did a one-eighty and headed for the phone. Setting down his glass, Tate moved, too. Their darting hands collided on the receiver, hers beating his by a nanosecond. Yanking the handset away, she jammed it to her ear.

"Who is this?"

"Donna?" A female voice croaked down the line. "Hallelujah! Do you realize I've tried to contact you all day?"

A ghastly sinking feeling dropped from the back of her throat to her heels.

"Donna, *Donna?* Are you there?"

She pried her tongue from the roof of her mouth to wring out two words. "Mrs. deWalters." She noticed Tate heading toward the champagne and her shock at hearing the other woman's voice segued into red-tinged rage. "Did you try this number earlier?"

"I left a message. Your cell is off, or out of range, or perhaps it's broken. I insisted your assistant divulge your whereabouts. Reception put me through to your room."

Though Tate purposely ignored her, she slid him a poisonous glare. So much for anonymity.

A sudden thought struck her. Did Mrs. deWalters have any idea who shared her reservation?

The older woman huffed on the other end of the line. "Clearly you've forgotten our appointment tomorrow?"

Donna's more immediate dilemma clicked back into sharp focus. Her mind flicked through a mental calendar. "We have an appointment Wednesday, Mrs. deWalters, not tomorrow."

"I told you last Saturday evening to call me Maeve. And we'd agreed on tomorrow, not Wednesday, to meet."

Donna stuttered as her brain froze and face burned. Maeve deWalters was wrong, but the grande dame also carried some important clout. Donna needed her ongoing financial support. Her pride had no place in this relationship. She would agree with everything, do anything, Maeve deWalters said.

Donna held the phone tighter. "Tomorrow... where and when?"

"Hardly matters now." She sniffed. "You're on vacation."

Oh God, she had to salvage this situation and quickly. "No, no. Not vacation. This is strictly business and I'm coming back tonight."

"Then why the reservation, pet? I mean, it's really none of my business..."

Donna enunciated each word. "I will be back by morning, Mrs. deWalters—"

"Maeve. I told you to call me Maeve." Her voice was frosty now. "Are you paying attention? You seem distracted."

Donna barely held off from screaming, first over the line, then at Tate. If he hadn't twisted her arm into coming here...if she hadn't been so gullible...

Curling her toes, she gritted her teeth and silently counted to three.

"I'll be there, Maeve. Perhaps we could have breakfast together somewhere nice then visit the properties—"

"The very reason for my call. I can't make it now until Wednesday. But you'd sounded so eager, I wanted to give you a hearing before I speak with my fund-raising committee first thing Monday. Yet I fear now I've caught you at an inopportune time."

Not an apology. More a dig.

Their misunderstanding needed repairing, but this conversation was only adding to the confusion. Besides, she was shaking too much to concentrate on anything other than the possibility of everything she'd worked for falling apart.

Maeve might discover she was here with her old enemy. The Registration Board might find out too, or the magistrate on Blade's case. This time last week her life had been sailing a crest. Tonight it was close to smashing on the rocks.

She tried to think calmly and control the quaver in her voice. "I'm about to leave to catch a plane, so, yes, perhaps it would be best to leave this conversation until Wednesday." As originally planned, she wanted to add.

A put-upon sigh followed. "Do put it in your calendar, pet."

Donna held off slamming the phone and walked straight to her handbag. Her cell phone's volume had been bumped down, probably pushed against something, and there was a stack of messages, several from Maeve as well as April, no doubt warning her.

Her hand shook. She wanted to hurl the cell at the wall, but it wasn't the phone's fault. Hell, it wasn't even Tate's. It was hers for being pathetically weak, buckling beneath his demands and coming here in the first place. A brief return to Eden was so not worth it.

Face burning, she whirled on him. "You listened to her message, didn't you?" Donna didn't wait for an answer. "Is there even a tiny part of you that cares about what you've done?"

He had sabotaged her position, jeopardized her goal, all to meet his own objectives. How typical. How very, very Tate.

His strong jaw kicked up. "Maeve deWalters is a crony who attained her position through marriage and her fortune through corruption. Believe me, you'd do better to look elsewhere for support."

Like from him? How laughable.

She marched for the bathroom. "You have no evidence of corruption or she'd be the first to know."

"And the public would be second."

At the bathroom doorway, she snapped around. "Because of media or family-feud justice?"

"A whole bunch of both."

With a purposeful gleam in his eye, he stalked toward her.

Swallowing hard, she turned away from him. "I'm getting out of here now before you really screw things up."

His arm shot out, caught hers and drew her close. As her clothes fell to the floor, he urged her against his chest. She didn't want him handling her, couldn't he see? Her body might betray her, trying its best to respond to his power, but surely he could read the expression on her face. Damn it, she was serious!

She struggled. "Let me *go*."

"You don't have to pretend," he told her. "This isn't Sydney, there are no public eyes upon us. We're completely isolated. You can hide from everything here—including yourself—if you want."

He urged her closer. She felt the hardness of his erection against her belly, and she smothered a moan before it left her throat.

His hand pressed a hypnotic circle at the base of her spine. "Be honest...when was the last time you felt so good?"

The answer was too easy: the last time they were here together. But things were different now. *He* might not have changed but she had.

How dare he play with her life? He might dislike the deWalters family, but his opinion mattered little where her life's work was concerned.

Determined not to let that fact fade beneath a haze of passion, she ignored the heartbeat pulsing a time-old message in her womb and settled her mind firmly on escape. "When is the next flight out?"

Grinning, he challenged her with his eyes. "We've missed it."

She didn't believe him. Still, this wasn't a major city with a revolving door of commuter fights. She needed an alternative.

"A private plane then."

His eyes flashed and too late she realized what she'd said. Automatically her heart went out to him. He avoided conversations about small aircraft. Too many bad memories. Knowing the story, she understood.

"There's the phone." He nodded his head to the bedside table. "I won't stop you." Yet his hands on her hips held her firm.

"A bus," she managed in a throaty voice.

"I'll beat you back to Sydney—" he nipped her ear "—and have had a relaxing couple of days to boot."

"Staying with you won't make a difference," she ground out. "No matter how much you push, I won't let you intimidate me."

"Is that right?" He sucked her lobe and her body glowed red-hot.

"I will give Blade a fair assessment," she said, stifling a moan, "nothing more, nothing less."

"Donna, shh. This isn't about work. What we're doing now is all about pleasure."

This situation had deteriorated so quickly. Why had she thought it would be any different? Tate was the one man who could evoke this delirious abandon in her. From the moment they'd met, she had wanted no one else.

If he looked at her with those hot eyes, reached for her with that hot touch, the fight was lost. That's why she'd refused to see him after their engagement party. He didn't need to know about that one weak moment a few weeks later when she'd gone to see him and had inadvertently witnessed just how little he'd missed her.

He ground against her, combing his hands through her hair. Cupping her head, he kissed her thoroughly. By the time she came up for air, her lips were on fire and her mind was mush. How she managed a threat of her own was nothing short of a miracle.

"Maybe I should go to the judge and tell him about your ultimatum."

The grip on her head tightened. "Not a good idea. You should avoid throwing suspicion upon yourself."

"And a weekend away together doesn't look suspicious?"

He released her to peel the robe from her shoulders so only the tie on her hips kept it from falling. As his chest grazed her tender nipples, she bit her lip.

His teeth skimmed her neck. "Your reputation will remain intact. No one will find out."

"Except the biggest gossip in Sydney."

He growled. "Maeve deWalters knows nothing."

Well, not yet.

She was walking a tightrope that could snap at any moment. Secrets had a habit of revealing themselves when least expected.

Hands skimming her sides, he lowered himself to one knee, gifting a kiss on each of her breasts, her rib cage, the square inch above her navel. She closed her eyes at the sensations. His method and skill were infinitely fine. Like champagne bubbles, he made her head spin.

Three days, he'd said. How could it hurt?

Her resolve gone, she sighed and held his head. "You won't leak anything to anyone. Promise?"

A hum in his throat, he parted the robe and drew a bone-melting line with his tongue between her legs.

"I promise."

Eight

If someone won't admit they have a problem, they're likely to continue making the same mistakes.

Late Sunday morning, Donna remembered that advice, wishing it didn't so aptly apply to herself. The irony was the more time she spent with Tate the more she could admit to the problem, and the less she wanted to do anything about it.

Lying sloped across a beach blanket, head in hand, she watched him dive through the rough foam-laced waves. The sun was warm on her skin. A picnic basket lay crooked in the sand beside her.

She would have a glass of champagne with lunch

and make love with Tate again after that—relive the incomparable thrill of joining with the only man on earth who could make her forget to breathe.

No one would understand. Hell, she didn't understand or forgive herself. She would still give Blade the assessment she believed he deserved—nothing would sway her there, not even Tate's diminishing threat of having that story aired. But if people uncovered this liaison, she wouldn't blame them for thinking all was not aboveboard.

Squeezing her eyes shut, she cursed under her breath.

These feelings for Tate were not only overwhelming, they were all-consuming. She knew she should be stronger, hated herself for being so damn weak. Only people who had experienced this same giddy sense of euphoria could possibly understand.

She didn't seem to have a choice, not here, where the past whispered at her ear and Tate was so alive and strong and real.

Tate jogged out from the ocean, kicking up water, smoothing hands back over wet hair, unconsciously exhibiting his incredible biceps. He looked unconquerable. Her lover. And she was—

Her heart rolled over.

His mistress?

He fell on his knees and, palms on thighs, shook

out his hair. Despite her mood, she laughed as water sprayed in an arc.

Sitting up, she wiped her arms. "Hey, watch it!"

His lopsided grin grew. "Or you'll do what?"

Or I'll burn tomorrow's flight reservations and beg you to keep me here.

She let out a breath and managed a smile. "You don't want to know."

"Bet I do." Eyes smoldering, he prowled toward her on all fours.

A nervous laugh bubbled up inside her. Yesterday he'd surprised her by buying her a bikini from the resort boutique. It was far more revealing than one she might have chosen herself. Now his finger hooked into the gold ring linking the top's black triangles and tugged. "How are you placed for skinny-dipping?"

He angled his mouth over hers—cold and fresh covering warm and willing. Moving closer, his back and head curled over her. When their lips softly parted, she was dizzy and his chest was heaving.

That finger, hooked through the gold ring, rocked her right then left as his hungry gaze devoured her. "I can't decide if I like this better on or off."

A glimpse of decorum struggled through the delicious thick fog of her brain and her hand stopped his. "We're in the open."

He looked around and shrugged. "No people here. Be adventurous."

That yanked her right down from the clouds. She'd been adventurous—reckless—enough. They weren't eighteen, with few cares or responsibilities. In fact, they each had enormous responsibilities and they were ignoring them all. But tomorrow—and the consequences—would come soon enough.

Nerves gripping her stomach, she swiveled toward the basket. "Maybe we should eat back at the bungalow." Suddenly she felt very exposed.

"I'm all for retiring indoors." His hand skimmed across the shoulder he'd covered with oil just thirty minutes before. "But the label on the suntan lotion said we're safe outdoors for a couple more hours." As his hand circled, then slid down her arm, a spellbinding sensation fizzed along her veins. His deep rich voice rolled over her. "It's up to you."

Both options were dangerous.

If they stayed out here amidst the swaying palm fronds and fresh salty air, she could see them getting carried away. If they went back to the hideaway, her bikini wouldn't last much past the front door. Instantly she would be washed away on a slipstream of rising pleasure. But the moment her parachute landed and her feet touched the ground, her mind would begin to work again—what they were doing, the trust she was breaking—and then she'd just want to die.

Nothing was worth the guilt, not even this glorious time in the sun.

Tate moved to sit beside her and swept the champagne bottle from the basket. "Can I tempt you?"

Her attention drifted up from his footprint left in the sand to his transfixing blue eyes. She blinked, then frowned.

"No."

He chuckled and made himself more comfortable. "Too early?"

"Better than being too late."

He purposefully set the bottle back on the checked cloth before looking at her. "I feel a discussion coming on."

Her heartbeat skipped but, after forty hours laced with scintillating sex, it was time to talk instead of touch.

His regard was casual yet steely. "Don't kid yourself this is like the first time. This doesn't have to end badly. What we've enjoyed here has been good for us both."

"What we've enjoyed here is *wrong*." Feeling ill, she dropped her head into her hands. "The board is already investigating one allegation against me. And then there's Maeve, who is more than a little unhappy with me. I can't afford any more slipups. If Maeve discovers I'm involved with the Bridges family…if she finds out I'm romantically involved with you—"

Did she need to finish the sentence? If Maeve found out, the ball of disaster would begin to roll downhill. She'd lose her funding, she'd lose her reputation, but worse, on a personal level, she'd lose her self-respect by being publicly caught in Tate's web again. Come to think of it, she didn't have too much self-respect left at this point anyway.

Tate's jaw shifted as he reached into the picnic basket and retrieved a wrapped sandwich. "I told you, Maeve deWalters is on her way out."

A set of tiny warning antennae quivered. That wasn't the first time he'd implied Maeve was crooked. Could there be more than malice behind it? Maybe she should take a breath and actually listen. Or, better yet, ask some questions.

"You're saying she's corrupt?"

He chewed and nodded. "Undoubtedly."

Her tone was dry. "Don't be shocked, but people might think you're corrupt trying to lever a court judgment."

"I'm not shocked." He swallowed. "I don't care."

Her teeth clamped down. "Why, pray tell, why is it all right for you to try and bend the rules and not Maeve?"

Not that she agreed anyone should be above the law, herself included.

"Your question concerns the difference between a woman skimming the cream off charity coffers to feather her own bank account and a brother doing what he can to protect his own against an unjust prison term."

"You maintain that Blade's innocent." While not a lawyer, she knew of several defenses against assault, one of them self-defense. But Tate was side-stepping her issue. "Why does that give you the right to manipulate me?"

He skimmed a hand through his hair and considered her for a long tense moment. "Would it help if I said I was sorry?"

She nodded. "An apology might help...if I thought you meant it. But at this point, I'm afraid I need a whole lot more from you than that."

He was still for a long agonizing moment, before he peered up at the sun through squinted eyes then nodded. "What do you want to know?"

"I want to know why you're so protective of Libby and Blade. And tell me everything this time— not the superficial lines you used to feed me."

His parents had died; he'd become his siblings' guardian. She'd always understood and appreciated the sense of responsibility associated with that. But instinct said there had to be more to Tate's obsession with keeping his brother and sister protected.

"You know my parents died in a private plane crash. I wasn't long out of college," he continued. "I wanted to start living my life. Do what I wanted to do, when I wanted to do it. It happened around this time of year—close to Christmas. I had friends to visit, but my parents called wanting me to come home for a couple of days. They had an important dinner to attend in the Blue Mountains, and Blade—" He cleared his throat. "He was going through a rough patch."

She pressed her lips together. Although her training said "listen," it was difficult to keep her emotional distance where Tate was concerned.

He concentrated on the sand. "I argued. Told them to get a sitter, if they really needed it for a nineteen-year-old. I didn't see why Blade couldn't look after Libby. Why call me?"

He blew out a breath. "I turned up late, groaning and dragging my feet. They wanted me there at three. I arrived closer to six-thirty. At that stage my mother wasn't looking forward to a three-hour drive that included winding mountain roads, and arriving past fashionably late. My father often chartered private aircraft. They thought a light plane would get them there in half the time with half the hassle." His mouth swung to one side. "You know the rest."

His parents hadn't been able to take their car. Instead they'd hired a private aircraft. For reasons never explained, the plane had crashed twenty minutes from its destination. And Tate had been left with a guilt he could never assuage. The mist began to clear.

A hopping seagull flapped and leapt high as Tate tossed his sandwich. "And you want to hear the kicker?"

"Go on."

"The party they needed so desperately to attend was at the home of none other than Maeve deWalters."

Donna coughed. Oh, dear Lord. "They were friends?" She'd assumed the families had always been at odds.

"Never friends. Business acquaintances. Maeve's third husband spent a great deal of money on advertising with my father's still-fledgling network." A muscle in his bristled cheek jumped. "The party had been cancelled. Dear Maeve hadn't bothered to inform her less important guests."

Little wonder Tate tortured himself and carried around a metaphorical knife for Maeve as well. He believed through his self-centered acts he'd deprived his siblings, and himself, of their parents.

Searching Tate's eyes, she wrapped her arms around his strong neck and pulled herself near. She murmured against his ear, "You need to let it go."

She wanted to say he shouldn't blame himself, but she knew self-absolution didn't come easily. Nothing, not even time, fully washed away the stain.

He took her shoulders and gently pried her away. His jaw had never looked stronger, shadowed with two days' growth of beard. His dusky pink lips had never looked sexier, slanted and resigned.

"I'm fine with where I am, Donna. I know what I want. What I need to do." He pushed to his feet, his smile convincing, invincible. "Right now, I need to go battle more waves."

When they made love that afternoon, it was just as soul-lifting, but, amidst the tangle of sheets, their joining also seemed changed, somehow deeper and more sensitive…as if a layer had peeled away and what lay beneath was still too raw to look at, too dangerous to speak of.

Landing in Sydney the next day, Tate was his usual charming self. After mentioning he would be in touch regarding the assessment Blade needed, she reaffirmed that should she provide one, it would be completely honest. She couldn't decide whether he looked amused or all the more determined.

When the taxi dropped her off and they kissed goodbye, she tried to convince herself it would be their last. The choice hurt unbearably, but surely it was wiser to be strong, end this relationship and avoid the train wreck that awaited them around their next clandestine bend. The weekend had been remarkable, but over time his demanding character would increasingly tear at her soul.

The facts remained: he wanted her continued affections and she needed to regain her self-respect.

She didn't return his calls. She needed time to set her mind straight. Yet by Thursday morning her inner struggle had only gotten worse. The urge to buckle and see him again was overwhelming.

Weeks after their engagement-party fiasco, she'd been gripped by a similar urge to surrender. To this day Tate didn't know that she'd seen him embrace and kiss another woman. Now more than ever she should remember not only how deeply he'd hurt her by consistently putting her feelings last, but also how easily she'd been replaced.

As she sipped coffee at her kitchen counter, she flicked through the morning newspaper. When a feature article caught her eye, she focused and scanned the lines. Her fingers gradually slipped and coffee streamed to darken the page. As her blood pressure exploded, one image crystallized in her mind.

Tate on his knees making love to her, murmuring, *I promise*. And lying through his teeth.

Nine

"I can't believe you went through with it."

Tate took in Donna's scathing words, studied the scowl on her face and, for the first time in years, didn't quite know what to do.

A maddening pulse beat in his neck. He loosened his tie and, without invitation, slid into the café's red-vinyl booth beside her. The close proximity had immediate impact. Her fresh-flower scent, the flow of silken fair hair, the—

At a flash of irritation, he flipped a hand. "Take off those dark glasses—" he needed to see her eyes "—and we'll talk about this rationally."

"Rational for you or for me?" The frames hit the table with a *snap*. "There's a mountain of difference."

She reached blindly beside her and threw the morning paper on the grey laminate next to some faded fake roses and an empty coffee cup. A headline was circled in angry red:

Couch Therapy—Be Careful Who You Trust.

Tears edged her eyes, but her mouth remained firm. "I tell you any assessment will be completely honest then I don't return your calls. So you decide to give me a taste of what's in store if I refuse to give you precisely what you want." She winced. "Do you know what hurt the most? You didn't have the decency to warn me."

"Because I had nothing to do with it."

He dashed the paper, and his need to hold her, aside. Three days without her body next to his had felt like an eon. How had he survived so long before?

She smirked, but he glimpsed vulnerability beneath the hard shell. "So it's a huge coincidence that you blackmail me, throw in a little seduction, and when I still won't come to heel, a sneak preview of your threat happens to show up in the broadsheets."

Logic. "Am I the only one who had access to information regarding the complaint against you?"

Her long lashes blinked. "No."

"Does the article mention you by name?"

A question mark formed in the shadows of those turquoise eyes before her beautiful mouth hardened again. "Doesn't mean you're not behind it."

"It also doesn't confirm that I am. In fact, if I were the instigator, I'd more likely leak the info just before my show's debut. With your story as lead, the ratings would soar through the roof."

Her eyes narrowed at his dry look before she pushed up the sleeves of her white blouse. Her lace bra was a tantalizing shadow beneath the silk. Despite her hostility and this less-than-conducive situation, his blood began to race.

"Maybe you leaked this now to leave me guessing," she concluded, sounding uncertain. "Too unsettled to rock your boat."

His eye line dropped to the slender waistband of her tailored red skirt. He'd bet she hadn't eaten before or after she'd phoned him in a rage. Coffee wasn't enough. A good breakfast would help settle her down. She liked flapjacks with syrup. He'd order two stacks.

Glancing around the mostly deserted suburban café, he tried to catch the attention of a waiter busy lining up soda bottles in the front fridge.

Her harsh whisper was a warning at his ear. "Are you listening to me?"

Turning back, he refrained from dropping his

mouth over hers to silence her. Kissing was what she needed. In fact, they both needed to get back to what they did so well, rather than arguing over an incident that couldn't be undone. If he could fix it, damn it, he would.

"I'll say it once more. I did not leak that story."

But in a way he was grateful to whoever had. Donna hadn't returned his calls since their return from Queensland. And this meeting had more easily opened up a way for him to get to her. They were good together; she knew that as well as he. Whatever had come before, they'd work through it— he'd make certain.

Her expression jaded, she fell back against the vinyl. "Yeah, you're just so principled. Guess I have nothing to fear by saying this then." She tipped closer to look him squarely in the eye. "Your lawyer needs to find another patsy. I'm off Blade's case. You can do what you want about it—badger, growl, charm, if you like. Tactics won't make a scrap of difference. I'm sick of bouncing on your string. As of this second, I'm getting on with my life."

His head cocked.

Hell, she thought she meant it.

But the past few days couldn't be erased. They were bound now, differently than before, and for more reasons than one. He angled around so his bent trouser leg rested on the seat and she couldn't misread or avoid the conviction in his expression.

"Blade needs you."

I need you.

"I told you from the start, Blade has to face the consequences of his actions." Her expression changed. "So do I. You say he's innocent. I know I am. The best we can do is sit back, keep our noses clean, and trust in the system."

Trust in the system? He thrust back his shoulders. "I can't do that."

"You're going to have to," she said simply.

He refrained from mentioning he wasn't sure if Blade's prior offense was admissible. Donna wouldn't sympathize. She still didn't know what had lain at the heart of the trouble the night of their disastrous engagement party. At this juncture, she'd be less inclined than ever to believe it.

"Don't you want to know where my brother got to last Friday?" That night Blade had left a message to say he was okay and not to worry. But Donna didn't know anything beyond that. "He met up with Kristin and they're trying to sort out their problems."

He hoped the subtext wasn't too subtle.

She shook her head a little too fast. "That's none of my business anymore."

His chest tightened as a frisson of annoyance

speared right the way through. "Like Libby wasn't your business anymore five years ago?"

Her eyes flashed. "She was seventeen when we broke up. I couldn't see her again—" Her voice caught before she began again in a calmer tone. "I couldn't see her again without seeing you. You know how much I cared for Libby. She was like my sister."

But not in the truest sense of the word. Donna had grown up in foster care. From what he knew of her experience, with the possible exception of Judith, she'd never had any real family. Donna didn't quite understand—and he was loath to point it out—that despite her fondness, she *could* walk away from Libby; he could not.

His focus wandered to her finely boned fist resting on the newsprint. That ugly, practical, black leather band was wound around her wrist.

He took her hand. "Where's my watch?'

Her dawning smile was almost sad. "It's so important to you, isn't it? Seeing your cuff around my wrist. Thinking you own me."

She was right, of course. He *did* want that sense of ownership. And he wanted *her* so much—but not too close.

The secret of success was delegation. He could do that with work, but personal matters were too important to farm out. Blade and Libby were enough. He didn't need the added worry of a wife, then, in the near future, another family to care for and angst over. Concerns over running a multimillion-dollar business were easier to handle than a crisis or tragedy involving kin.

Before the breakdown of communication three days ago, he'd thought he and Donna had come close to an understanding. Together they could share the good times without the complications.

He wanted her to understand, but the perfect words wouldn't come.

He held her eyes with his. "I want you to be part of my life."

She looked at him with genuine pity. "A narcissistic comment if ever I heard one."

His touch trailed her red skirt's seam. "Don't pretend you don't want me, too." Their chemistry was through the rafters. Even here, now, he grew hot.

His hand was on her thigh before she stopped him.

"I might want a million-dollar necklace," she told him, "but I don't break the shop window to get it."

"We don't have to be bad for each other." He wound her hand around his and squeezed. "After this court hearing is over—"

"What? We'll continue to sleep together and live happily ever after?"

Her lifeless tone and glistening eyes made him think.

Who made rulings on what constituted a fairy-tale ending? His idea was two people who needed each other, every day, every night. God knows, he and Donna could make each other happy.

She disengaged her hand and bumped against him. "I have to get to work."

He eased out from the booth. "I'll drive you."

"Do me a favor." She collected her sunglasses and slid out, too. "Don't do me any favors."

Her phone rang from inside her handbag. All thumbs, she rummaged inside and stabbed the cell phone button too late. She studied the ID screen and cursed, then cursed again.

Not difficult to guess: Cruella De Vil.

Straightening his tie, he schooled his features. "Did you meet with deWalters yesterday as planned?"

He'd put money down that Maeve had got the days mixed up again. Witch.

Donna snapped her cell shut. "That's privileged information."

He didn't like her around that woman. Concern or control, didn't matter what you called it—he simply knew what he knew. When the lid blew he didn't want Donna drenched by the fallout.

He slipped a bill from his wallet and set it under

the rose vase. "How much do you need toward the maintenance costs for your project?" The wallet slid back into his jacket's breast pocket. "I haven't made my donation yet."

"I don't want your bribes. Stay away from me and my project, and that includes its benefactors."

Tate's jaw shifted.

He couldn't do either.

He collected the newspaper, slotted it under his arm and followed her to the door. She went left—sexy red heels clicking on the pavement—and he eventually went right.

For the next half an hour, he paced his office like a caged tiger. By the time he opened his private locked cabinet, his head was pounding.

Don't get emotional, think with your head.

Carefully he drew out two files, one marked Blade/Donna, the other deWalters. After a deep breath, he crossed to his desk and picked up the phone.

Donna would soon find out…this time he *would* go through with it.

Ten

Laughing, Donna threw her arms around Libby and held on tight. How wonderful to see her again and so soon. When she and Tate had their big bust-up last week, she'd been determined not to let this renewed friendship with the younger woman lapse. As it turned out, Libby had the same idea.

Tate's sister drew back, her pretty face bright and violet eyes thankful. "Are you sure you can spare the time? Buying furniture for my new apartment isn't exactly urgent business."

Cheerful for the first time in days, Donna linked an arm around Libby's waist and walked beside her into the enormous furniture retail outlet, which on the day before Christmas Eve was decorated with festoons of tinsel and silver holiday bells.

"I'd love to help." She surveyed the orderly displays of dining suites, lounges and beds, interspersed with festive trees draped in blinking lights. "Are we going ultra contemporary?"

"I'm not sure what I want yet. Everything's a little up in the air." Libby chewed her lip. "No surprise, but Tate was not too pleased by my announcement."

Holding down a deep breath, Donna continued to walk. Though she didn't want to hear about Tate, she knew Libby needed to vent. She had missed this sisterly connection, particularly now when other pieces of her life seemed to be falling apart.

Libby steered them down a wide aisle toward the dining room section. "Tate didn't take my moving out too well. I'm twenty-two, he had to know I'd leave the nest soon. But he's been so grumpy lately, what with Blade's trouble and the schedule for this new show giving him grief."

Donna's mouth twisted. The grumpy crown would fit just as well on her head. Maeve deWalters kept setting back appointments and yesterday the Registration Board had informed her that a hearing before the Professional Standards Committee was going ahead. Given she was innocent and had hidden nothing in her response to Hennessy's allegation, she could only surmise the board was being extra vigilant due to that disturbing newspaper feature.

Her cheeks flushed with embarrassment whenever she thought of it.

The night of the benefit she'd acquiesced to Tate's "request" that she interview Blade, but she'd also made it clear any assessment would be unbiased. Had he shown some muscle by organizing a hint of what was in store should she continue to hold out? But if that were true, surely he would admit that he'd somehow prompted the newspaper article. Or maybe she'd been right and he'd meant to confuse her.

Oh, hell, she'd been so angry and upset and tired of being pushed and pulled, she didn't know what to believe anymore.

Libby stopped by a chiseled stone dining table with a gold wire reindeer centerpiece. Looking coy, she ran her finger along the rectangular glass top. "Do you want to talk about it? I've heard it helps."

Donna was taken aback. "Talk about what?"

"If I had one guess why you're so preoccupied, it'd have to be over my big brother. Am I right?"

Donna strolled around her. "No."

But that was a lie. He hadn't phoned since that day at the café and she hadn't contacted him. A clean break was exactly what she'd wanted. Yet every night she found herself tossing and turning, reliving in her mind those three sensational nights with Tate. She could smell mango and briny air even now. If she closed her eyes, she could feel his hard-muscled body sliding against hers.

Libby hooked her French-manicured fingers over a chair back. "Don't make the same mistake Tate does. I'm not a child. Maybe I can help."

Donna paused. Libby may not be seventeen anymore, however, blood was said to be thicker than water. She'd like to have that much faith in her friend, but could any member of the Bridges family be trusted with such a confidence?

Libby rounded the chair and sat down. "You helped me so much when I needed you. Maybe there's something I can do for you now. Let me try." She extended her hand. "Please."

Oh, hell. She did need someone to talk to. Desperately. She couldn't talk to colleagues. None of her current friends even knew about Tate. And Libby did know everything…or almost.

Crumbling, Donna sat down, too. "Your brother and I…" Her throat convulsed and she swallowed. "Well, we've been seeing each other again."

Libby was quiet for a long, thoughtful moment. She looped a fall of sable hair behind an ear. "I presume when you say *seeing,* there's more to it than that."

Beneath the crush of guilt, Donna exhaled. "More is right and, for so many reasons, I need it to end."

"Because of the conflict of interest with Blade's assessment?"

"I told Tate a week ago to find someone else."

Libby's brows jumped. "Brave girl."

That pretty much said it all.

"Tate is just so wrong for me."

Wrong for any woman who didn't want to be dominated by a strong male.

Libby leaned forward to take both of Donna's hands. "Tate's a good man. He just has a hard time understanding that doing the best by those he loves doesn't mean he gets to rule their lives. My brother doesn't like making mistakes, and he can't stand the thought of anyone he cares about suffering for a mistake, either." She shrugged. "He tries to fix things so we don't have to."

Donna had to smile. Tate's flaws sounded justifiable coming from Libby's forgiving mouth. But the sad truth was Tate didn't listen. He simply did what he deemed necessary and no one else's opinions mattered.

From her perspective, that just didn't work. "Tate needs someone who is willing to have all their decisions made for them." And their feelings disregarded in the process. "There are women who would gladly hand over the reins to a powerful, attractive man."

But not her. She wanted to feel safe, not manipulated.

Libby seemed to choose her words carefully. "I don't think Tate wants any other woman."

"Give him a few days."

"He hasn't had a serious relationship since you two broke up."

Eyes burning, Donna dropped her gaze. This was harder than she'd thought. "I appreciate it, Libby, but you really don't have to try to make me feel better."

"It's true!"

Donna clenched her jaw, but in the end she couldn't hold it back. That horrible secret had been bottled up so long, she felt set to burst.

She willed her chin not to tremble. "I saw Tate kissing another woman less than a month after we broke up." After that heartbreaking night when he'd left her all alone to face their concerned guests.

Libby's brow buckled before her eyes went wide. "Oh, Lord, you must mean Madison, that personal assistant."

"I don't know who the woman was. I only know

I saw the two of them, lips locked, in his car out front of your house."

The corners of Libby's mouth tipped up. "You'd come back to make up with him?"

Hell, why not be totally honest and finally say the words aloud?

"I told myself I came over to see that you were all right. But that was only half of it." She felt her stomach twist. "I was weak." And, man oh man, had she been stupid.

Libby was shaking her head. "Tate never dated that woman. Madison was a gold digger. She kept inviting herself over for so-called business dinners. She made it well-known, even in front of me, that if Tate was available so was she. She must have tackled him in the car. I wouldn't put it past her. I remember he fired her. He didn't say why, but Blade and I knew."

The surrounding noise and bustle receded into nothing. Donna's ears began to ring. Libby was telling the truth, that much was obvious.

All these years, she'd believed it had been "out with the old and in with the new." That he'd found another woman within weeks of their breakup. What else had she been wrong about?

Libby unfolded to her feet. "I'm leaving with friends tomorrow for two weeks in Bali. Blade's holed up with Kristin somewhere." One fine eye-brow arched. "I'm thinking Tate could use some company."

A whisper-thin glimmer of hope struggled through the dark. But a past misinterpretation didn't pardon Tate's current frame of mind: basically he had coerced her into doing Blade's assessment. Then he'd manipulated the situation and her feelings in order to sleep with her. But maybe he'd already had his fill. "He hasn't called once in over a week."

Libby inclined her head. "My bet is that he's—to use his word—*regrouping.*"

"Or flat out finding a replacement for Blade's assessment as well as for his own bed." Donna cringed. "Sorry, you didn't need to hear that."

"I'm sure that's not it." Libby's expression deepened. "My brother is stubborn and has real trouble accepting that he can't keep us wrapped in cotton wool, but that failing comes from a very good place. I think he needs you to help him dig that good place out."

Wishful thinking or wise words?

Donna leveled her friend a look. "How old are you again?"

"Old enough," Libby laughed, "and anytime now Tate will have to accept it."

For the remainder of the afternoon, Donna tried

to concentrate on furniture, but facts kept rolling around in her head.

She was off Blade's case and free from the ethical dilemma. Tate hadn't fallen for the next blonde who had sashayed into his life after their broken engagement. No evidence supported her belief that he had leaked information about Hennessy's complaint.

But the biggest problem remained. Tate's king-of-all bearing. The I-know-what's-best-so-don't-bother-asking attitude. No getting around the fact that he had threatened to expose a weakness, even if initially he'd bought the rights to that story to help not harm.

Perhaps if she tried to put the past behind them...if she gave Tate this one last chance...if she completely opened her heart to him and dug really deep...

Perhaps.

Eleven

Tate's front door chimed, resulting in an entire chorus of "Jingle Bells" booming through the empty corridors of his house.

How had Libby talked him into that?

Camped out behind his study desk, he ran an eye over the script he'd worked on most the afternoon. He'd been in "the zone"; he did not appreciate being yanked out.

Buttoning the bottom half of his white collared shirt, leaving the tails hanging, he studied the title. *Good Deeds or Tainted Trust.* Not bad. A "sensational" edge. Alliteration helped. He had a couple more weeks to get everything right, but no longer than that. The show's preproduction was way behind schedule, and this series of stories was a leading contributor to the delay.

He'd procrastinated long enough.

On his way to the front door, the bell rang again. Cursing, he picked up pace.

The housekeeper was off visiting. Blade was happy someplace with Kristin. Libby was on a plane bound for Bali. God, he hoped she put locks on her suitcases.

He could think of only one person he wished to see and he hadn't worked out the best way to make that happen, particularly when a truckload of mud was about to hit an industrial-size fan.

Ruffling a hand through his hair, he swung the door open. Surprise and instant arousal struck with simultaneous brute force.

Looking fragile, Donna smiled and cleared her throat. "I, um, heard you were alone tonight so I thought I'd drop in."

With a bottle of champagne, no less.

Breathing again, Tate opened the heavy door wider. Her long, tanned legs were bare beneath her short pink dress. One of her manicured feet, in flat white sandals, stood slightly pigeon-toed. Sweet Lord, she looked delectable.

His racing desire struck a pothole. If she knew what he was working on, she'd likely smash that bottle over his skull. And he couldn't keep it from her forever.

One sandaled foot edged back. "If you're busy…"

Snapping out of his stupor, he moved forward to thread an arm around her shoulders. Her golden tan from their weekend away still glowed.

He guided her into the foyer. "I'm not busy." Not anymore. "Let me take that."

Only slightly hesitant at the intimate contact, she handed over the bottle and rubbed her hands down her dress. Her big eyes blinked as if she had something to confess. He'd keep his own confession for much later.

Closing his fingers around hers, he drew her down the wide hallway toward his private sitting room.

A smile lifted one corner of his mouth. "I didn't expect to see you."

She almost met his eyes. "We're both without family this year so it seemed…right."

Tate nodded. This time of year he missed his parents most. He'd often wondered what it must be like to have no memories of family at Christmas— or anytime, for that matter. Was it similar to never tasting chocolate and therefore never missing the treat? Or more like being deprived of food and being aware every day that you were starving? If anyone had the answer, Donna did.

She'd only spoken of her time in foster care once. Libby, Blade and a couple of their friends had seemed most interested. Donna was still unaware of how her recollections that day had unwittingly contributed to Blade's trouble on their engagement party night. Better now it should stay that way.

He led her into the salon with its own wet bar and marble fireplace, though summer Down Under was no time to build crackling hearths. He switched on the low-voltage downlights to take an edge off the shadows. Crossing to the room's far side, he opened up the full-length concertina glass doors and invited in the night air and a panoramic frame of twinkling dark velvet sky. Then he left her standing, hands laced in front, while he moved to the bar to uncork and pour the champagne.

He returned to her side, he paused to inhale her rose-petal scent, then pressed the flute into her shaky hand. He focused on her parted lips as he sipped before finally speaking. "I take it you're over your suspicion."

Her mouth was pressed tight. "Tell me one more time you had nothing to do with that newspaper article."

The hopeful tone of her voice jacked up his pulse

rate. He wanted to close his eyes and run his tongue around her mouth till he could taste her right down to his toes.

Instead, to appease her, he repeated, "I had nothing to do with that story. But you already know that, or you wouldn't be here."

"Actually this was Libby's idea," she said. "I spent yesterday afternoon helping your sister choose furniture for her new place. Seems your little chick has flown the coop."

Nonplussed, he shook his head. "Libby has her job and part-time university. Living here, she doesn't need to worry about paying bills or maintaining her car or cooking or laundry—"

"I think she's looking forward to experiencing all of those things. There comes a time in every person's life when they need to leave and a parent has to let go."

He studied her—so knowledgeable, yet she had no firsthand experience of being a parent, or of knowing her own. Driving the family bus wasn't nearly as easy as some made out. Donna would realize that when she had children of her own.

Chest catching, Tate shook off that left-field thought and moved slightly away from her.

She followed. "So Blade is still hiding out somewhere with Kristin?"

Should he sit on the couch or be far less subtle? They both knew why she'd come. The champagne was good but having her legs coiled around his hips was going to be far better.

In the soft glow, he made himself comfortable sitting on the plush white rug, one arm resting on a raised knee, the other arm propped behind. "Blade hasn't told me where they're staying. He wants complete privacy, away from media spotlights, to see if they can figure out where to go from here."

"Is he okay with your barrister arranging another psychologist for his assessment?"

"More than happy. In fact, he was insistent." When her eyebrows nudged together, he explained. "I came clean about our Queensland jaunt. That I'd organized everything and you, more or less, had little choice but to come along for the ride."

Her smile was curious. "Sounds as if you're developing a conscience."

He'd developed a conscience years ago. That had been the start of his problems.

Still standing, she swallowed more champagne. "I hope everything works out for him."

Tate was certain the assault charges the cameraman from that opposition network that had brought against Blade were garbage. Still, knowing the legal system, the outcome of Blade's day in court would be hard to call. Staying out of jail seemed all the more important to him now that Kristin was back in his life.

Tate scowled. "He'd have a better chance if Cruella deWalters could keep her big beak out of things."

Donna swirled her glass and grinned. "Cute nickname."

Not cute; fitting.

With a tilt of his chin he indicated she should join him. "Have you finalized any agreements with dear Maeve?"

Donna hesitated then carefully eased down beside him, half an arm's length away. "Not yet."

"Maybe she won't commit." He set his glass down.

"Don't say that. I understand the full history between you all now, and I sympathize. But her financial support and name are vital to my project. No one else has come forward to offer that level of assistance."

He had—at least offhandedly that day in the cafe. And maybe that was still an option. If she was still speaking to him in a month's time.

He moved closer to her, then asked, "When do you need Maeve's pledge?"

"By the end of January."

Just before ratings season kicked off. But tonight he'd forget about work.

Knowing he wasn't the only one wanting to put an end to the anticipation, he eased the glass from Donna's hand and set it beside his own. He brushed her cheek with the back of his hand before moving lower to caress her breast. He angled his head and lightly kissed her lips.

She moaned softly against his mouth before she slowly drew away.

"Tate, I won't pretend. I want to be with you again, so much. But we need to talk first...about us...our future."

He grinned. "I'm interested in what's happening now."

He kissed her again and the satisfaction of her response spread like wildfire within him, sparking the urge to skip foreplay and take her without delay.

When their lips parted, her gaze had lost three parts of its determination. "We should talk."

He tasted the slope of her jaw then growled close to her cheek. "I can't forget those nights we spent together in Queensland. Can you?"

She sighed. "I'm here, aren't I? But I need to sort out what happens next."

So he did.

His tongue trailed down her throat. "So am I moving too fast?"

She noticeably shivered before she sighed again

and, finally giving in, slanted her head to allow better access. "Always."

The rug was soft, the lights low, no one would interrupt. He braced her back and, tipping his weight, eased her down.

"I've missed you."

So damn much. Thank God tomorrow was a holiday. He hoped it rained so they could lose themselves amongst the bedclothes clear through into Boxing Day.

She craned to meet his mouth at the same time her hands moved beneath the open vee of his shirt. When he deepened the kiss and her fingers clutched and stroked his chest, a strained shirt button popped. Fever growing, he grabbed one side and tore the shirt fully open. Bunching a handful of her dress, he wrangled with it until the cotton came off over her head.

His erection throbbed against his zipper at the sight of her, sans bra, her tiny pink panties so sexy he could almost leave them on.

He cupped her breast and lovingly looped the beaded peak with the tip of his tongue. She moved beneath him, holding his head with one hand, shucking the shirt from his right shoulder with the other.

"I want to be here with you like this," she

murmured in the throaty voice he adored. "But you have to know…I need more."

His tongue stilled before finding its rhythm again. He moved his palm down her belly, beneath the pink lace triangle, between her warm thighs.

"Need more what?" His teeth grazed her nipple.

On a soft groan, she massaged his hair. "More than sex."

Hearing that word leave her mouth shot a double-barrel blast of desire through this system. Pushing off on one elbow and a knee, he found his feet, unzipped and discarded his blue jeans.

His voice deepened. "How much more?"

Her slender throat bobbed as she swallowed. Her gaze lingered before climbing to connect with his. "Maybe more than you're prepared give."

He knew where this was leading and why she was saying it now. Commitment. She'd more than implied that was the last thing she wanted from him, yet it was abundantly clear tonight that she did. But they'd gone down that path years ago and it had ended unhappily. This time he wanted to keep their relationship uncomplicated, without discussions about wedding bells and, later, diapers. He had all the responsibility he could handle with Blade, Libby and the network. He did not want more. But he did very much want this. Donna, here in his arms.

After grabbing some silk cushions off the couch, he joined her again. She rolled in and nuzzled against his chest. Taking her hand, he molded her fingers around his shaft. As she stroked and mind-blowing sensations multiplied and grew, he held her tight and admitted, "I'd give you everything if I could."

Locking her leg over his, she tilted her face and kissed him with such meaning, he couldn't help but be shamed by his past treatment of her. He hadn't wanted to use pressure the night of the benefit. He hadn't wanted to put other considerations before her feelings, now or in the past.

When her mouth broke gently away, her nose rubbed the tip of his. "What about love?" Her question reached down and twisted in his chest. "Do you love me, Tate?"

He eased her hand aside and pulled her panties down and off her legs. Positioning them face-to-face, he eased into her. As she arched beneath him, he trailed fingertips down her cheek, his mouth sampling her texture and scent in their wake.

Donna was the only woman who could make him forget all the headaches milling around outside—Libby leaving, Blade's trouble, the new show, deWalters and her scams. But he still had sense enough…

Confessions of love now might lead to promises he couldn't keep.

She locked her left arm under his right and trailed her fingers up and down his back. "You told me once you loved me."

Frowning, he increased his rhythm.

His feelings were different now. More intense, perhaps, yet...changed. He was certain of nothing except the taste of her, the feel...the heat she swaddled around his entire being.

Lightning flashed hot through his veins. Breaking the kiss, he bit down hard. Filling his lungs, he clenched every muscle around the maddening, luscious need to explode.

"I want you in my life," he repeated.

"Enough to try again?"

As she whispered in his ear, he finally gave in to the urge and let go. Pinpricks of light converged in his head then zapped through his bloodstream. As the tsunami surged, he gathered her up and spilled into her; felt her come along with him.

When the colors faded from his mind and his surroundings began to materialize again, he had only two thoughts. One, that had been a remarkable orgasm, and two, "I didn't use a condom."

Twelve

Donna was gradually floating back to reality when she heard Tate's words. Cuddling into his toned chest, she opened her eyes to find Tate's face blank with shock.

He searched her face. "I've always used protection. I've never forgotten before."

Her finger stroked his chin's raspy cleft. "I arrived out of the blue. It happened quickly."

Actually their arousal had been meteoric. Undeniable. Even now, she couldn't get close enough.

His face darkened. "That's no excuse. Are you protected?"

She shook her head. "Sorry."

But at this point in her cycle, it was unlikely she would conceive. And yet...

Although she'd had no intention of having un-protected sex tonight, now that it had happened one couldn't deny the idea of being pregnant with Tate's child had its appeal. She was twenty-eight. Tate would be her only lover; no one could overshadow or replace him. She wanted a family. God, she'd wanted that for as long as she could remember.

But he hadn't answered her question. Was it possible to overcome their difficulties and really try again? Get married? Have that family?

Brows knitted, he rolled to partially hover over her. His ocean-blue eyes infiltrated her soul. "I'm sorry."

At his gruff apology, her throat closed off. She guessed that reply in part answered her question. Clearly he was nowhere near as sorry for her as he was for himself.

Edging away, she grabbed his shirt and kept her voice light. "It's a shared responsibility, Tate. As much my fault as yours."

He'd lifted her to such heights so quickly that she hadn't considered protection. For the first time ever, they had slept together as a husband and wife would, a couple who felt sheltered by each other and wanted children. Ultimately that's what two people who felt this way were meant to do—marry, have a family. But Tate, it seemed, wasn't so sure.

Her mind spinning, she absently slotted her arms through his shirt. The lower buttons were missing. Still glowing warm inside, she wrapped the fabric around her middle.

Her focus landed on the tranquil nativity scene set out beneath a miniature Christmas tree on the mantel.

She eased to her feet. He was so quiet. She sensed the tension reeling off him.

Her fingertips trailed the tiny barn roof. "Do you want me to go?"

His graveled voice came from behind. "Of course not. I'm just…getting my breath."

Collecting the miniature manger, she inspected the swaddled baby inside. An intense sense of destiny built then washed over her. If she were pregnant, how would Tate react? Faced with the reality, surely he would come around.

Although he was overly diligent and, yes, frustratingly arrogant in some ways, no one could say he wasn't a conscientious substitute father. But Blade and even Libby were finding their own ways now. With them living their lives, Tate should feel free to concentrate on his. If he were to become a real father, wouldn't he naturally put her and their baby first?

Donna sighed and replaced the manger.

Oh, her imagination had run away. Chances were she wasn't pregnant, but at least she knew she was ready.

If Tate asked her to marry him again.

She turned to him and realized she needed a minute on her own. "Can I use the bathroom?"

Back in jeans, he finger-combed his hair and joined her. With his hand on her shoulder he pressed a kiss to her temple. "Is there something we should do? There's an all-night chemist down the road. Don't they have a morning-after pill now?"

The flush—hurt laced with irritation—doused her body. Weaving the shirt protectively around her waist, she hugged herself. "I don't know." She didn't care to discuss it. "Do they?"

"Maybe we should jump in the car and—"

Dodging his attempt to caress her, she moved toward the bathroom.

"It only takes once, Donna."

"Not at this time of the month." She bit down against rising emotion. *Don't worry, Tate. You're safe.*

His voice was husky, low. "We'll find out for sure soon, then."

Yes, they'd find out soon and only one of them would get what they wanted. Usually that was Tate.

* * *

Christmas day, she woke in Tate's bed, wrapped securely in his big protective arms.

Before she had time to reflect on her mixed feelings from the night before, he reached for the side table and presented her with an exquisite bottle of French perfume tied with gold ribbon. Taken aback, she blinked away happy tears, unraveled the ribbon and sprayed the subtle floral fragrance in her hair.

Coming close, he murmured that he'd known it would suit her perfectly. And he wouldn't hear of her feeling bad over not having a gift for him; he had all he wanted this Christmas.

Despite the faint undercurrent of unease—his concern over their forgetfulness the night before—it was the best Christmas she'd ever known. Just the two of them, all day, all night, with a fridge full of holiday food and lazy hours spent by the pool, then in bed.

The dream didn't last nearly long enough.

By midweek he was back at the office, but with Libby overseas and Blade still with Kristin, when they came together in the evenings, the time was their own. Yet every time she tried to bring up the question of their future, he would change the subject, usually kissing her until she forgot everything but the pleasure of his mouth on her body. Clearly he was avoiding the issue. Although there were times when Donna was convinced she ought to, she couldn't find the wherewithal to push the point.

Early in the new year, however, her happy bubble burst. For better or worse, she knew Tate's would, too. The board was going ahead with the investigation against her, but that was only the start.

Stomach in knots, Donna arrived late-morning at his office. His assistant informed her that Tate was downstairs preparing for an edit session. After riding the lift, she tracked Tate down to an editing booth. Through the small square glass, she saw he was alone, sitting before a panel of hi-tech equipment and monitors, absorbed in his notes. Preparing her speech, stomach twisting more, she was about to enter when Blade rushed past down the hall, obviously without seeing her.

Her smile was thoughtful.

Once she'd harbored so much anger toward Tate's brother. She'd blamed Blade for their breakup, although she could admit now that final night was a bomb that had been ticking at the end of a long-lit fuse. She hoped for both Blade and Kristin's sakes he would be found innocent of the assault charges that had been brought against him when he'd been harassed by the media and had shoved an overzealous cameraman out of his way. Everyone deserved happiness.

Putting Blade's indiscretions out of mind, she filled her lungs and swung open the door. Tate's frown as he peered up from his notes dissipated before returning with a vengeance. Eyes suddenly dark and eyebrows slashed together, he pushed aside his notes, leapt from his seat and stood before her, hands locked eye level on either side on the jamb.

His grin seemed strained "Hey, what are you doing here?"

She blinked several times. She wasn't imagining his agitation. Maybe she should wait until tonight. But she couldn't.

Easing back her shoulders, she tried on a teasing smile. "No kiss hello?"

He dotted a welcome on her cheek as his hands dropped and he spun her around. "We'll get out of this stuffy booth and have a coffee."

His words were clipped, his expression…almost guilty. Then she saw the image, in triplicate, on the editing screens.

A withering, dizzy sensation came over her. Digging her heels in, she skirted around Tate and stared, gaping, at the monitors. Her voice all but lost, she pointed a finger at the screens.

"What's Maeve deWalters doing up there?"

Maeve's bright red hair was as elaborately coiffed as ever. The shot looked like a recent portrait had been freeze-framed and captured behind a mock-up of crude jail bars.

From the doorway, Tate exhaled heavily then cursed under his breath. "Well, you had to learn sometime."

As nausea rose and damp prickled across her forehead, she inched around. "Learn what?"

One stride and he crossed the space between them. He held her shoulders with branding hands as he seemed to will her to remain calm.

Her legs felt boneless. If he hadn't been holding her, she'd have fallen in a pile. The life force seemed to drain from her, along with every ounce of belief she'd ever had in him.

In them.

"You're really going to do it, aren't you?" she asked over the lump in her throat. "You're going to do a story on Maeve and maybe destroy me in the process. I suppose you have the Hennessy story lined up next."

Hunching over her, Tate's fingers dug into her arms. "I'm not trying to destroy you. I'm trying to *save* you."

"Then why didn't you have the decency to tell me instead of letting me find out like this?"

"I tried to tell you."

He meant the conversation that night in the bungalow? "You said you thought Maeve was corrupt. That I'd do better to look elsewhere for support. You didn't say you had hard evidence and were taking a deep breath, getting ready to shout it to the world."

"It's high time someone did. Maeve deWalters was well on her way to being crooked when my parents died. These days her financial advisor and offshore bank accounts help make the funneling of funds so much easier."

She crossed her arms. "What evidence do you have?"

"Enough, and from a reliable source. But I have to keep this quiet. The release needs to be timed well for two reasons."

"The first would somehow revolve around your need for revenge."

He ignored her gibe aimed at the role Maeve deWalters had played in his parents deaths. "This is part of my job. Hard journalism is what this show's about. This story will come out either way. Question is, do we air it first or will somebody else get the privilege?"

Years of frustration and hurt swelled inside her chest. The ache was so great she thought she might burst.

"Then I suppose congratulations are in order. Too bad I get trampled along the way."

She'd mistakenly assumed that if Blade and Libby relied on themselves, Tate would be left to focus on their life as a couple. She'd thought he would have time for her now—that he would naturally consider her feelings.

She'd forgotten about his work. Her feelings would always come second to his precious television network.

Her vision blurred with brimming tears. "You haven't changed."

She'd hoped that her love could transform him. That was just wishful thinking. One person couldn't change another, she knew that better than most, yet the exhilaration of being close to him again had left her blind. Her love for Tate wouldn't change him. Nothing would.

Not even a child.

His chin edged up. "I have a duty to the public. I can't sit on this or sweep it under a mat."

"I understand you're on a timeline. Can't have the King beaten at the post now, can we?"

He growled out an impatient breath. "You're lining up to sign with Maeve. Auctions, dinners, special events. After she takes her cut, I doubt a third of the contributions would make it to your project."

He honestly didn't see. "This isn't about whether Maeve deWalters is corrupt. I'm upset because you had no intention of discussing this story with me until after it had aired. You go straight ahead and do what *you* think is right, and I'm supposed to forgive you after the fact. But even if I didn't like what I heard, I deserved to know about this story."

He continually took for granted that she would accept being kept in the dark and looking like a fool to boot. Never again.

He cursed under his breath and rushed a hand through his hair. "I was going to tell you about this story. I just needed…the right moment."

"It's a little late," she blurted out. "Maeve and I worked out details this morning, right before I received a message from the board to attend a meeting tomorrow. I assume the Hennessy investigation is going ahead."

Tate froze then trailed a weary hand through his hair again. While she trembled, she imagined his mind ticking over.

"All right," he said. "First things first. Maeve. You don't want your name linked in any way with hers. The taxation and other departments will run fine-tooth combs through her books and anyone associated with her. We'll see my lawyer, get you out of this. I'll fix it."

The booth extension rang. Tate looked at it, back at her then snapped up the receiver. Donna couldn't help but smile at the irony—commanding, arrogant and predictable to the end. The third worst day of her life and still Tate couldn't let a phone ring.

"Bridges here." His square jaw tightened. "Put her through." His attention landed on Donna. "I was expecting this call from Bali. Libby left a message a half hour ago. Molly said she sounded worried. If she's somehow landed herself in trouble with the Indonesian authorities, I need to know."

Donna didn't have time to wonder whether Libby was in some kind of trouble before Tate covered the mouthpiece with a palm. "I thought you might have some other news," he hesitated, "about the other night."

What he meant was—*about the mistake*. When they'd loved each other so well, so completely, protection had totally slipped both their minds. Yes, indeed, she'd come to see him about that, too.

His brow creased as he studied her face. "You've found out?" His expression said, *I'm here for you.* But beneath the concern she read more clearly, *I'll fix it.*

Her answering grin felt cut from dry ice. Just eleven days had passed since that night when she'd told him it was late in her cycle and not to worry. But three home tests conducted on separate days

confirmed suspicions. She was late. She was pregnant. She was sure.

She slanted her head and manufactured a dismis-
sive face. "All clear. Nothing to worry about."

Nothing you want to hear or concern yourself with.

He closed his eyes and exhaled as if to say "Thank
God" a moment before he had the receiver more
firmly to his ear. "Libby—that you? What's wrong?"

When his tone leveled and she was certain Libby
was all right—it sounded as if she only wanted to
stay another week—Donna walked out.

She felt numb inside, more alone and vulnerable
than at any time in her life. Nothing Tate said—no
mortal thing he could do—would make a difference now. He'd hinted that day at the café that he
would make a donation to her safe house project. It
killed her to ever think it, but right now she would
almost rather her project fail than be beholden to
him. She'd held her heart out to him and he'd
robbed her of everything.

Well…not *everything.*

Thirteen

Tate watched Donna turn and just missed catching her arm as she left the booth.

Damn! They were nowhere near finished their conversation. On top of this deWalters mess, Donna had just told him she wasn't pregnant. After days of wondering, he now knew she wasn't carrying his child...

"Libby, if everything is okay, I need to go. I'll see you in a week."

His little sister was all grown up and making her own decisions. Right now he had enough on his plate sorting out his own life.

On the other end of the line, Libby's voice

sounded concerned. "Is something wrong? Every-thing okay between you and Donna?"

"It will be."

Although, given the gutted look on Donna's face just now, maybe he was kidding himself. Had he lost her for good this time?

He hung up. Two strides put him at the doorway, but Blade appeared out of nowhere to block his path.

His brother held up two hands. "Whoa! Where's the fire?"

Tate sidled out the door. "I'll explain later." He needed to catch Donna before she left the building.

"Sure. Just thought you might like to know our barrister called."

Tate stopped and turned. "What's the problem now?"

"No problem." Blade crossed his arms and rocked on his heels. "I'm a free man! The prosecution withdrew the charges. Must have seen they couldn't prove their case and didn't want to waste any more time or money."

"Thank God that's over." He'd always known there was no real case.

Never again did he want that kind of worry, and he was certain Blade wouldn't create it. A rare kind of peace seemed to glow from his brother since

Blade and Kristin had begun dating again. Tate prayed it would work out for them and the world would leave them the hell alone.

Blade slapped Tate on the arm as he passed. "I'm off to celebrate with my girl."

Tate rotated to watch his brother amble down the corridor. "We've got a busy day ahead."

As soon as he finished speaking with Donna, he had to get back to it. He was up to his eyeballs. He had no choice, and he needed Blade's help.

Blade edged around. "Mate, I love my job but I love my lady more. We have our life back. If that's not worth taking the afternoon off, I don't know what is. You must feel the same now you and Donna are an item again." Lifting his chin to loosen his tie, Blade looked around. "Could've sworn I saw her around earlier." He seemed concerned now. "Everything okay in lovers' lane?"

A phrase was still resonating through Tate's brain—*I love my lady more*—when he snapped back and waved his brother off. "Fine. Everything's great. You go."

"Might see you tomorrow then." With a curious look, Blade headed off again.

"I'll be here." Like every other day, even most weekends, although he had enjoyed that brilliant seasonal interlude. Having Donna snuggled up or laughing beside him over Christmas break had left him feeling more refreshed, more himself, than he had in years.

Oh, God. *Donna.*

He strode back into the booth and dialed reception. Apparently Donna had just walked out of the front exit. The receptionist had seen her jump into a cab. Dropping the receiver back in its cradle, he glanced up to see Maeve's hideous face and teased red hair blasting out at him from the monitors.

Welcome to the rest of your week.

He set his hands on the back of the seat as his mind filled with a montage of other images—his parents hugging him goodbye, Blade waving goodbye, Libby saying goodbye, Donna meaning good—

The images imploded and he slammed the chair against the desk.

Donna was right, and wrong. He did want revenge on Maeve deWalters; he longed to see that witch behind bars where she belonged. And he also wanted to keep Donna safe from Maeve's influence, but without any unpleasant scenes beforehand or the chance of Maeve being tipped off before everything was set to go. To his mind, if he aired this story without Donna's prior knowledge, she would simply have to see reason and accept that he'd had no alternative. Then again…

He thought the same way on their engagement party night, as well as all those other times he'd let Donna down because he'd been convinced she would understand about priorities, which often meant his siblings or his work. It was no secret that he liked things done his way.

But when all was said and done, why should Donna understand or accept how he'd gone about this? She'd said he hadn't changed. He wouldn't disagree that his habit of acting first, talking later, could be labeled as arrogance. He was paying for that today. Fate had handed him a second chance with Donna. But in trying to control the agenda yet again, had he blown whatever future they might have had together?

He surveyed the claustrophobic booth.

This was the sum of his adult life. Trying to make it up to Blade and Libby, trying to appease his conscience, and for what? Gratitude? Admiration? Or for absolution and the privilege of returning home to a huge empty house each evening, and for what? When did it end?

Visualizing that empty house disintegrating around his ears, he moved into the corridor. People rushing to shoot a news update or hurrying tapes down to preproduction didn't register. Nothing registered but one monumental, all-encompassing mistake.

He'd tried so hard to make up for what he'd lost that given the speed with which Donna had left a moment ago, he might well have lost the one person who meant more to him than anything on the planet. He was deeply sorry his parents were gone. He loved Blade and Libby, but his work with them was pretty much done. He should feel free. Instead he felt empty. Like that house. He'd felt emptiness the moment Donna had said they wouldn't be parents.

He wouldn't be a father...

Setting his jaw, he headed down the corridor.

Who was he kidding? He couldn't work today anymore than Blade could. He needed to see Donna. He was certain she believed him about Maeve de-Walters's corruption; she knew he wouldn't risk his reputation unless he had strong facts that would stand up against scrutiny. But as she'd said, Maeve de Walters's illegal activities weren't at the heart of their problems. He had to figure out some way to make Donna trust him and assure her that he would never put her second again.

Thirty traffic-weaving minutes later, he was home and standing at the foot of his bed. Fresh on the satin quilt he smelled her scent. Bouncing off the walls he heard her laughter, but...

He spun a tight circle.

He and Donna and *here* didn't work.

Light reflecting off the side table caught his eye. He came close and softly smiled...her gold bracelet watch. Collecting the jewelry, he let the smooth links slip through each set of fingers while he worked out what was missing, how to make it right.

Unevenness beneath the watch face made him look. Etched on the gold lay the inscription he'd quoted to the engraver all those years ago before the trouble had set in. He stared at the single word and concentrated.

He needed to reclaim that time. Needed to get her back.

Forever.

Fourteen

Two days later, in an up-market suburban restaurant, Donna sat wringing her hands. Maeve deWalters was due to arrive at any moment. Though the meeting wouldn't be a pleasant one, Donna doubted it could be worse than her anguish when she'd walked out on Tate.

Rather than receding, the pain had grown worse. He hadn't pursued her, hadn't even called. Given his recent record in such matters, she guessed she shouldn't be surprised.

Heart thudding low in her chest, Donna collected

her dinner napkin and absentmindedly wound the starched linen around her fingers.

She could live without his embrace. Could live without his sexy smile. Heaven knows she *couldn't* live without her dignity. Once again Tate had placed his interests before her feelings. She didn't want to continue being Tate Bridges's mistress, but more so she couldn't live with wondering when and how he would humiliate her next.

Libby had said Tate was a good man. That he merely had a hard time understanding that doing the best by those he loved didn't mean ruling their lives. Whether or not that was true didn't matter. Bottom line was, he continued to hurt her. If she persisted in seeing him, she was condoning his behavior and had only herself to blame.

Visible through the wall-to-wall window facing the street, a dark rolling blur caught her attention. The gleaming wheels...those number plates...the gunmetal-grey paint. Pulling up at the curb outside was Tate's European convertible.

Adrenaline flooded her system.

This wasn't a coincidence. Had April told him she'd be here? Or was Maeve the person Tate had come to hunt down?

A prim voice at Donna's side made her jump.

"I must confess," Maeve said, placing her pocketbook on the table, "I'm pleased you called to arrange this meeting."

Her mind racing, Donna glanced between her company and the convertible. Tate had emerged from the driver's side, looking edible in tailored dark trousers and button-down shirt. His hair rumpled in a stiff breeze as he analyzed his sur-roundings, checked his watch then shut the door.

Swallowing hard, Donna looked again to Maeve. "It's about our agreement."

She needed to wrap this up quickly. Get out of here fast. The last thing she needed was Tate hurling a live grenade into the foxhole.

With a disenchanted air, Maeve eased into the tapestry-covered seat. "Precisely what I wish to discuss." She flicked a hovering waiter away then clasped her age-worn hands, and their long red tips, beneath her chin.

"I am loath to bring it up, however, I believe you've been consorting with those horrible Bridges boys." Her hazel eyes glowed. "A rather obtuse pastime, you'll agree."

In Donna's peripheral vision, she saw Tate slot his sunglasses into his shirt pocket and breeze around the building's corner, out of sight.

"How…" Donna paused, swallowed. "How did you know?"

Maeve arched an eyebrow. "Pet, you can't keep secrets from me." She sat back, not amused. "Naturally this changes our relationship."

Picturing the scene about to explode, Donna nodded. "More than you know."

His face dark, Tate stopped at the maître d's podium and Donna withered in her seat. She prayed he wouldn't turn this into a public incident.

After flinging a determined glance around, Tate strode over. Maeve had begun a speech, of which Donna had heard not a word, when he appeared by their table like a knight drawing his sword—or bringing it down.

More than ever, his dominating presence sent electric impulses hopscotching over her skin. Though she'd have done anything to prevent it, she quivered with the urge to kiss the bristled shadow of his jaw...hear the rumble of his rich voice against her ear.

"Hello, Maeve." His voice today sounded ominously deep.

The doyen's mouth stopped moving. She blinked then pivoted around. Her souring expression shrank in on itself like an apple speed drying in the sun. Finally she flicked her hand and feigned an inspection of her menu.

"Please leave. No one invited you." Accusing hazel eyes slid up to scorch Donna's. "Unless..."

Tate ignored the dismissal. "This meeting is over. Donna is unable to proceed with any agreement, verbal or otherwise."

Donna half expected a camera crew to race out. She knew how Tate's business mind worked. High-stakes confrontations such as this made for excellent promo vision. However, as much as the realization would prick his ego, this meeting was not about Tate or his precious show.

Although her breathing was anything but even, her tone was surprisingly calm. "This is none of your business, Tate."

Take your commanding good looks and insufferable sex appeal and go—just *go*.

Maeve sneered. "Are we rehearsing for one of your network's soap operas, Mr. Bridges? *Love Conquers All,* perhaps?" Eyes bright, she drummed her nails atop the menu. "I see you're as impudent as your brother."

Tate's dark eyes simmered at the slur against Blade and his—in Maeve's opinion—unwelcome attachment to Kristin. "You can hang up your broom there, Maeve. You have no power over them anymore."

A corner of Maeve's mouth ticked as her eyes narrowed to vengeful slits. She sliced her attention back to Donna. "As I said, highly obtuse." She collected her pocketbook. "I'm pulling my support as of now, and not purely due to Mr. Bridges's uncouth behavior." Her tone was one of manufactured regret. "I understand misconduct charges are being heard by your peers."

Donna's cheeks toasted more with every word. Not in humiliation but in anger.

"Actually the board has decided no disciplinary action is necessary." They'd thought it fair and reasonable to inform her in person that the complainant in question had lodged similar grievances against two other reputable professionals. All the charges had proved to be unfounded. At least one turn in these crazy few weeks had gone her way.

Tate's hand brushed her arm as his expression melted with relief. "That's great news."

Great was an understatement. Now he genuinely had nothing to hold over her head.

Smug, Maeve pushed to her feet. "We all know the saying. Where there's smoke..."

Tate nodded. "I know of at least one instance where that's true."

Donna's patience broke. "Can you both please just be quiet!" She retrieved an envelope from her bag. "Maeve, to make it official, this letter states I no longer require your support with regard to The Judith Safe House Trust."

Maeve sputtered. "You're dismissing *me?*" Her jowls wobbled. "How dare you!"

Tate stood beside Donna. "Save your energy, Maeve. You'll need every ounce soon enough."

Donna silently ended the sentence. Maeve would need her strength when the authorities caught up with her money-laundering schemes. She wondered how the redhead would do without her hairdresser in jail.

Maeve blanched. "And just what is that supposed to mean?"

"Watch the news and find out," Tate happily replied.

Running a calculating eye over them both, Maeve straightened and stormed out.

When Tate focused his full attention on her, Donna shivered in her seat. Despite everything, she glowed inside when his encouraging eyes smiled down. "You made the right choice."

As his finger curved her jaw, she longed to lean into his caress. But she wouldn't make the same mistake again. Twice was shameful enough.

She collected her bag and got to her feet. "What I did had nothing to do with you." Well, not in the way he might think. "Your problem with Maeve might have a personal origin, but you wouldn't air a story that wasn't fully grounded in fact. I'm not foolish enough to put my pride before my foundation's best interests."

She owed it to Judith as well as so many other unknown women who would one day need that shelter.

Tate tugged his ear. "I have it on good authority the story about Maeve will hit the air by the end of the week. Our news department will cover it, but unfortunately that's a little early for our debut show to compete with."

Her gullible heart contracted. "That story meant a lot to you."

He rolled back one big shoulder. "There'll be other stories."

As that edict sank in, Donna inwardly cringed. Lots and lots of other stories would always mean more to him than she did. She was through having her feelings trampled on. She needed someone who thought enough of her to discuss important issues, not a man who hogged the reins, made all the decisions and was proud of it.

Biting down to stave off the hurt, she edged past. "I have to go. Good luck, Tate."

As she moved off, she sensed him striding behind her.

"Do you have an appointment?"

At the counter, she signed her account. She set down her pen and faced him. "That's none of your concern."

"I'd like it to be."

Unwelcome arousal flashed through her, but she reached in extra deep and found her resolve. "And I'd like to keep this polite. Excuse me."

She continued on out the door and into the muggy street. Overhead, grumbling thunderclouds rolled in from the east.

Tate was by her side. "I have something to show you."

Focusing on the noisy traffic, she spotted a cab. She moved to the curb. "Not interested."

Stepping in her path, he cut her off. "Donna… I'm sorry."

Raw emotion—swift and cruel—sprang up to sting her nose and strangle her aching heart. She sighed. "Even if I believed you, Tate, don't you see? It's too late for apologies. Whatever we shared couldn't last. Obviously you don't want to make a commitment and now I don't think you should." He tried to interrupt, but she held up a hand. "You have your family and your work. That's enough for you. I'm sure you won't have any trouble finding someone else to warm your bed."

The cab pulled up. Moving around Tate, she tried to slide inside but he blocked her path.

"Do you know why Blade got into a brawl the night of our engagement party?"

Her breath caught in her chest. Why on earth was he bringing this up now?

She stretched to reach for the cab's door handle. "I don't need to know."

"That night one of Blade's friends had taken great pleasure in running your reputation down."

She heard the words but they didn't make sense. Confused, she slowly shook her head. "What are you talking about?"

Tate reached over and pounded on the cab's roof, sending it away. Then he came closer. "You remember talking about your foster care days in front of Libby, Blade and his friend during that Australia Day barbeque?"

It seemed so long ago. They'd all been laughing and sharing, and she'd felt this overwhelming need to divulge her past, to connect and feel part of their circle—their family.

She nodded. "I remember."

"Early on the evening of our engagement party, Blade's university friends were having a drink and discussing how well suited Blade and Kristin were. They agreed Maeve should've been pleased her daughter had found such a catch. Then that friend from the barbeque—"

Tate's jaw hardened, as if he were debating whether or not to go on. He lowered his voice.

"Blade's friend went over the top, spouting off about water finding its own level. How Kristin and Blade were social equals, but he couldn't see why I would be interested in you, someone who'd been dropped at the church stairs and had no background, no pedigree." Tate blinked twice. "Blade said his silver-spoon friend called you a bony lost puppy looking for a home."

She felt slightly light-headed. How cruel to hear those words aloud…and yet that's exactly how she'd felt. Though she'd never known it as clearly as this moment. She didn't belong anywhere, not then, and in many ways not even now.

Exhaling, she looked Tate in the eye. "So Blade hit him."

"I didn't condone that behavior," he told her. He took her arm and began to walk with her. "But I understood. Blade told his friend you were the kindest lady he'd ever known. How you'd told him that if ever he needed to talk to someone, you were always there."

They reached Tate's car. Facing her, he grabbed both her hands. "That boy kept ribbing Blade. On top of all the trouble with Kristin, Blade's lid popped. The boy's father was a retired cop. I had to call in some mighty big favors that night."

Donna's eyes squeezed tight. "Why didn't you tell me?"

"I put off calling you that night, hoping it would be wrapped up quickly. I was wrong. When I did phone, you didn't answer my calls. The next day you barely spoke to me, other than to say it was over. As time went on, I didn't think burdening you with those details would make a difference."

Her head was reeling. "All these years, and Blade had only acted to protect me."

But if she'd known the facts back then, would it have made a difference to her decision to stop seeing Tate? As heartrending as Tate's admission was, she couldn't be sure it would have. Tate had put his sibling and work commitments ahead of her many time before that episode. His absence that night had merely been the final straw.

There was always some sound reason behind Tate's actions. Her hurt stemmed more from his inability to see that she deserved to be treated with respect instead of being kept in the back row. She couldn't go on that way, not knowing exactly where or how she would fit in with his plans.

Tate opened his passenger door and set his warm palm on her back. "Drive with me. There's more you need to know."

Fifteen

Donna wasn't certain how far they drove. She felt the cool wind funneling through her hair, saw the heavy rolling sky above. And knew Tate, powerful in the driver's seat—speeding up, slowing down, changing gears—was, as always, fully in control. She felt anything but.

As Tate took a corner, she studied his stone-carved jaw. Ripples of stark desire, interlaced with dread, swam out from her center. She'd made some horrible mistakes. Was she making another one?

When he'd asked her along for this drive, every-thing inside of her had screamed no. But he'd said there was more she needed to know. In light of what she'd finally learned today, she wouldn't rest until she knew it all.

The car swerved off into a quiet dead end over-looking a deserted stretch of beach. As the tires rolled to a stop, intermittent dots of cold rain splattered on the bonnet and fell on her lap. The approaching storm's salty gusts blew icily on her arms and face.

Seconds after swinging out of the driver's side, Tate opened her door, but she hesitated taking the hand she knew as well as her own. "This isn't the best day for a stroll."

He frowned. "You're right. It's about to pour. We should find some shelter."

Before she could suggest they put up the top and leave, he folded her hand in his. As his familiar masculine heat soaked through and her defenses teetered on a cliff, he led her to a picket fence painted a holiday turquoise-blue. Without a pause, he swung open the hip-high gate.

Taking in the private landscaped gardens and the serene Queenslander-style home before them, Donna tugged back. "We don't want to bother anyone."

All species of palms rustled around the enor-mous three-sided verandah. There wasn't another house for miles.

"Whoever lives here obviously likes their privacy," she said, as the drops fell harder, plink-plonking on the high-pitched corrugated roof. She tugged again. "Let's get back in the car and go somewhere else."

A smile lit Tate's face as he cast an eye over the wide porch stairs and white and turquoise trimmed front door. "It looks kind of friendly to me."

A wind chime hanging above the door tinkled in the strong breeze and a delicious fruity scent filled her lungs. Behind a blossoming frangipani tree, she spied another tree laden with heavy bunches of ripe fruit.

Mangos.

When he drew her into the yard, this time her feet made the decision for her.

He indicated a slight incline decorated with a colorful garden display. "Now there's something you don't see every day."

Holding back the hair blowing over her head, Donna took in the stone sundial then read the single word created by swirls and patches of scarlet ground-cover roses. The petals, which by their decoration must have been freshly planted, seemed to grow larger and brighter the more she stared. Her heartbeat knocking at her ribs, she could do no more than breathe out the word.

"Forever."

Her gold bracelet watch…the inscription. Donna

held her stomach. But what did it mean here, today, in that windblown pretty flower bed?

Afraid to ask, but too curious not to, she looked up and searched Tate's eyes. "I don't understand."

"I was wrong, Donna. Wrong and arrogant and stupid."

The penny dropped. "This is your house, isn't it?"

"No. This is *our* house."

She bit her lip and edged away. "Please don't do this. On the surface this might look romantic, but deep down it doesn't mean anything. I know who you are and I know you can't change." Tate wasn't happy unless he was fully in charge. She couldn't deal with that anymore.

"People *must* be able to change, or you'd be out of a job."

He was twisting things. "That's different."

"It's only different because after the Maeve de-Walters episode you don't want to take another chance on me?"

"It's more complicated than that. You've proven time and again you'll do what you think is right without considering me or anyone else. In a costume drama that might be heroic, but in real life it doesn't work. You don't even respect me enough to answer whenever I've asked lately about our future. It's pretty obvious what you want from me, and it's not marriage and it certainly isn't children." Her voice caught on the final word.

He took a moment then spoke. "Blade is taking over full responsibility for the current affairs show. I signed off on it yesterday. From now on, it's his baby."

She shook her head. That show meant too much to Tate to hand over. "I don't believe you."

"In fact, Blade is now joint CEO."

She blinked several times. Tate would never surrender that much control.

He seemed to read her mind. "At first I thought it would be hard to ease back, but actually it felt so good that after I spoke to Blade, I rang Libby and promoted her out of children's production to help share the responsibility. She was thrilled. I, on the other hand, am taking an indefinite sabbatical. As of this moment, you are my main and only concern."

As much as she wanted to, Donna couldn't buy it. "If that's true, I'm happy you feel confident enough to share the network's load with your brother and sister. But if this is some kind of scheme to get me back into your bed, you're missing an important point. I don't want to continue with our affair. I will not be your on-the-side lover. Not for one day. Certainly not forever."

"Which brings me back to the flower bed." His arm wound securely around her as he walked with her up the incline. "You'll understand when you see the top half."

Quizzing his eyes, she gradually let her vision wander back to the garden. Above *Forever,* above the sundial, the flowers spelled out a question—two words that blocked her throat and flooded her body with disbelief and terrifying hope.

His deep voice rumbled gently like the thunder overhead. "Would you like me to read it for you?"

A raindrop wet the tip of her nose as, gaze glued to the display, she pressed her lips together and, speechless, nodded quickly.

Her blurred vision panned over each letter as he drew her close and murmured, "Marry me."

She turned into him, hiding her hot face against his chest. His arms immediately folded her in close.

"I bought this house yesterday," he said. "I thought we could live here together—you, me...our own little family."

The vee of his hand supported her head as his mouth lowered until his lips hovered a hair's breadth from hers. "Forgive me, Donna. Be my wife."

A tear escaped. "You want a family?"

His loving smile wrapped around her heart. "The moment I realized we hadn't used protection that night, although I wasn't ready to admit it, I think I knew. I love you, Donna. I want to build the rest of my life around you." He claimed the kiss she'd secretly ached to surrender all day.

As he pressed her close, the world dropped away and she found herself floating atop a cloud. A sparkling jet of sensation flew up from her toes, sending her giddy with desire and so much more. When he gently broke away and she felt the earth beneath her shaky legs once more, her mind cleared enough to ask again.

"You're *really* sure?"

"About a family?" He contentedly studied her face. "One hundred percent. I'm sorry I went about it the long way. Truth is…I was worried I'd disappoint you, make some fatal mistake and never be able to make it up to you. But I won't let that kind of thinking get in the way again. I want to be a part of you, to feel *complete* with you—if you'll have me."

"You want to be a parent."

He grinned. "I'm going to throw away my cell phone, moor a boat outside our door and teach my son to fish like I always wished my father had taught me."

"And if you had a daughter?"

"I'm sure a girl can learn to throw a line." He kissed her nose. "Girl or boy, one of each or more, I'll be happy."

She called upon all her courage and faith.

"That's good news, because when I said I wasn't, actually I was. Or rather, I am—" she released the word "—pregnant."

A second later, she was swept up in the cradle of his arms, twirling through the air. When he stopped, she was laughing and he looked as if he'd been given the world on a plate.

His chest expanded as he inhaled deeply. "I'm going to be a father."

She nodded.

"We're going to be a family."

Beaming, she nodded again.

Drops of falling rain clung to his lashes. "But you still haven't answered my question. Donna, I love you."

Her reply was the truest words she'd ever spoken. "I love you, too."

"Will you marry me?"

She searched his eyes. Yes, he wanted a wedding as much as she did, but his gaze told her more than that. Tate hadn't changed. He'd simply found a part of himself that he'd lost long ago—Tate before his parents' accident, before he'd felt obliged to give and be more than anyone expected. She saw that awareness shining in his eyes and knew the man who had proposed today would be the best husband and father he possibly could be.

Nevertheless, she couldn't help but tease him.

Still in his arms, she drew a lazy fingertip around his jaw. "I'll marry you on one condition."

Studying her expression, he arched an eyebrow. "I see…an ultimatum. You want my donation for your foundation? Consider it done."

She glowed inside. "Thank you. But that's not it."

His chin kicked up. "Let's have it then."

He'd played his little game. She'd play hers.

She wrinkled her nose. "I'm not sure. We're out in the open."

His smiling eyes assured her. "We're the only ones here. I promise, you're safe."

"Maybe we should go inside." She grinned. "Can I tempt you?"

Tate murmured, "Always." As the rain came down her chest, his mouth claimed hers again and Donna knew in her heart finally she was home.

* * * * *

FREE

2 STORIES AND A SURPRISE GIFT!

We would like to take this opportunity to thank you for reading this Mills & Boon® book by offering you the chance to take another specially selected 2-in-1 volume from the Desire™ 2-in-1 series absolutely FREE! We're also making this offer to introduce you to the benefits of the Mills & Boon® Book Club™—

- ★ **FREE home delivery**
- ★ **FREE gifts and competitions**
- ★ **FREE monthly Newsletter**
- ★ **Books available before they're in the shops**
- ★ **Exclusive Mills & Boon Book Club offers**

Accepting this FREE book and gift places you under no obligation to buy; you may cancel at any time, even after receiving your free shipment. Simply complete your details below and return the entire page to the address below. You don't even need a stamp!

YES! Please send me 2 free Desire stories in a 2-in-1 volume and a surprise gift. I understand that unless you hear from me, I will receive 2 superb new 2-in-1 titles every month for just £5.25 each, postage and packing free. I am under no obligation to purchase any books and may cancel my subscription at any time. The free books and gift will be mine to keep in any case.

D9ZEE

Ms/Mrs/Miss/Mr..........................Initials ....

BLOCK CAPITALS PLEASE

Surname ....

Address ....

....

....Postcode ....

Send this whole page to:

The Mills & Boon Book Club, FREEPOST CN81, Croydon, CR9 3WZ